FRANCESCA
Of <u>Lost Nation</u>
A Novel

Greetings from Home Farm,
Lost Nation, Iowa, 1947.
Enjoy!

Lucinda Sue Crosby

Special thanks to Editors
Laura Dobbins and Elizabeth McAdams

This book is a work of fiction. Names, characters, places, and incidents either are products of the author's imagination or are used fictitiously. Any resemblance to actual events or locales or persons, living or dead, is entirely coincidental.

Copyright © 2010 by Lucinda Sue Crosby

All rights reserved, including the right to reproduce this book or portions thereof in any form whatsoever.

First printing 2010

For information about special discounts for bulk purchases, please contact ldobbins444@gmail.com

Designed by Laura Dobbins

Editors:
Book Editor Elizabeth McAdams
Beaumont Hardy Editing
jane@beaumonthardy.com

Contributing Editor Laura Dobbins
ldobbins444@gmail.com

Printed in the U.S.A. by
Morris Publishing®
3212 East Highway 30
Kearney, NE 68847
1-800-650-7888
www.morrispublishing.com

Manufactured in the United States of America

ISBN 978-1-4507-0167-9

Companion Song

A song called, "Stories They Could Tell," has been selected as a companion piece for "Francesca of Lost Nation." The author of this book, known as Cinda in music circles, co-wrote the song with Grammy Award songwriter and Bluegrass recording artist Carl Jackson. It is performed by Christian artist Renee Martin and arranged by Jackson.

His eyes are dimmed with age; his speech is slow
He can't remember half the things he used to know
His golden years have come and gone but still he lingers on
Alone and lonely in a world he used to own
Not the fault of the man he outlived his useful span

CHORUS: *Oh the stories he could tell*
The comings and the goings of a long life's ebb and swell
And if we cared enough to ask him, he might dare to dwell
On the stories he could tell ...

Her hair is iron gray; her hands are still
All her pretty things are listed in her will
Her mind at times is fooled, she thinks her son is off at school
Confused about the family she used to rule
Not the fault of the man he outlived his useful span

CHORUS:

BRIDGE: *Some day we'll be right where they are*
Watching out the window for that one familiar car
As young'uns crawl upon a knee, the future weds the past
For an hour of the present that flies by too damn fast

CHORUS:

© *1999 Lucky Cinda Music (ASCAP) and Colonel Rebel (ASCAP)*
To learn more about this concept or to purchase the song, please visit: www.LuckyCinda.com

ACKNOWLEDGEMENTS

To HB who first recognized the promise of this work and to LD who helped bring it from the possible into the real.

For and to
Francesca and Babe
with love and a thousand thanks

Foreword

My name is Sarah, which is a Hebrew name and translates to the word "princess." Of course, my German-American family was actually Presbyterian.

As a young girl, and throughout much of my life, I had the honor and privilege of knowing and loving a most remarkable, graceful, vigorous, resilient, eccentric, stubborn and fascinating woman.

She was never petty. She was never dull.

This is our story.

Chapter 1
Morning Music

I write of a morning in Eden ... or, more precisely, in Lost Nation, Iowa in June of 1947.

A pale melon of sun peeked over a strand of rolling hills and, safe and sleepy in my bed, I could hear our red-shouldered hawk calling to its mate.

It was another sunrise, a heavenly first-of-summer dawn of the most memorable year of my childhood. Adventure awaited me. The ancient oak down the hill beyond the weathered split-rail fence begged a climbing. I could also hear the cool depths of the fishing pond whisper my name. But first, the aroma of sweet cornbread, just done, tickled my nose. All other plans would have to wait.

In the glory of my nine soft years, I loved the unfolding of this new day. I could already hear my father's off-key hum as he shaved himself. My mother, I knew, had been awake one whole hour, making magic in the kitchen on her vast black stove. She cooed to it and wooed it like a lover and in return, it always delivered up to her fine hands a golden bounty: Thanksgiving turkey stuffed with cornbread dressing, sourdough griddle cakes and Sunday chicken dinner with au gratin potatoes. Better than a pirate's treasure. Better than a king's ransom.

My room was white-washed pine. The wood floor was covered with a rug woven by my Grandmother Francesca's graceful hands. I remember the many months she worried over it. On my eighth birthday, when she presented me with her prize, I received it with a proper reverence. No queen ever got more on coronation day, so delicate were the stitches, so fine and pearly the threads.

I never called her anything but Francesca, for that was her name to me. Not Grandmother, not Nanny, or Gran, not even Frances ... but Francesca. Especially Francesca when the giggling got to us. My grandmother was regal. She was leggy and gracious and full of life.

Since it seemed that Francesca must be awake on this fine day, I slipped from underneath an ancient coverlet that was light as air. It had belonged to Great-Great Grandmother Mendenhall, and I loved its worn softness. I tiptoed down the hallway to Francesca's boudoir.

Of course, it was really just a bedroom, but Francesca's spirit made it seem much grander. Armfuls of summer blossoms cascaded out of old wine decanters. I can still remember the faintly odd scents which filled the air: Witch hazel; rose sachet and spice oranges, all capped by the aroma of lilac powder.

In the same way I did each morning, I tapped lightly on her door, once, twice, three times. I heard her stretch lazily, rustling under her often-washed sheets. A low voice called out softly. "Who is it?"

And I answered, in as stately a voice as possible, "Madam, your chariot awaits!" With the tingling anticipation that I felt every morning at Francesca's private chambers, I listened for the invitation. Heart beating, toes curled under, I finally heard the words that never failed to delight me: "Come in, Sarah. I have missed you all night long."

As I opened the cracked walnut door, which smelled of lemon oil, I was blinded by the sunlight that streamed in through open-weave curtains. Francesca never pulled drapes against the outside world.

She didn't "put any faith" in drapes. Sunlight and moonlight were made welcome to fill her boudoir however they pleased.

"It's going to be hot today; I can already tell," said Francesca with a sigh.

My grandmother thrilled to the spring rain, to the winter sleet and snowdrifts, but she disdained the humid, baking days of the Iowa summer.

"Well, we'd better begin what we're about while I still have a breath left in me," she said and then sighed again.

That's when I kissed her, right on the top of her gray-brown head.

"I'll bring café au lait," I promised, already skipping to the narrow rear stairway to the kitchen.

My mother was standing in front of the black stove, whispering encouragement.

"I need you to be just a little hotter now. Yeeesss ... my, my, that's perfect."

Without interrupting her flow of praise, Mother pointed to a rosewood tray in the center of a long trestle table. Covered with a fine lace cloth and set with see-through porcelain cups, the tray looked like an outsider. It was a touch too exotic, a touch too elegant for a farmhouse ... much like Francesca.

The dining set was a part of the honeymoon treasure Francesca and my grandfather Cox had brought back from New York City.

Cox and Francesca were married for many years. High school sweethearts they had been, different from one another and from everyone else in Lost Nation. They argued and danced and high-kicked their way through life like a pair of matched grays. Francesca was always the wood nymph, cool and moon-covered; Cox was the imp gambler, reckless and roguish. They lived honestly together, yet there was a separation, too, if that's possible ... each respecting above all else the right of the other to grow. Their marriage wasn't a match made in heaven by any stretch, but it was lively and full of surprise.

Cox died in 1943, and I'm not sure that Francesca wasn't still mad at him for leaving. Her father had warned her forty years earlier that would happen, and it galled Francesca that Cox had eventually proved the old man right, even if it took untimely death to do it. Francesca was no fan of "untimely death."

Mother was at the stove, cooking, and I heard her humming the words to one of my father's favorite tunes: "Cool Water."

Her voice, unlike Daddyboys' raspy, wrong-noted instrument, was low and firm.

She poured coffee from the spotted-metal pot into the two cups on the tray and added warm milk still smelling of hay and cow. From the tin breadbox, I snuck two crumbly squares of cornbread and topped the feast off with a crock of butter. I kissed my mother then and hugged her.

She hugged me back in the sweet but dismissive way mothers do when their minds are occupied. That's when it struck me that something wasn't quite right in the house this morning. But for the life of me, I couldn't put my finger on it.

I took up the tray — swept it up, really — and with a great flourish and a curtsy, I took the meal Mother had prepared for Francesca and carried it carefully up the back stairs. Then, with one foot in front of the other, I made my way down the center of the hallway. It was important, staying to the center. I never wanted to offend one side by showing too much attention to the other. For the same reason, I sat on all the chairs in the parlor, even the scratchy horsehair sofa, in rotation and never wore a shirt more than one day at a time.

I set the tray on the floor by Francesca's door and knocked again.

"Madam, your morning sustenance."

"Do come in," said Francesca as she opened the door for me, taking the heavy tray and setting it on the delicate walnut dressing table by the window.

There were thirteen antique silver frames on that table, each one containing a photograph of members of our family. The only one not represented in the collection was Francesca's own sister, Maude. My grandmother had a prejudice where Maude was concerned, and it didn't do to ask about it. All you'd get for your trouble was a frosty stare. No, it didn't do at all.

As we nibbled and sipped, I watched Francesca finish her morning toilette. She was wonderfully long-limbed. As a girl, her legs had been judged the best in the county by the group of boys she'd grown up with. But she would have preferred to have had the beautiful face of her sister Maude and often said so. (I would have traded mine for Maude's too, for that matter.)

But even in her workaday outfit of any old shirt and patched cotton trousers cut off at the knees for coolness, you couldn't get around Francesca's lithe shape and queenly bearing. I'd seen pictures in *LIFE* magazine of Princess Elizabeth, the future monarch of England. But I thought Francesca was much better suited to the job, both in appearance and personality.

I sat on the bed and watched as Francesca brushed her bobbed hair in her usual off-hand manner, despairing of the wisps that formed around her forehead in the humidity.

Francesca had taken to wearing her wedding ring around her neck on a gold chain. She fingered it contemplatively as it caught the light from the window. She sighed and turned abruptly to face me.

"Is there something odd going on in the house this morning?" she asked.

"Yes," I whispered.

So she'd noticed it, too. I shouldn't have been surprised, because Francesca was as canny as Sherlock Holmes.

"Listen," she said.

We could hear my father's scratchy baritone struggling:

"Quand il me prend dans ses bras
Il me parle tout bas... hmm hmm la da da di...
La vie en rose ..."

Now that was certainly odd, since Daddyboys — that was my father's nickname and how I referred to him — was a true-blue Country Western music fan. His all-time favorite was Roy Rogers and the Sons of the Pioneers.

"I don't get it," I said.

"It must be a mystery," said my grandmother, teasing me, because she knew I didn't like to be in suspense. I always wanted to find out right away what was going on. I thought my mother had been acting occupied while cooking breakfast. Now my father was singing strange songs. It was all too puzzling.

"Let's talk to Daddyboys right this minute," I said.

Patience was a quality I possessed only in dribs and drabs. Francesca, on the other hand, was a great one for the proper thing in its proper time, and she had the patience of a stone carving.

Christmas presents on Christmas morning, never Christmas Eve. Lunch after noon, never before, no matter how much your stomach growled. Resolutions harvested when the moment was ripe, never until. So it was with mysteries.

But suspense in our own household was more than I could endure and I wanted to know everything now. Whining, however, would get me nowhere. My father was not to be questioned, and that was final.

"Stop sniveling, Sarah," Francesca warned. "He'll tell us when he's good and ready. I'm perfectly content with that."

"What if he doesn't?" I continued to persist.

"Then you can ask him," was all Francesca offered as a response.

Impasses like these were a frequent pitfall in my conversations with my grandmother. She had many of the qualities of a fairy-tale princess, not the least of which was imperiousness. I got my pig-headedness from her, make no mistake. We might easily have gone on this way for an hour without either one of us giving in. We'd done it often enough in the past.

But, like the Indians say, "Those who fight and run away, live to fight another day."

So I threw my hands in the air and turned the conversation around a corner.

"What chore shall we do first?" I asked.

Francesca lifted her pug nose toward heaven.

"Why, whatever you like, Sarah," she purred, magnanimous on the field of battle, victorious.

Chapter 2
Summertime Chores

He was the premier mechanic in a twenty-mile radius. My father enjoyed a thriving business and he also often burned the midnight oil. Sometimes, Daddyboys would stay at the shop for fourteen hours at a stretch, keeping the town's outlandish cross-section of cars, trucks and tractors in good running order. In the summer, when the touring season was at its height, he had more work than he could handle.

My mother was a cook of considerable repute. I swear her pie crusts melted on contact with your tongue. In fact, Daddyboys insisted that she'd made a pact with the devil when it came to flour — "No lump would ever dare show its ugly face in her gravy," he'd tease. Her biscuits were light as air; her canned fruits and vegetables were spiced with unusual seasonings of her own devising. She spent her days with her beloved stove, creating delicacies that sold briskly at Porter's Emporium, Lost Nation's sole general store.

It was up to Francesca and me to keep the farm running while my parents worked, so most of the daily chores on our property fell to us. We fed and curried the horses, RedBird and Miss Blossom. We also cared for the chickens and tended to the flower and vegetable gardens.

Our apple trees were harvested by next-door neighbor Joshua Teems and his sons, Isaac and Jacob.

Mr. Purdy, the butcher, dressed out the occasional sheep or pig I raised as a member in good standing of the 4-H Club. Butchering days were painful. I raised those animals practically from the day of their birth, and by the time they had grown to eating size, they'd become the dearest of friends.

Whenever Daddyboys loaded the truck for a mournful trip into town, I hid out down by the pond, so as not to hear the awful squealing and bleating that echoed in my head long after the truck was out of sight.

These woebegone episodes of mine prompted my grandmother to cluck her tongue and pronounce that I would never be a farmer's wife. "Too much poetic soul," she would observe, not unkindly. Prophetically, as an adult, I don't eat anything with four legs.

Thankfully, there would be no butchering today. Instead, Francesca and I would take a delicious detour from our chores.

"Let's ride RedBird and Blossom to the swimming hole," I suggested, already skipping down the back stairs. I knew exactly what Francesca would say, which she did.

"But of course."

In the kitchen, Francesca and my mother exchanged polite greetings.

"Good morning, Rachael."

"Good morning."

Their relationship was not distant, exactly. It did, however, exist on rather strictly defined terms. They were generous to and thoughtful of one another, but I never saw them in one another's pockets.

My mother was practical and outspoken; my grandmother was grand and outspoken. My mother was rooted to the earth; her mother's feet always rested on a mountain top, the better to look down upon your little world and keenly observe every single thing that happened in it. My mother was business-like to the point of briskness and rather cheerful. Francesca was ... well ... more like an empress in a folktale. She was cooler, deeper. By some accident of birth, they had been thrown together like clashing colors in a crazy quilt.

"Wherever did that come from?" Francesca said, pointing to a tiny replica of the Eiffel Tower that sat rather haughtily on top of the ice box.

"Why, I'm sure I don't know," my mother answered. "I thought maybe Sarah put it there."

"I can't reach that high," I said. "Besides, what would I want with that old thing?" Of course, whatever I may have said, my interest was piqued. I have always loved a mystery.

Mommy smiled and took my face in her flour-scented hand. "It's amazing that you can reach that high when spice cookies are cooling there. My daughter, the 'stomach,'" she said with a shake of her dark blond hair.

Rachael could be warm and kind, but she could be stern, too. I learned to address her according to her mood, which is why sometimes I called her "Mommy" and other times it was "Mother."

Today she was on a very even keel, quite unlike Daddyboys' unusual antics and newfound love of popular music. Maybe we were about to find out what in the bejesus was going on.

At that moment, my father breezed into the room, wearing a Sunday shirt and smelling faintly of vanilla. He grabbed my mother and began waltzing her around the kitchen.

"Clay," she sputtered, "what on earth? What has gotten into you this morning? Surely you don't plan to go to work dressed like that?" Francesca and I traded knowing looks. Something was definitely up.

With a little huff, Mom pulled away from Daddyboys, who laughed, kissed her loudly on the cheek and disappeared out the back door. Wham, went the screen.

"I wish he wouldn't slam it like that," Mother sighed, staring after him with a frown.

My grandmother returned her attention to business.

"What can we do for you today, Rachael?"

There was a long list. Mary Porter was coming at ten to pick up the pies, and Mrs. Sweeny would be there in the afternoon for the laundry.

"I think the peas are ready, too," said Mother. "You could clean and shell them. And shuck the corn, will you?" My mother looked at me sharply. "Just don't eat all the peas."

"Don't worry; we won't," said Francesca as we went out the back door and down the stoop.

"And don't let the screen door ..." It was too late; slam!

The barn stood across a side yard, where grass struggled to find the sun under a broad elm. Francesca whistled softly, and RedBird nickered from her stall. Anyone who saw those two together, the woman and her horse, would have sworn they'd been sisters in another life. When Francesca communicated with her mare in that quiet way she had, RedBird's ears pricked up. They gazed into one another's eyes like long-lost friends. No matter how far out in pasture RedBird was, when Francesca whistled, that horse would come running. Francesca rarely used a saddle and never a bit, preferring a simple hackamore.

"After all," she'd remind me, "you don't steer with your hands. Just a little knee pressure suffices."

Let's just say I hadn't quite mastered that technique. Francesca said it was because the riding was still primarily in my head.

"It needs to come right from your blood, from all your muscles, from your heart."

Francesca was a great one for doing things from your heart. Things you'd never thought of as having anything to do with your heart. Like schoolwork and sewing and even weeding.

After we replenished food and water for RedBird and Miss Blossom, Francesca helped me saddle up. With a click of her tongue, she set RedBird into motion, and Blossom followed alongside and slightly behind.

Miss Blossom was under fourteen hands, fat and dappled. She'd had a hard life. You could tell by the scars on her knees. By the time Daddyboys bought her from a scrawny, mean-looking little man named Hoffstedder at the county fair three years back, she'd sunk pretty low. She was skinny and saggy in the middle, and there was dullness in her eyes that made my stomach knot. Under Francesca's care, Miss Blossom had regained her weight and had even developed a sunny disposition.

Daddyboys was against purchasing Miss Blossom at first.

"I don't know, Frances," I remember him saying. "She's the right size for Sarah, but I don't trust that look in her eyes."

But I, in the odd way of some small children, had fallen in love with the ill-used pony, convinced that if I didn't have her for myself, no one would ever love her again.

"Please, Daddyboys? Oh, pleeease ..."

Francesca had been quietly studying Miss Blossom for some minutes while my father contemplated the matter. She stepped up to the mare's muzzle and blew softly into her nose. Miss Blossom snorted back, softly.

"Well, now, Clay, I appreciate your feelings. You know I do. But I have a sense about Miss Blossom."

Francesca's instincts about horses were similar to my father's own senses about machines. He bought Blossom without uttering another word.

Sitting in the saddle now, looking down at Blossom, I couldn't help but think how really great a horse she'd turned out to be. As we trotted down the gravel drive to the road, Francesca interrupted my thoughts. "Which way should we go?"

"Let's take the long way. I'm not too keen on seeing Isaac or Jacob."

"Does someone have a little crush on someone?" Her eyes were twinkling devilishly. I was no fool, even at that tender age. I deftly rerouted the conversation. "Daddyboys has a secret! I'd give dollars to doughnuts to know what it is."

Francesca pursed her lips slightly and turned things over in her mind for a moment or two. Then, "Yes, he's got something up his sleeve. You know, Sarah, there's more to your father than meets the eye. I wonder ... It's going to be an interesting couple of days."

She began to hum *La Vie en Rose* softly.

Chapter 3
Unexpected Delights

My family lived on a piece of land that had once been part of a much larger tract. Francesca's forebears had begun arriving in Lost Nation in the 1850's, having survived a treacherous migration from Essen, Germany. Their stories, which were handed down by the generations with assorted embellishments, were hair-raising and full of ingenious creativity.

Farmers they had been in the Old Country and farmers they would be in the New. With their detail-oriented industriousness, the German settlers, many of them Pittschticks, were soon enjoying a vigorous prosperity and did so for about seventy years. But then, the Great Depression hit hard.

The family dug in for a grim battle with the American economy but came up losers. Little by little, bits of land were sold off from the thousands of acres that had been Home Farm, until only the last twelve were left. With farming no longer a career option, the Pittschticks became mechanics and teachers and Presbyterian missionaries traveling into the darkest regions of Africa — and California — to spread the Gospel and save so-called lost souls.

By 1947, Francesca, Rachael and I were the only descendants left out of a once-thriving colony of cousins. Home Farm, as it was still called, was not jointly held by my parents; it belonged to my great-aunt and grandmother equally and would one day belong to my mother and me. As my Grandpap had been a Schneider and my dad a Morgan, they were not eligible to inherit.

This morning, Francesca and I rode along the western boundary of Home Farm on Thunder Ridge Road, the main drag into and out of Lost Nation. There was supposed to be an actual Thunder Ridge up in the hills somewhere, and I'd always wondered where it was and where the name came from.

My grandmother, who loved thunderstorms, with their great booming claps and corkscrew lightning bolts, insisted that those hills were the site of ghostly native rites. According to her busy imagination, long-dead Indians, their spirits keening and hollering, danced around spectral campfires. And it was true that whenever the thunderheads rolled in and draped our uplands in the purples and earth-tones of Apache blankets, I swore I could hear those phantoms in their celebrations.

RedBird was a whiz at anticipating Francesca's moods. With scarcely any prodding, she took the path that led down to the fishing pond. It was swim time!

We tethered the horses and stripped down to bathing suits. In a flash, I was up to my ankles in the chilly water, but no matter how quickly I moved, Francesca always seemed to get there a tad ahead of me.

I was what my grandmother called an "inch-by-incher," letting one part of my body at a time become accustomed to the shivery cool. Francesca (who had worn bathing suits under her farm clothes for decades) always dove right in head first, with little regard for the temperature of the day or the water. Never a fan of the Australian Crawl, she dog-paddled a little, and we started to splash one another, with me shrieking every time the icy droplets hit my still-dry back.

Suddenly, I glanced beyond Francesca and spotted what looked like a dead crow floating across the water. There was a rookery on our property, and since this was the time of year when fledglings were learning to fly, we found the noisy black birds — adults and youngsters — in the darnedest places. But this was the first one I'd ever seen in the pond.

Francesca took up the still form in her right hand and held it up to her ear like a sea shell.

"It's still alive," she said.

"Can we save it?" I asked.

Without answering, she waded over to the bank, took up her soft cotton shirt and gently dried the still body. Francesca peeked under its wing and discovered down, which meant this was not a crow at all but a baby raven.

"What should we do?" I asked.

Francesca determined we'd return to the house, where we could better tend the tiny, sopping survivor.

"Sarah, you carry it now."

This was an unwelcome surprise. I was not allowed, by parental edict, to touch any of the chick hatchlings, for fear I'd be too rough and hurt them somehow. At age five and in a fit of love, I had smothered one to death with my tender but heavy-handed caresses. What if something bad happened now?

When I felt prickling behind my eyes, I screwed my brows together and forced my eyes into slits to hold back the tears.

Reading my mind, Francesca put her free hand on my shoulder.

"It's time you left that nonsense behind. You, of all people, who wouldn't hurt a fly or eat a farm pet even if you were starving."

She looked into my eyes and smiled, but I didn't smile back. I took a deep breath and set my mind to the task.

Using a stump as a boost, I scrambled up onto Miss Blossom's saddle, finding the stirrups with my feet. Francesca handed me the baby raven, gathered up our clothes and hopped up on RedBird.

We started off, with Francesca leading Miss Blossom by her reins. I paid no mind to anything but that tiny living bundle cradled in my hands.

We rode onto Thunder Ridge Road and saw a cloud of dust closing fast. When I heard the rattle-a-tap of the truck, I realized that it must be Hunny Clack out early with the mail.

In the days before the war, Greely Clack had been the Postmaster of Lost Nation. When the draft scooped him up along with my father, they were sent to Camp Dodge, Iowa's only military training installation.

During the First World War, Camp Dodge had been one of sixteen national training centers and was deactivated shortly after the Armistice. But when World War II broke out, the federal government dusted the place off, swept out the mothballs, patched up the roofs and commissioned it as an induction center.

Daddyboys' tour of duty took place from 1942 to 1945, in the lower 48, mostly as the head mechanic of motor pools. He was happy enough doing what he loved to do, what he figured he'd been born to do. But his best friend had been restless.

As soon as Greely got through basic training, he requested a transfer, hoping to get to any place with some "real action." He was eventually posted to England, where he helped censor GI mail, mostly striking out any references to the soldiers' whereabouts. Greely Clack's ultimate task was to make sure General Eisenhower's D-day plans stayed a secret, and Greely Clack did his job. In the event any American mailbags fell into enemy hands, they wouldn't learn one single thing from correspondence passing under Clack's watchful eyes and black laundry marker.

With Greely overseas and Lost Nation needing a post person, Hunny applied for the job and got it. A small, round woman with a fresh-scrubbed complexion, her hair was honey-colored and usually hung in a fat braid to her knees. It was her crowning glory and the source of her nickname.

It took Hunny a while to comprehend the postal way of doing things, but eventually she mastered the job and enjoyed her independence and new-found standing in the community.
When Greely finally mustered out of the Army, it was impossible for Hunny to consider stepping back into the shadows. Instead, she declared she would share the job with her husband, who knew better than to object. And since the Census Bureau predicted Lost Nation's population would be increasing, the county Postmaster kept them both on.

Rattle-a-tap, RATTLE-A-TAP! The truck got louder as it got closer.

Although our exchange with Hunny Clack was less than two minutes, it seemed an eternity to me, and all I could do was stare at the little bird.

The window of her truck was already rolled down when she screeched to a stop alongside us. Peeking through instead of over the steering wheel, she waved and grinned.

"Hi ya," she called over the noise of the still-knocking engine. "you headin' back to Home Farm?"

Francesca nodded.

"Great! Can you take this with you? It's for Clay."

Francesca nodded again as Hunny handed a larger-than-normal envelope.

"It's special delivery. It must be important. Hope it's happy news."

As Hunny drove off with another cheerful wave, Francesca turned to me. "You know, Sarah, the war was a terrible thing for most people. But it was quite a boon for Hunny Clack. Hmmm ... I wonder if this ... has anything to do with your father's little game."

"Of course it does," I answered fake-nonchalantly, pretending to think about something other than the bird in my hand.

Francesca then said idly, "Would you say you were about as tall as Hunny Clack?"

"Gee, Francesca, she's practically a midget! I'm at least as big, probably bigger." I carefully shifted the baby raven from my right hand into my left. "Who'd write Daddyboys and have it be so important, and all?"

Francesca examined the envelope and noted the return address: New York City.

"We have relatives in New York," she observed.

"But if someone died, or something, wouldn't they telephone or send a wire?"

"Absolutely. How's that bird?"

"It's moving its claw, the right claw! What should I do?"

"Don't do a thing, Sarah. The life's coming back into it little by little. The legs will move next."

And they did.

We rode along like this all the way back to Home Farm. Hovering between panic and despair, I'd pester her by observing every tiny change in the raven's behavior. Francesca continued to assure me that everything was going along perfectly and not to worry. She had the patience of a tomcat stalking a lizard.

When we finally reached Home Farm, the raven was beginning to squirm. I was terrified I'd have to squeeze it to keep it from falling to the ground.

Francesca herded the horses into the paddock and ran into the house for a dish towel. She arranged it across the wicker table, and I carefully set the raven down on top of it.

It was beautiful, with feathers so glossy black they looked blue. It kept looking up at me, cocking its head quizzically this way and that, as if trying to make out the secrets of Home Farm ... of which there had certainly been a sufficiency that morning.

Francesca brought out a saucer of water along with an eyedropper and quenched its thirst in this way. "Now, it's up to the raven. We'll keep an eye on it, and I'll ask Rachael to watch it from the kitchen."

My mother wasn't the kind of person to take this type of duty very seriously. She seemed rather indifferent to animals and their feelings unless she was folding parts of them into pie dough. She wasn't cruel or unthinking; she was just so brisk and busy, up to her elbows in flour and mixing bowls and recipe cards.

I watched through the back door screen as Francesca spoke to Rachael with low tones and animated gestures, pointing in the direction of the raven. I snuck closer, so I could hear.

"It's important, Rachael. I want you to mind that bird and no nonsense."

Rachael nodded absently, and Francesca gripped her shoulders.

"Are you listening? I know this is your busiest day of the week. But if anything happens to that bird out there, I will make your life a misery. And you know I can do it."

This time, I saw Mother's eyes focus, and she shrugged off Francesca's hands. There was an odd expression on her face that met somewhere between annoyed and unnerved.

When my grandmother rejoined me on the porch, the raven was attempting to stand.

"I want to call him Humphrey," I said.

"You do?" She looked puzzled for a split second before saying, "Well, of course you do. Humphrey will be fine here for a while. Let's go find your daddy."

My father worked out of his garage, which was in reality just a drafty converted barn that sat at the southwest end of our property. Two driveways led to it from Thunder Ridge Road, one bypassing the main house completely so that we were seldom bothered by Daddyboys' customers.

A walk to the garage always took longer than expected, because Francesca stopped every few feet to examine a strand of sweet peas or a young bed of oregano, muttering mental notes to herself all the while.

"This one needs feeding. I'll have to pinch this back. Crikey! How did this get so dry?"

To her, gardening was like minding a brood of naughty children. Where Mommy cooed to and seduced her stove, Francesca scolded and praised her plants by turn, attempting to keep them in some kind of mystic balance.

Daddyboys was giving the once-over to Mr. Blackfeather's 1913 Ford. Everyone in Lost Nation was amazed that the ancient contraption still ran, but my father was a genius with all things motorized. When he swore he could fix an airplane engine with a screw driver and a coat hanger, most people believed him.

Mr. Blackfeather was Lost Nation's barber. His face was as fierce as any Indian chieftain's, making him quite a sight when wielding his straight razor. In fact, I often wondered why our neighbors trusted him to use that glistening blade so close to their necks. But as he was the only barber in Lost Nation and environs, they didn't have much choice.

As we approached the garage, I could hear the men talking.

"I know you can fix it, so you fix it," Mr. Blackfeather said with deliberate intention.

"It's not that simple, Tom. I just don't know where I can get the brake fittings I need."

"You'll get 'em. You will, because you always have. And if you can't get 'em, you'll get 'em anyway."

Tom Blackfeather loved that old collection of nuts and bolts. For years, my father had tried to talk him into getting a new car, or even just a newer car, one he could depend on. But Tom refused to contemplate such faithlessness. So the old black Ford kept breaking down, and my father kept patching it up.

Daddyboys sighed. "I can't get to it today, Tom. But if you can leave it with me, I'll start first thing in the morning."

"Okey-dokey. I brought Totem. I'll just ride 'im on home."

Totem was Mr. Blackfeather's paint pony. On any given day, you'd see it trailing along after the old Ford, connected by a long rope. Totem was a lot more dependable than the car and didn't seem to mind the cloud of gas fumes that spewed out from the exhaust.

As Tom swept out with a solemn nod to us, Daddyboys saw the package in Francesca's hand. His face changed color, paling noticeably.

"What is it?" he asked.

"It's from New York," Francesca answered.

"Open it! Open it!" I couldn't contain myself a second longer. Daddyboys took the manila envelope and turned it over gingerly in his hands, like it was filled with explosives. Finally, he held his breath and slit the flap open. Then, he smiled, a dazzling light-up-your-eyes smile that made you want to please him and hug him. Without a word, he folded the letter back up and began to hum an old favorite, "How You Gonna Keep 'Em Down on the Farm."

"Is someone gonna tell me what's going on here?" I asked rather bluntly.

But Daddyboys was lost in his private thoughts, meaning there would be no revelations from him until he decided it was proper.

I kicked up some dust on the dirt floor of the garage.

"Sarah!" Francesca shouted as she pulled me outside into the daylight.

"What?"

"Happiness is a treasure, Sarah, especially someone else's. It is therefore civilized behavior to think carefully before you set about spoiling it."

She took me firmly by the hand and walked me back to the porch, where Humphrey was showing signs of a complete recovery. He was about to become a moral lesson, though I'm sure he was ignorant of the fact.

"Let's take Humphrey as a for-instance," Francesca began. "What if your mother had been too busy or too unconcerned to watch him, and he'd fallen over the side of the table and been eaten by the Teems' cat?"

"Francesca!" I protested.

"It would have hurt you. Your mother realized this fact and took a little bit of care about it. Just a little bit of care is all that's required most of the time."

As you can see, Francesca used peculiar discipline. She never griped at me for not making my bed or for tracking mud across the kitchen floor or letting the screen door slam. Her concerns had more to do with spiritual tidiness. She gave me a walloping great hug and finished up with, "I love you, Sweetchild. You're going to grow up to be the cat's pajamas!"

Humphrey began some serious cawing. He seemed to be expecting some kind of answer. And sure enough, within a couple of minutes, he got one. It must have been his mother squawking back from the elm, obviously urging him to fly to her. Humphrey was still a little the worse for wear and moved like Joshua Teems after a jug of hard cider. But the mother bird persisted. Pretty soon, she was joined by a fistful of other adult birds, and they all began calling. Whenever Francesca started to approach Humphrey, they screamed at her to keep away. Humphrey became more and more agitated and finally flew up to join them. An immediate quiet settled down on Home Farm, which led me to think those ravens knew exactly what they were doing.

In fact, about three days later, the entire rookery gathered together and began to caw, just at sundown. Neither Francesca nor I had ever heard them do that before. We decided they were singing a psalm of thanks for the miracle of the return of their beloved brother Humphrey from the land of the dead. It gave me the goose bumps.

That night at dinner, Daddyboys came to the table dressed in a suit and tie and polished shoes! He brushed past Mommy several times and hummed into her ear. When he took her in his arms and began dancing her around the room, she decided she'd had enough.

"I'm tired of this mysterious behavior!" she said, using her hands for emphasis. "Staying up late at night; writing at all hours; singing French songs; wearing Sunday clothes, and now all this dancing. Clay! What is going on around here?"

My mother could be loud and physical on occasion. Frankly, it ran in the family. But my dad didn't pay any attention. He just smiled and shrugged himself loose from her grip. He went to the Victrola phonograph in the parlor and turned up the sound so we could hear a new Edith Piaf recording.

She was performing a tune she'd written in 1945 that went on to become known as her signature song. But for the life of me, I couldn't understand why my father was attempting to sing it now as he pirouetted across the room.

"*C'est toi pour moi, moi pour toi, dans la vie Tu me l'as dit ...*"

Then, he gathered up the tiny Eiffel Tower on top of the ice box and proceeded to place it ceremoniously in the middle of the trestle table. I figured he'd gone right around the bend, like his Aunt Beedie, who sometimes thought she was Catherine the Great.

Though my mother was clearly irritated, Daddyboys was not deterred; he kept right on dancing and singing:
"*It is you for me, me for you, in the life you said it to me...la vie en rose.*"
Then, my father began to laugh. It was a rumbling laughter that came right from his toes. He gathered Rachael up as easily as a doll and set her gently on a ladder-back chair. As he gathered himself together, we all waited excitedly for his news.

I held my breath. You could have heard a biscuit drop. Francesca sat calmly, but the flush on her cheeks betrayed her curiosity.

"Rachael, I've won a contest," Daddyboys beamed with delight.

"A contest, Clay?"

"Yes, a contest, in *World Travel* magazine. You know, sweetheart, the one you always pore over at Purdy's?"

My mother sighed in relief and clapped her hands. "And you've won a subscription for me; is that it? How lovely!"

"No ... not exactly. I won a trip to Paris."

The words hung suspended in the air. My mother seemed unable to speak for an eternity. "Paris. Paris, France?" she finally whispered.

"Umhmm. Paris, France. That's right; that's right! We'll make a stop in New York and then board the Queen Elizabeth, which will sail across the Atlantic all the way to Cherbourg, a lovely town in Normandy. Then it's on to Paree where we weel stay at a luxe otel," my father said with a hand flourish, using a French accent for emphasis. Then he fingered an imaginary moustache, puffed out his chest like a rooster and practically burst his shirt buttons.

"During the war, most of the great steamships were refitted to carry troops. Now, they're being reconverted, so, to generate interest in overseas travel, cruise ship lines have been running promotions, many in the form of contests. *World Travel* co-sponsored this publicity campaign, and I won it! I won a trip of a lifetime!"

Mommy sputtered, "This is why you've been prancing about? But how, I still don't ..."

"It was an essay contest: Dreams of Paris. Of course, I added a little something to my title ... I called it: Dreams of Paris, Dreams of Love."

"And you didn't tell me? Exactly how long have you known?"

"They wired a couple weeks ago, I guess. But it wasn't final until today." My father was still grinning. Then, Mommy got the giggles. She started laughing uncontrollably and holding her sides, pointing at my father and shaking her head. She tried to speak. "You ... essay ... Paris, France?" was about all I could decode before Mom had to run upstairs to the bathroom.

Daddyboys looked a little shaken by this response, so Francesca stood up and put her arm around his shoulders.

"No two ways about it, Clay ... I'm stunned. Obviously, Rachael is, too. But we're all proud, so very proud," she said, and she kissed him on the cheek. "Now, why don't you go on upstairs? I'll bet Rachael is settled down by now." Francesca gestured toward the staircase. "Go on," she said quietly.

Clay took the stairs three at a time.

Long into the night, I heard playful noises coming from the master bedroom. At one point, I even heard the unmistakable pop of a champagne cork. Now, you may think I didn't get a wink of sleep with all those goings-on. And you'd be right. But this celebration was better than sleep. It was like having the most wonderful dream while you were still wide awake.

Chapter 4
Bon Voyage

With only eight days left before my parents' departure, there were a million things to attend to. We actually had lists of lists. And let's not forget the blizzard of special delivery letters: one from Daddyboys to Mr. Toynbee at *World Travel*, formally accepting the award; another from Francesca to our relatives in upstate New York, telling them Clay and Rachael would be passing through; and still another to Great Aunt Maude and Great Uncle Harry, who were asked to visit and help out with Daddyboys' business ... not to mention keeping Francesca and me out of trouble. Fat chance!

Travel documents needed signatures; a money draft had to be drawn up and trip reservations needed verification. My parents would also linger an extra day in Manhattan to hammer out the rest of the "particulars" with the editors of *World Travel* before venturing across the pond.

Our usually silent phone didn't stop ringing. People we hardly knew called or stopped by, trying to sell my parents luggage, wallets, passport holders and cures for Montezuma's Revenge. Then, there was the constant stream of unsolicited advice: don't drink the water; watch out for pickpockets and don't spoil those European waiters and bellhops by over-tipping.

Daddyboys was clearly enjoying the spotlight. We did boast a pretty good newspaper in Lost Nation, the *Daily Pulse*. But in our tight-knit community, the grapevine was the fastest way to get the word out. I recall a time when word of mouth caused 1,000 people to gather at one of the neighboring farms to witness a gizmo dreamed up by a local. He'd designed it to pick up and drop mail sacks in one fell swoop. Apparently, he'd worked on the darned thing for nearly a decade. That was considered really big news.

These days, however, the folks just wanted to gaze upon the town's newest celebrity, whose face and prose would grace the feature page of a big-time magazine. While my father was basking in the radiance of his growing notoriety, Rachael also looked to be caught up in the excitement. This surprised me. For once, she didn't seem to care a whit about letting her beloved stove go cool for hours at a time.

She and Francesca also metamorphosed into each other's constant companions. Together, they redesigned and altered everything "decent" in my mother's closet at least twice.

Shopping trips were high on the list. Hats, gloves and shoes were waiting to be tried on and purchased, not to mention two new sets of suspenders in gray and blue for Daddyboys.

"And you need proper lingerie, Rachael," Francesca pronounced. "No daughter of mine is going to Paris without a few frilly underthings. They'll add to your confidence."

While my mother made a series of ruthless packing decisions, Daddyboys finalized arrangements for help at the garage while he was gone.

Uncle Harry would take on the occasional major mechanical problems. But my father also wanted to bring in someone who already knew the day-to-day ropes and could help Harry out with the nuts and bolts of routine maintenance. For that, there wasn't anyone better than Abraham Lancer, the solitary taxicab driver in Lost Nation as well as the head of the only black household.

Abraham often worked with my father during the winter months, when farm vehicles got their annual overhauls and the taxi business was slow. So it was decided; Abraham and Harry would be looking after things, with Uncle Harry expected to drive over from Des Moines in a couple weeks.

The idea of his visit, however, was sure to unsettle Francesca.

My Great Uncle Harry Schneider had lived a rather steady sort of life with just one or two major hitches in the proceedings. He was born and grew up on a large and successful farm across town from the Pittschtick place. Early on, all the boys in the county were well aware of the real treasures of Home Farm — two little girls who grew up to be Maude of the gorgeous face and Francesca of the regal limbs. Harry was no exception.

It was common knowledge that my Great Uncle was the catch of the county, being the eldest son from the wealthiest family in the area. He was an earnest, sober and patient man who early on showed a gift for both fixing machinery and fiddling with numbers. One thing was sure — he had no interest in farming and so would have to find his own way in the world.

It was impossible not to like Harry. He was not effusive, yet he got along famously with the highborn and the lowbrow. And for a time, Harry and Francesca seemed to be deeply and truly in love.

I wasn't there for the courtship but was told bits and pieces of the story many times. Everyone in Lost Nation had an opinion that colored their own incontrovertible set of "facts."

The tale in a nutshell: When sixteen-year-old Harry first noticed that the budding fourteen-year-old Francesca was no longer a child, she was receptive to his attentions. In a matter of weeks, they were considered "an item."

Like many young people in the throes of first love, the couple dated for the remainder of their high school years and even spoke about marriage and raising a family one day.

But Francesca was a most unusual woman for her time. She was determined to attend college instead of settling down immediately after graduation — an unheard-of choice for well-bred young ladies from Iowa farm communities. And to be honest, she was quite well known for her stubborn streak, along with an inclination to speak her mind.

Though older and more experienced, Harry was also much more traditionally minded than Francesca. And though he'd fallen head-over-heels for her, this intersection of character and circumstances caused a rift between the two. They had a rather noisy public falling out at Porter's Emporium on a May afternoon that sent them irrevocably on their separate ways. To my knowledge, neither ever disclosed the specific cause of the breakup, which remained a secret between them forever.

But Harry didn't leave our family circle altogether. Instead, he took up with the younger and less strident sister, Maude. It was the scandal to hit Lost Nation that year.

When it came time for Harry to choose a career, Maude made it abundantly clear she would not countenance becoming the wife of a "grease monkey."

That left Harry with only one choice, really — accounting.

After earning his degree, he married Maude and landed a good job with a large company in Des Moines. Within seven years, he'd started his own firm, and it seemed they were successfully settled into wedded life, if not exactly bliss.

Francesca had a "slogging, soul-searching" time, recovering from the heartbreak of losing her first love, but she went on to college, where she earned a Bachelor of Arts degree. While there, she soaked up a wide range of courses about the art and history of the big, wide world and slaked her hunger for knowledge of other cultures both ancient and contemporary.

She also eventually found comfort in the arms of another man, perhaps one who reminded her of Harry ... his younger brother, Joseph Robert, aka Cox or J.R.

Although Francesca married Cox and went on to enjoy a satisfying life with him, I know that Harry was never too far from her thoughts. Sometimes, I'd see a particular faraway look in her eyes, and I could tell just where she'd escaped to. And then, she'd tell a part of the whole sad story over again, as if by sharing one more time, she could somehow desensitize the jolting electric current of the memory.

Over the years and with a tremendous investment of time and energy, Harry's accounting firm became stunningly successful. At age 55, he was able to sell it for a tidy sum, allowing him and Maude to revel in a rather luxurious "semi-retirement."

But in a karmic twist of fate, Harry's innate love for engines of every description bloomed once again. He began to collect antique automobiles he delighted in restoring himself.

Needless to say, Maude was not thrilled by the ensuing turn of events. However, it did mean that Uncle Harry's "bent for incessant tinkering" (that was Maude speaking) would be perfect for the aging collection of cars and tractors to be found in Lost Nation.

"It'll be just like a vacation," he observed in his quiet way during a telephone conversation with Daddyboys.

* * * * *

By now, you have enough information to imagine the undercurrents when, without any warning, Maude arrived at Home Farm on Friday by herself. For Francesca, it was one lousy surprise, to put it gently.

I'd almost forgotten how fashionable Maude was, for an Iowa great aunt. She had a little way of draping a scarf or trimming a hat with pheasant feathers that reminded me of picture spreads I'd seen in movie monthlies like *PHOTOPLAY*.

Seeing her fashionable sister arrive unexpectedly like that, you could have toppled my grandmother over with a puff of smoke.

Francesca knew what was right. She was always more than happy to explain it to anyone who would listen. To be fair, she made a real effort to practice what she preached. But no amount of effort on Francesca's or Maude's part, however heroic, was going to make their coming together anything but strained.

My grandmother's eyes naturally lit up whenever she greeted Harry, but this business with her sister conjured up a whole different set of rituals.

"Maude, dear," my grandmother said unconvincingly.

The two women stood for a moment, stock-still, hesitant, and stiff. Then Maude hugged Francesca, whose arms remained at her sides. There was an air-kiss worthy of a couple of lock-jaw Connecticut debutantes, and Maude swept into the house, calling, "Rachael? Rachael, where are you?"

Right under Francesca's sniffing nose, Maude took Rachael firmly in tow, and my mother's wardrobe was made over yet again. This time, though, my mother seemed more pleased with the results, which rattled my grandmother.

Maude was a very sweet person. I thought her a little naive, but she was quite grand in her way and very artistic. In fact, she taught me to draw and broadened my appreciation for painting. I got along with her swimmingly. She sometimes put on airs, of course, but I always found the stories of her travels and lifestyle exciting. She and Harry had wandered a good bit through the years. They'd been to Europe, Canada, Mexico and toured extensively through California. They even had plans underway for a trip around the world.

Maude's experience made her very free with advice about what Rachael and Daddyboys absolutely must see and do during their "sojourn to the continent."

My grandmother's only trip outside Lost Nation had been her honeymoon with Cox to New York, so she had few observations to contribute during the animated exchanges. But Francesca still managed to make her feelings known.

She sat too quietly, studiously working on a needle-work pillow which read, "Silence is Golden." It was a pillow I had seldom seen before Maude's arrival and after her return to Des Moines, it vanished for good.

As Maude continued to expound, my grandmother continued to stitch, accompanied by little sighs.

On the eve of my parents' departure, Francesca organized a going-away celebration. She festooned the house with French sayings written on long pieces of butcher paper. She had studied the language in college and was pleased as punch to translate for everyone who would listen.

It seemed like the whole town turned out to wish Clay and Rachael a Bon Voyage. Uncle Harry even managed to make it over from Des Moines.

Of taste bud-tingling food, there was plenty, and a number of our friends and neighbors contributed to the feast.

Rachael made her famous fried chicken and steamed our entire first crop of asparagus. The Tycorns brought hand-churned ice cream; Mrs. Sweeny baked her double devil's food chocolate cake; and Abraham's family contributed candied yams that melted on the tongue. The Purdys provided a sugar-cured ham, and the Porters served German potato salad. I think they used dark lager in the dressing.

As for spirits, Joshua Teems brought a large barrel of hard cider, which the men drank neat and the women softened with lemonade.

Of course, no going-away party would be complete without gifts, and Hunny and Greely Clack had a special one to offer. They'd managed to put together a gigantic telegram, on extra-long paper, which was titled: "Lamour Toujours."

I wondered if this was a reference to Dorothy Lamour in the "Road" pictures. But Francesca, lording it over everybody, translated the message with full body movement: "Love Always."

Uncharacteristically, she was snippy about the missing apostrophe in the word, *l'amour,* and no one dared contradict her.

There was more company at the door.

It was Sheriff Daniel Mosley and his wife, Starr, who was Mr. Blackfeather's eldest daughter. Standing hunched over and hidden behind them was Daniel's older brother, Matthew, a barnstorming pilot who'd recently moved to Lost Nation to recuperate from a terrible plane crash. The poor man was a mess. There were crisscrossing stitches straight across and slightly underneath his hairline, set off by a gruesome set of bruises in various shades of purple and green. He was gaunt and slack-limbed, and his energy level dragged much like his broken leg. He limp-shuffled along, leaning heavily on a wooden cane.

Why anyone would drag a sad-faced man like that to a party was a mystery to me. He cast a definite pall over the festivities. We were all polite to him, of course. Francesca even attempted to draw him out a little. She had always possessed a compelling empathy for injured creatures of every description.

Thankfully, he had the presence of mind to keep to himself and spent most of his brief visit sitting on the porch, sipping from a hip flask. When the Mosleys left shortly after supper, the party breathed a collective sigh of relief.

I was not allowed to drink alcohol, but in all the confusion, I managed to sneak a gulp or two of that stomach-warming brew of lemonade and cider. At first, it made me giggle, but after the third guzzle, everything and everyone in the room had turned sideways. I squished myself into a corner and sat quietly for a while, trying to deep-breathe my way back to normal vision.

After dessert, Isaac Teems struck up some music on his fiddle, and Francesca joined him on the upright piano for a spirited rendition of one of her favorite popular songs, "Ac-cent-chu-ate the Positive."

Daddyboys also managed to get Rachael and Maude to sing a duet as he growled his way happily across their pretty harmonies on the song, "Don't Fence Me In," until the room exploded with laughter.

Francesca was forced to provide piano accompaniment or spoil the evening, which she could not bring herself to do. So she played the song as properly as she could with clenched fists.

The evening ended with my father waltzing my mother around the living room to the tune of "*La Vie En Rose.*" They were lovely, like newlyweds. It must have been just like the first time they ever danced together, and I got a little lump in my throat watching them.

My parents looked fine side by side — the tall, thin, broad-shouldered man and the small, plump blonde woman. I realized that my parents were in love. It was something I had never considered before, picturing them in a romantic way. Suddenly, I understood that they had a deep feeling for one another that had very little to do with me.

Without warning, I burst into besotted tears. The combination of hard cider and the realization that my parents were leaving for a wonderful adventure without me was just too much.

Mommy rushed over and hugged me, and Daddyboys said maybe it was time little ones should be in bed. He scooped me up and carried me to my room, cradling me tenderly in his arms. They undressed me as I hiccoughed and sobbed and waited at the side of my bed until I quieted down.

As I began to fade off, I heard my mother say, "She looks so small, doesn't she, Clay? I'll miss her terribly." And then, I was asleep.

* * * * *

I still felt dizzy and queasy the next morning as I eased myself gingerly out of bed. I found Francesca in the kitchen with my parents and Great Aunt and Uncle gathered around the dining table. They were looking over the checklists one more time, giving a final look-see to passports, travel arrangements, phone numbers and the magazine's address.

"Good morning, Sarah dear," said Francesca, without looking up. Then to Daddyboys, "Do you have your money? Now, you be careful with that. There are pickpockets all over the big cities these days!"

Turning to look at me for the first time, she asked, "Sarah, what on earth? Are you feeling ill?"

"I'm fine," I mumbled. Everyone was now giving me "the look" — very much like the one doctors display when confronted by an interesting diagnosis. Aunt Maude poured me a glass of orange juice, which tasted just right to my dry mouth but gurgled down in my stomach.

Francesca went on, "Perhaps you should consider a money belt, Clay."

"Don't be silly, Francesca," Maude broke in. "Paris is a very civilized place."

"So was Ancient Rome, and look at what went on there!" Francesca pointed out and went on with the list. "Take some American bathroom tissue. Yes, you'll need it; believe me. Do you have your motion sickness pills and your tickets? I think that does it."

My stomach was still leaping and swaying when Mother shouted from the front door: "The taxi's coming!"

Maude and Harry were also leaving but would be back in two weeks. That made saying good-bye even harder. I clung to my parents tightly and started to cry again. In a soothing manner, Daddyboys promised to bring me presents from Europe and reminded me of the amazing adventures I would have with Francesca.

That turned out to be the second biggest understatement of 1947.

With a last volley of waves, they were all gone.

Francesca and I looked at one another for a moment before I dropped my chin to my chest.

"Look at me, child," my grandmother said softly. "Mark my words; it's going to be one helluva of a summer."

Chapter 5
Surprise Visitors

Lightning bolts sizzled across the sky, and the rain poured down in buckets as a string of thunderstorms hit Lost Nation near the end of June. The weather delighted Francesca. She would stand on the porch, watching the spectacle, breathing deep, letting her soul soak up the cool. Inside, as she cleaned and cooked, she hummed to herself in rhythm with the rolling claps of thunder.

These were the days when any self-respecting child had to get busy thinking of ways to entertain herself.

In the front parlor, next to the large stone fireplace, my grandfather had built an indoor-outdoor wood box. Under the eaves of the house, a substantial pile of firewood was always stacked, dry and ready for use. This was an efficient storage arrangement in a place where unexpected snow clouds could breeze in and unload in a matter of a few minutes.

At this time of year, the tin-lined wood box was empty. On drizzly days, I'd spread a comforter, open the outside door and laze away the hours, reading or just watching the massive cloud formations roll through. Now that I was almost ten, my little haven had grown cramped. But it was still a good way to pass the daylight hours that were too wet for outdoor activity.

I was an avid and precocious reader. That summer, I had taken a serious step up in material, thanks to Francesca's enthusiastic ministrations.

She'd graduated from the State University of Iowa, one of the most forward-thinking schools of its time. State U was the first public university in the country to admit men and women on an equal basis. It was also the world's first university to accept creative work in the arts (including literature) on an equal basis with academic research. It was just the kind of environment in which Francesca could thrive.

Even after she'd married Cox and rerouted her energies into gardening, her tremendous respect for and love of the written word was always a hallmark of her happiness. She made sure she passed these feelings down to me. Starting on my fifth birthday, she'd drive me once a week to the library, and we'd pick out children's stories and biographies together.

I was currently working my way through *A Tale of Two Cities*, a historical novel by Charles Dickens set in Europe during the French Revolution. Francesca had carefully explained the many threads of plot which the author wove expertly in and out of the fabric of his writing. I was madly in love with Sidney Carton, that heroic ne'er do well and pictured myself as Dr. Manette's hapless daughter, Lucy, saucy ringlets and hoop skirts included.

I was gazing adoringly into the gun metal sky at an imaginary portrait of Monsieur Carton when a sudden gust of wind began slamming the outside door of the wood box. The noise jolted me back to Lost Nation from the Bastille. In fact, I was so startled that I hit my head hard on the wood box ceiling. But even the sharp pain I felt was instantly forgotten when I noticed an animal the size of a fox and about the same color red digging in the garden.

No. Not a fox. A dog! A little red dog!

It was obviously having a whiz-bang time and seemed to relish the destruction of Francesca's prize roses. I took out after it, yelling and waving my arms like a lunatic — straight into the middle of a particularly heavy downpour. Nobody but Francesca dared touch those bushes, because they had been brought over from the Old Country more than a hundred years ago. The stupid creature was killing a family heirloom!

After a minute or two, I managed to shoo it out of the side yard and across the property, where it disappeared into the curtain of rain. Then, the front doorbell rang.

Sheriff Daniel Mosley had a presence that filled up most doorways. He was a tallish, well-built man with dark hair and light eyes. He sported a trim moustache, and his boots were always see-your-face polished.

Daniel and Francesca had carried on a mild flirtation for years, each referring to their relationship as a "mutual admiration society." Since the sheriff was obviously happily married and Francesca was also at least 15 years older than he, Daniel's wife remained untroubled by a little innocent fun.

"Daniel, what a nice surprise," Francesca said happily. "For Heaven's sake, take off that wet coat. Hang it there on the hook. Sarah, get us all some bath towels, and try not to puddle so much."

We settled comfortably in the kitchen, where Francesca poured out two mugs of coffee. She automatically put cream and sugar in front of Daniel. Remembering little preferences like that was one of her gifts.

"You still have the best legs in the county, Frances," Sheriff Dan said.

"It's a little hard to tell in this get-up, Daniel. And I'm sure you didn't canoe all the way out here on this frightful day to talk legs. Though, of course, I'm always enchanted to hear your expert opinion."

"Truth is," Daniel said, looking more serious, "I got some information over the wire this morning, and I thought you should hear it personally. An arsonist named Eisenstaedt escaped from the Anamosa State Penitentiary sometime yesterday — nobody knows exactly when. He might've gotten away in a meat supply truck, of all things, and he could be heading this way. Seems he spent some time here years back and may still have family in the area. We're looking into that now."

I wasn't familiar with the word "arsonist," so the sheriff explained it was someone who set fires on purpose.

He continued, "The two of you are living out here alone for most of the summer, and I got to thinking about it ... and ..."

"I can certainly handle a gun, Daniel, if it comes to that," Francesca said.

"I know it. I've seen you shoot skeet. But I'm a little worried about you two all the same. Home Farm is pretty isolated, you know. I hate to think something bad might happen to a woman with the best legs in the county. It might just ruin my day."

They grinned at each other.

Dan sipped his coffee and was silent for a moment. Then, he shifted in his chair. "My brother, Matthew ... well, you met him ..."

"Yes," she answered. "That poor man."

"Well ... He's going to be here awhile, visiting. Can't fly, you see, till he's healed up. He's been staying with Starr and me, but I think he might do better ... that is ... you two'd be a lot safer if he came to stay out here. Just for a while. To keep an eye on things ..."

Francesca raised her right eyebrow.

Sheriff Dan headed her off at the pass. "He wouldn't be in your way. You can see he's a quiet one, and he'd only have to stay until we find Eisenstaedt." He cleared his throat and took another sip of coffee.

I could see Francesca "cogitating." She was an independent woman and proud of it. But she wasn't stupid.

"When he's healthy, does he look anything like you?" she asked.

Sheriff Mosley laughed. "Well, most folks say he got the handsome in the family."

Francesca walked over to the kitchen sink and stared out the window.

"I'll be expecting him this afternoon," she said.

A brooding, injured stranger was coming to visit. For how long, nobody knew. While I wondered what that would be like, Francesca was more concerned about where he would stay.

The Main House at Home Farm was a rambling two-story dwelling with seven bedrooms and three bathrooms. Three of the bedrooms were rarely used, in an effort to cut down on housekeeping chores.

"Why can't he use the downstairs guest room?" I asked. It was light and airy with an inviting featherbed atop an antique four-poster.

Francesca said she thought he might need some privacy. "And it might not seem proper. You know how the townspeople are here, Sarah, nannygabbers, many of them. He may be Daniel Mosley's brother, but he is, after all, an unmarried man. It might not look ... appropriate," she concluded.

"Appropriate" was a favorite word of Francesca's, especially when she was prepared to explain only half of something I wanted to know more about. It meant that no matter how I wheedled her, I couldn't make her cough up the real skivvy. So I busied myself helping Francesca prepare the Bridal Cottage for our new houseguest.

In the old days, it was customary for the Pittschticks to invite their newlywed children and spouses to live at Home Farm. Family was everything; the more the merrier is how they looked at it. So with each new marriage, a snug new home was built. When children came along, a room was added to the couple's cottage. Of course, not everyone stayed, and as people moved or died, lodgings changed hands. Most of these "bridal cottages," as they were called, had been sold along with the land after the Depression. But we still had one. It was located between Main House and Daddyboys' garage. It hadn't been used for years, so there was no telling how many pounds of spider webs and dust would have to be scoured away.

Clay and Rachael and I had lived in the cottage from the time I was born until my grandfather, Cox, passed away. Francesca was lonely and had insisted we move into the big house with her to "take up some of the silence."

The cottage drifted into neglect. My grandmother was convinced, however, that we could bring it back to life, just like Jesus did with Lazarus.

The rest of the day was spent lugging mops and pails and boxes of soap flakes through the rain. I'm sure we tracked as much mud in to the place as we mopped up. You could write your name in the dirt on the windows, which I did five or six times. We chased out some mice and cleared what seemed like a wheelbarrow of dried animal droppings. Some of the cobwebs were five feet long and made my skin crawl when I ran through them. But I did it just the same, screaming like a banshee from the nerve-tingling pleasure.

"Sarah! The mice have gotten to this coverlet. Be a darling girl, and fetch me another from the linen closet." This entailed running to Main House, which meant tracking in more mud, which then needed to be mopped up.

It took about three more hours to get the cottage spic and span, but it was worth the effort. The woodwork fairly glowed. Francesca put her thin arms around my shoulders and hugged me as a reward for a job well done.

Bark! Bark! Just as we finished up, we heard the unmistakable sounds of a dog. It was my little destroyer of heirloom roses, back for another assault! For some reason, it was running crazily around the yard in circles, yapping and yapping. As we ran to Main House, it followed us. Right up the porch stairs. Looking ever so bedraggled, it stood there wagging its tail, flinging muddy droplets all over us with every swish.

"It's some stupid old dog and he's after your roses and I've tried to chase him away, but he won't go! Stop it, you stupid dog!"

"Hush, Sarah."

I swear the dog stopped barking and sat down.

"What a good girl," Francesca went on quietly as she cautiously approached the stray. "That's a good girl. No one will hurt you. Here, girl. Come here, girl."

And the dog went right over to my grandmother and sat on her shoe. Francesca took the dog's face into the palm of her hand and examined it, looking into its deep brown eyes. How often I'd seen her commune with animals in that way.

My grandmother guessed the dog was about a year old. "It could be part herding breed with a touch of Labrador," she mused. "Look at the fine black hairs sprinkled across her back."

To me, it looked like a mutt and nothing but a mutt.

"A very special mutt," she said and added the dog was smart as a whip and possibly a good swimmer. "See the webbed paws?"

Where had she come from? Francesca and I'd never seen her before, and we knew all our neighbors' pets.

Francesca blew softly into the dog's snout. It made a joyful yelping noise and stood on its hind legs, bracing against Francesca's pant leg.

"Sarah, I think this dog wants something from you."

"From me? You're the one she's pawing. She doesn't even like me. She practically bit me earlier."

Francesca drew her eyebrows together. "Perhaps it was a simple misunderstanding. No collar. Hmm. Well, if we're to do the right thing by her, we'll have to call her something. Why don't you name her? I think she'd like that."

"Why should I? Muddy old thing."

"Be my Sweetchild."

There it was — her big weapon. It wasn't fair using that pet name, as it put me at a disadvantage. It was blackmail.

"Penny?" I offered grudgingly. "How about calling her Brandy? Maybe we could call her Pepper or Tracey?"

Francesca shook her head once, no.

"Then, how about calling her Babe?" I asked.

Oddly enough, my grandmother was keenly interested in a half dozen great athletes. Her two favorites were Il Bambino, The Sultan of Swat, and Babe Dedrikson Zaharias.

Bambino, better known as Babe Ruth, was a gifted New York baseball player, acclaimed for his home run-hitting power, as well as his feisty personality and enormous appetites. Zaharias was a versatile champion, achieving outstanding success in a number of sports, most particularly swimming.

So the name "Babe" was by way of being appropriate.

"Here girl. Here, Babe," I ventured. To my utter astonishment, the little red dog trotted over to me and sat down on my left shoe. I melted. And so "Babe" it would be.

Just then, we heard the rumble of an automobile. A long, fancy, silver vehicle pulled onto the gravel drive from Thunder Ridge Road.

Our houseguest had arrived.

Francesca walked over to greet him. I followed close behind, my new best friend at my heels.

Chapter 6
Unfamiliar Territory

It was a glorious machine — long, sleek and meticulously polished. It certainly hadn't been left out in the rain. Even from where I was standing, I could appreciate the depth of the perfectly painted silver-gray metal.

Francesca motioned him to a spot behind the house under the elm.

Matthew Mosley looked just as broken-down and diminished as he had at Mom and Dad's party. If anything, I noticed his skin had developed a definite pallor underneath his tan, the mark of a body whose caretaker was careless.

He was neatly dressed; his shirt and trousers had seen an iron recently. One pant leg was split below the knee to accommodate the cast. His energy was low, and his vitality seemed pent-up, like a sleeping tiger. You could sense the raw power hidden deep inside. Even at my age, it was impossible not to be aware of the strength that was, for the moment, disguised by the fragility of the man.

He was better-looking than Sheriff Dan, but only just. Matthew was slightly finer-featured, with more elegant bone structure. He had the same general coloring, brushed here and there with gray. His eyes were pale like his brother's, but Matthew's were dulled by pain, and there were worry creases etched in his forehead.

He didn't appear at all grateful about his new home. In fact, he acted downright sullen.

Francesca didn't appear terribly concerned and behaved in her usually gracious manner. She actually opened his car door.

"We've decided to put you in the Bridal Cottage. You'll have more privacy there," she said.

No comment.

"It's down this gravel drive. Perhaps you'd like to park closer to the cottage to unload your things? It's the first building you'll see on your right ...," she gestured.

No comment.

I was still gawking at the car.

"What in the name of heaven is this?" I spoke my enthusiasm out loud. "It's ... too much!" I tap danced around the classic auto, touching the chrome and looking at my reflection in the glistening paint job.

Francesca held out her hand. "Welcome to Home Farm."

Matthew looked at it like it was radioactive. She drew it back like it was on fire. They stared at each other for a long, long minute.

"Afternoon," he finally mumbled. I decided he reminded me of Gary Cooper — the strong, silent type.

He shifted his weight from the left foot to the right. "I won't need any help, Mrs. Schneider, or anything to eat later."

He then turned to me and said, "It's a Duisenberg, from Germany."

* * * * *

We watched from Main House porch as Matthew hobbled back and forth, unloading his suitcases and a few boxes. His cast rendered him unsteady.

I went into the kitchen for a glass of sweet tea.

"Babe, come back here!"

It was too late. She had slipped out the screen, run across the yard and grabbed Matthew's pant leg, growling like a tiger.

When he tried to kick her away, he fell on his backside and into a mud puddle. Though he'd missed her by a mile, Babe hightailed it back to the porch, her tail now between her legs.

That made me angry. "Did you see ...?" I started in a huff.

"Yes, my child," Francesca responded soothingly. "You have to take into account each animal's pain and treat them both accordingly." Then, she turned her face away, and I saw her shoulders quiver, her head bobbing up and down.

Matthew had finally stood up, with a third of him covered in black ooze. He did look comical. But never mind! I thought our houseguest was mean. "Babe is just a puppy. He could have hurt her. He better be planning on taking his meals alone."

"He's probably depending on it," Francesca said. But she wound up cooking dinner for three just the same.

Francesca had always prepared food with gusto. No careful measuring for her — a handful of this and two dashes of that! She was a very good cook but not a great one. With some things, like chicken and dumplings, she excelled. But after Grandpap died in '43, she lost her appetite for several months, and her love of all things kitchen disappeared with it. At the time, it seemed only natural that Mother should take up the slack. Rachael had always adored the odors and rigors of the kitchen and had somehow mastered the great black stove, a feat Francesca had given her little help with.

For some reason, that night was different. Francesca had a new zeal, or maybe it was a return of the old calling. And her meal would not disappoint; the chicken was crisp, the dumplings light as air and the country gravy smooth and creamy.

As Francesca bustled capably, I figured it was time to peek in on Matthew Mosley. Dinner wouldn't be for a while, and I wanted to know more about this mysterious man. At least that's how I convinced myself it would be alright to spy.

From the cottage window, I watched him unpack, placing only one article of clothing in the closet or bureau at a time.

When he finished, he set up a small portable phonograph near the fireplace and mixed himself a drink. He stirred something into the Coca-Cola. With the window closed, it was difficult to hear the music, but it sounded like "Sentimental Journey." He must have liked it a lot, because he replayed it five more times as he continued to sip and stare into space.

When I had enough spying for that evening, I went back to the house, where Francesca was already setting the table. When she asked me to run over and invite Mr. Mosley to dinner, a tinge of guilt came over me but not enough to tell on myself.

Matthew was still playing the phonograph, but this time it was a different song, something about a "Buttermilk Sky." I peeked through the screen door and saw him gimping around. Then, without preamble, he howled like a wounded animal. I heard the sound of glass tinkling to smithereens on the oak floor, accompanied by some inventive cursing. In fact, he strung a few words together I'd never heard before.

I curled my toes, took a deep breath and tapped lightly on the door. I swallowed and whispered that supper was ready.

No answer.

I tapped again, slightly louder this time.

He opened the door with a bang.

"Yes! What is it?" he snarled. I could see shards of glass splayed out behind him alongside an empty bottle. I was unnerved.

"Uh, my ... a ... grandmother ... she made some supper. She ... that is, we thought ..."

Then, I froze and just stood there. He stared through me. I wanted to run, but I couldn't make myself move.

Then, he looked down on me and suddenly no longer seemed angry. I mean, it was like a curtain swooped down — boom! It was like snapping your fingers, and a different guy popped out.

"Supper? Yes. Hey, about the dog, I ... that is ... Supper sounds nice. Let me just wash up, and I'll be along," he finished, almost gently.

Dinner was exceptionally quiet. When Daddyboys was home, we would play silly games.

Matthew wasn't the game-playing type. He shoveled his food, barely taking time to taste any of it. He didn't say anything at all during our meal, even when prodded quietly by Francesca. When he finished, he stood up, rinsed off his plate and put it in the sink.

"Excuse me," was all he said. Out the back screen door he went. Slam! Just like that.

Babe had stayed clear of Matthew during dinner but now returned to the kitchen to be with Francesca and me. Within a matter of seconds, we had developed one super-duper case of the giggles. It's something that runs in our family, and once we start, we can't stop. Every word, sigh or movement becomes another trigger for increasingly loud laughter. We had worked all day and were bone-weary. Dealing with the tension Mr. Mosley carried around with him was the straw that broke the camel's back.

Our eyes were wet with tears, and I even accidentally spurted a mouthful of milk at Francesca. Babe licked it up off the floor, which caused me to nickname her the "Vacuum Cleaner." That set us off again. We left the dishes until morning.

* * * * *

Francesca and I lay across her bed together, watching the moon hang like a pearl in the black velvet night.

I wondered if my mother and father were looking at it, too.

"They're probably drinking champagne and dancing the tango," Francesca said. "They've been sitting at the Captain's table, I'm sure, as they are celebrities of the cruise."

All at once, I missed them terribly and sniffled twice, which caused Francesca to stroked my hair.

"We'll have our own adventures," she offered.

"As good as Paris?" I sniffled again.

"Indeed," she whispered.

We spent the next few minutes writing down a list:

I was going to learn how to drive.

"Really?"

"You're definitely tall enough. Let's see ... We could look for Thunder Ridge and catch the Indian spirits dancing."

"I don't see how. No one else ever found them."

"Ah, but we're not ordinary mortals." She touched my nose.

"And we could forget about doing chores for a day or two."

"No *chores*?"

"I ask you ... what's an adventure with chores?"

I could have schemed like that all night, but Francesca said it was time for me to brush my teeth and get ready for bed.

"Where will Babe sleep tonight?" I asked innocently.

With a serious tone, Grandmother offered several solutions, including tying the dog outside on the porch. I didn't like any of the ideas.

"Sarah, where do you think Babe should sleep?" She knew exactly how I would respond.

"On my bed. Just until we can build her a doghouse and get her settled. I'll put a sheet over the covers, so ..." I said, grinning, "... no dog hairs."

Francesca pretended to be surprised by this solution. She blew me a kiss and gently reminded me that we needed to try and find Babe's owners.

"We'll post some signs and ask around tomorrow," Francesca said and closed the door to my room.

Suddenly, the thought of losing this little dog, this mutt, left me heartbroken.

Maybe no one will claim you. I love you, little red dog.

Chapter 7
New Confrontations

By the time Babe shot out through the screen door the next morning, Francesca was already sitting in her glider, sipping freshly made coffee. The kitchen was spotless.

"I would have helped you," I said as gave her a hug.

Francesca shook her head. "It was clean when I got down here this morning."

Daddyboys would have said the "Dish Fairy" had dropped by. Mr. Mosley didn't look anything like a dish fairy. However, some things didn't deserve too much attention, especially when we were about to launch into our first Wild And Amazing Adventure. WAAA!

As we had determined the night before, Francesca called Abraham's son, Lincoln, to help out with the chores.

* * * * *

You can never tell when any old ordinary moment is going to run haywire.

My heart was racing. I had been taught, reminded, schooled, educated and warned not to get behind the wheel of any vehicles on our property, especially the ones in Daddyboys' shop. But Grandmother insisted it was time I learned to drive.

"What if I bash it, or something?"

"We'll cross that divide when we hurtle through it."

"Have you ever taught anyone how to drive before?"

"You're my first victim."

I sensed a recipe for disaster but said nothing as we walked toward the Dodge pickup. Babe jumped in first and plopped herself on the passenger side.

The truck was old, Francesca explained patiently, and already had more than its share of dents, so I wasn't to worry. She drove to an open pasture near the fishing pond, carefully explaining all the mysterious workings as we bumped along.

"This is the gear shift. Of course, you can't get into gear without engaging the clutch. This is the clutch, you see. It's right next to the brake pedal."

I examined the equipment I was supposed to maneuver but wasn't sure my legs would be able to reach.

"You push it in with your left foot, firmly but slowly," Francesca went on. "And this is the accelerator pedal. It makes the car go forward. Except, of course, it doesn't work that way when you're in reverse. Try not to confuse third and reverse gears, or we'll be leading with our gluteus maximus."

I'd watched my parents drive oodles of times and always imagined how nifty it would be to toddle down the highway with the air blowing through the wind wing and the radio blasting. But the reality was intense.

Of course, Francesca was not fazed and continued her litany: First, second and third gear. It's a snap.

"Now, to drive, you use your right foot for the accelerator and the brake, but squeeze; don't pump. It's just like your father's 410 over-and-under trigger." At this point, Francesca's mind veered at a right angle.

"That reminds me," she said, "I need to get that gun out of storage and clean it. I guess I'll have to start keeping it under my bed." Then, her thoughts leaped back to the task at hand. "Well, I think that's it. Now, you try it."

She had me rest on her lap, so I could reach the pedals. My arms were twitching. I could barely see through the windshield. Francesca nudged me and whispered she would help me.

Turning the ignition on wasn't too bad. Okay ... okay.

"Push the clutch in, and shift it into first," Francesca said calmly.

The horrible grinding sound sent chills up and down my spine, and the truck bucked like a champion bull. Babe yowled and tried to crawl under the seat. I yanked the door open and jumped out, accidentally kicking Francesca's shin as the engine died.

She tilted her head down at me and said soberly, "I believe you were in the wrong gear. Let's try it again."

The last thing I wanted to do was to get back into the truck but she called me "Sweetchild." And you know how that goes.

After an hour or so, I was starting to get the hang of it. In fact, I was doing so well that Francesca thought it was time to venture away from the field onto the driveway. Still struggling with the pedals I could barely reach, I looked down just for a second. That's when it happened.

CRASH!!

The jolt, however, was nothing compared to the explosion out of Mr. Mosley's mouth. He'd pulled into the property at the worst possible moment.

"Dammit! What in the most fired blazes of Hell do you two think you're doing? Son of a bitch if I'm not one!" He yelled a ton of other things — including some of those interesting, unfamiliar phrases he'd used before.

When I saw Mr. Mosley get out of his car, I slunk down onto the floor of the truck next to Babe.

"Jesus have mercy on me! I have driven this car all over this country. Nothing ever happened to it before! How could you be so careless? So stupid!"

Francesca wasn't above railing at her own family on certain occasions, but she couldn't stand for someone else to do it.

"There's absolutely no reason to behave like a screaming Mimi. It was an accident," Francesca defended me. "And the damage ..." She bent over and peered dramatically at the offending mark, "is miniscule."

"Why in the Hell were you letting that child drive in the first place? It's asinine ... completely asinine!"

Grandmother swallowed some anger before responding calmly.

"It is the custom hereabouts, to introduce young people to the mysteries of driving early. The practice has saved many lives in an emergency and will doubtless save many more!"

This was an exaggeration and Matthew called her on it.

"Bull!" he fumed.

That's when they had their first stare-down. Francesca always won these competitions, even when she broke away first. It was uncanny.

She took on a statue-like stillness. He started strong, refusing to give in. Finally, with three deep breaths, she condescended to speak to him. "We apologize for the state of your car. But you have to admit, the dent is practically unnoticeable. It was an accident, purely and simply. Is there anything else?" Francesca asked. Her voice warned him there had better not be.That sent Matthew storming off.

Babe and I hid in the wood box for an hour or so. That's when I overheard Francesca on the telephone.

"It's just not going to work out, Daniel. I can appreciate...That's not fair, Daniel. You know that I couldn't ... You don't understand ... But he ... but I ... oh, brother. Okay! I'll give it one more *week*," Francesca said, slamming down the receiver for emphasis.

I opened the wood box door. "Are we getting rid of him?" I asked hopefully.

Francesca didn't even hear me, as she was talking heatedly to herself.

"What a baboon! The man's insane, gone completely round the bend and will never return. And his brother isn't any gift, either."

She clattered the dishes as she put them away and slammed the cupboard doors as she continued ranting: "It was an accident!"

Bang! More clatter.

"The way he spoke to me!"

Another Bang!

"The way he spoke to you!"

Clash! Bang!

"How did I ever let myself get into this?"

Clatter! Bang! Now, she was working on the pots and pans.

"Matthew and Daniel Mosley can both go straight to Hell!"

Bang!

I sat silently, waiting for Francesca to calm down, as I knew she eventually would. She wasn't one to hold a grudge ... unless Maude was involved.

"Maybe we can have Lincoln fix the dent in Matthew's car," I suggested, when relative calm had been restored to Home Farm.

"I suppose so, although it's more than that cretin deserves," she sniffed.

Lincoln didn't think the dent would be too much trouble.

"Sure is a shame someone marked up this beautiful car," Lincoln remarked with a grin. "Look here, hardly even scratched the paint. You must have been travelin' kinda slow."

A plumber's helper was all that was necessary to make the car like new again. Save for the few scratches we waxed out, you couldn't even tell the Duisenberg had been hit by a delinquent child driver.

* * * * *

When the mail came, a little past noon, there was a letter from the Waldorf Astoria in New York City, one of the most famous hotels in the world.

> *Dear Frances and Sarah,*
> *How we love you both and miss you dearly...*
> *The traffic never seems to stop here. You awaken to its rhythm in the early morning and it rocks you to sleep at night. Your mother and I became instantly accustomed to the sounds and hardly notice them after only 20 hours!*
> *The smells overtake you on every street corner, where small groceries, called "delicatessens" flourish, selling exotic delights from many cultures.*
> *The city is patrolled by men on horseback and your mother and I took a ride through Central Park in a hansom cab, pulled by a sweet-coupled bay ...*
> *We set sail tomorrow.*
> *Love to you both, from our hearts to your hearts.*

After reading the letter two or three times, I folded it carefully and put it into my treasure chest. I still have all the letters I received from my parents that summer.

I wasn't so keen on our next chore. It was time to post notices around and about that we had found a small, reddish female dog. The good news was there would be no truck-driving lessons for me today.

Instead, we saddled up RedBird and Miss Blossom and ambled down the highway, nailing the flyers on telephone poles and fence posts as we went.

I fastened mine where I thought it would be difficult, if not impossible, for anyone to see. Francesca noticed but said nothing.

When we returned to Main House, Matthew Mosley's car was gone, an occasion for gentle rejoicing on my part.

Since Lincoln was still at the house doing chores, we invited him to have lunch with us — left-over chicken and mashed potato sandwiches — open-faced ones. Although this was a common meal in Lost Nation, I haven't seen it anywhere else. Their loss!

As the afternoon heat swelled, it was time for a swim. Using the shortcut, Francesca beat Babe and me to the pond. As per usual, she dove in head first while I wriggled in one inch at a time. Babe delighted in the water, too, slapping at it with her paw, barking as she played.

It was the perfect, glorious, lazy afternoon. Nearing sundown, we dozed underneath the oak, letting the warm air dry us. It was positively paradise ... or so it seemed.

At first, I thought I was imagining it, since Francesca didn't stir. It felt like someone was watching us.

What was that?

I heard a twig snap. That's when Babe took off barking, tearing in the direction of the escalating noise. It sounded like someone stomping quickly through the undergrowth. I started to go after Babe, but Grandmother grabbed my arm.

We gathered our things and made our way back to Main House as quietly and quickly as possible. But just a short distance from the house, we heard another sound, this one sharper and much closer. We froze.

Francesca took my hand and silently mouthed one word to me, pointing toward the house, "Run!"

As I took off, someone jumped into the clearing, aiming a twenty gauge at me. I started screaming.

"It's okay, Sweetchild," Francesca said, running up to me to hold me.

It was Matthew.

"Are you two alright?" he asked as he walked over to us.

In a month of Sundays, I never thought I would have been relieved to be startled by Matthew Mosley holding a weapon.

"Someone was here," Francesca explained.

Matthew nodded. "Yep. Last I saw, Babe was chasing after a man, heading toward Lost Nation. I whistled her up, but I couldn't get her attention. Ah, here she is."

Babe trotted over to me and sat down in a puffing heap. I knelt and hugged her hard around the neck.

"Good girl! What a good girl!" I looked up at Matthew and took a deep breath. "Was it the man that burns houses?"

"Could be."

"Do you think he'll be back?" Grandmother asked.

"Well, I made sure he saw me with my shotgun. That ought to discourage him. Just the same, we should telephone Daniel."

"Yes, of course. And thank you."

"Nothing at all, ma'am."

He suggested next time we went swimming, to take some extra precautions.

Sheriff Dan stopped by that evening to look around the grounds but didn't see any traces of an intruder.

"Still, I second Matt's advice. Take a little extra care, you two."

Then, Sheriff Dan rubbed his hands together.

"Starr is off visiting her mother, and that means our stove is cold tonight. What's for supper?"

* * * * *

My childhood was filled with adventure. I'd knocked down a hive once, by accident, and was chased by some angry bees. I'd broken my finger, swinging on the rope that hung over the fishing pond, and I'd gotten myself scraped and bruised, with the breath knocked out of me a number of times. I'd even fallen off a horse. But except for the occasional nightmare, that experience was the first time in my life I could ever remember feeling real terror.

Chapter 8
Starting Over ... Again!

Midweek was the best time to market, according to my grandmother. She and Rachael relished attending to this pleasant chore, because it "added some welcome distractions." Though today I would have the honor of accompanying Francesca, I wasn't the only one going.

We stood on the stoop of the Bridal Cottage, taking in the empty booze and beer bottles.

"Humf," Francesca grunted.

The windows were closed, but the panes fairly shivered with the raucous snoring coming from inside.

I saw a tell-tale twinkle steal into Francesca's pale blue eyes. Though her actions often surprised me, I had learned to accept her eccentric "inspirations" unquestioningly by the time I was three years old. So what the heck we were doing disturbing a cantankerous man while he slept off an entire bottle of hard liquor was a question I kept to myself.

KNOCK! KNOCK!! POUND! POUND!!

That should have awakened a hibernating bear, but it didn't seem to affect Matthew Mosley. Francesca banged on the door harder, with enough vigor to startle a granite boulder.

With a growling "What the Hell?" followed by a crashing sound and more curse words, Mr. Mosley seemed to have risen at last. He flung the door wide and stood at the entrance bleary-eyed and bedraggled in a rumpled robe.

I had never seen a hangover in action before. It wasn't pretty.

"Sorry to disturb you. Sarah and I are going into town. Can we get you anything? Or would you care to ride along?" Her words were sweet, her intention not very.

He stood silently and glared at Francesca.

"Can we get you anything?" she repeated.

"Give me a moment," he said and slammed the door shut.

"We'll be waiting by the truck." With a toss of her head, she turned and strode back up the drive. I swear I heard her whistling.

While Mr. Mosley was still about as amicable as a rattlesnake, he had turned out to be someone we could count on. That won him some points.

He'd also stopped objecting to my driving the truck around the place. Even so, Babe and I avoided him as much as possible. Francesca, on the other hand ... looked at him with an alert attention I didn't like.

We entered Lost Nation grandly in the Duisenberg. You should have seen the heads turn! For some strange reason known only to our resident flyboy, he'd insisted we take his car. I felt like the Lord Mayor of London heading up a parade, and by the time our "chauffeur" dropped us at Porter's Emporium on Main Street, we had left a sea of gape-jawed Iowans in our wake.

Matthew went on to visit his brother while we entered the general store. Porter's Emporium sold just about anything you could think of: canned goods and meat, clothing and paper products, treats and fresh-baked pastries (often whipped up by my mother). The heart of the place was a small wooden table surrounded by chairs, where the coffee pot was always full and the gossip flowed.

The Porters had been in Lost Nation almost as long as the Pittschticks and much longer than the Schneiders, Grandpap's people.

Chet Porter came from British stock. His house boasted several fine pieces of rosewood furniture and Royal Doulton china his forebears had brought over generations back. He was tall, skinny, sandy-haired and soft-spoken. And what beautiful manners!

His nose was exactly the same shape as Princess Elizabeth's, and he insisted he was distantly related to the House of Windsor, which Francesca doubted.

His wife, Emily, was just like a bird. She had fine features, glossy black hair and a pointed way of looking around that reminded me of Humphrey, the crow. She and Hunny Clack would have been co-winners of any enthusiasm contest anywhere, anytime.

If you can imagine, Emily was the perfect cheerleader type and had actually been head Spirit Girl at Lost Nation High back in the early 1900s. She and Francesca had grown up together. They'd been best friends throughout school and shared a number of my grandmother's wilder excursions, including one outing where they mooned the governor.

They also bobbed one another's hair and painted one another's toenails, thereby driving both sets of parents to distraction. They loved the movies and agreed that Scarlett was a "silly twit," as they put it, for not latching on to Rhett Butler with both hands.

These days, the girlfriends weren't so much in each others' pockets, but there was a lively banter they shared that kept the connection between them strong.

"Isn't this a surprise? It is so nice to see you, Francesca. And Sarah!"

"It's Thursday, Emily. I come to town every Thursday. It'd be a lot more surprising if I didn't."

"You'll cut yourself one day on that sharp tongue of yours."

"No doubt, but you'll be there to sew it back on again!" They laughed loudly and hugged.

Francesca got out her list, and the two women began to gather up our order from the meticulously organized shelves, each product sorted alphabetically by brand name.

"Sarah, dear, what do you hear from those world travelers?" Emily asked.

"Daddyboys said New York is nothing but smells and sounds. He and Mommy took a hansom cab right through Central Park!"

"Clay Morgan has a deep stretch to his soul. I always said so," Emily replied.

"You never said anything of the kind, Emily. I suppose you're still out of bleach?" And on it went like that between the two of them.

In one corner of the truly general store, Kett Purdy had set up a meat counter, a nicety that made shopping so convenient, it was a practice later adopted by the supermarkets.

Kett was a medium man. He wasn't thin or fat. He wasn't short or tall. His disposition was even-keeled. He wasn't the brightest man, but he wasn't dumb, either.

He was your average Joe in spades.

Butchering was his specialty, everything from dressing venison to cleaning trout. Of course, he bought beef, lamb and chicken from the local farmers to sell to the city people. But he didn't mind helping the farmers out, even when they were eating from their own stock.

Kett was married to the reclusive Mary. It was common knowledge that his wife was a little like my Great Aunt Beedy, the one who sometimes insisted she was Greta Garbo. The butcher never hid the situation. It would have been futile in Lost Nation, where word of mouth spread rumors and facts faster and farther than a tornado could spread cow patties.

Francesca always made it a point to ask Kett about his wife while she did her shopping.

"I need a pound of bacon, some stew meat, a roast and a nice sausage. How's Mary? Is she having a good spell?"

Kett appreciated people asking about his wife.

"Actually, she's on a definite upswing these days. I may even persuade her to join me at the July Fourth picnic."

Independence Day celebrations were a delicious excuse for flag-waving, barbecuing, and parading. As in most rural areas and smaller towns, Lost Nation was a place where people invented their own entertainment, with many traditions dating back to before the turn of the century. Annual celebrations or monthly events like ice cream socials, oyster suppers, church teas, school events and town plays were big deals and filled everyone's calendars. Lectures were also commonplace, with political debates being a perennially hot ticket.

Francesca and Kett exchanged opinions on the weather, the Clinton County Fair car races and the G.I. Bill while she stacked the neatly wrapped meat packets in her shopping bags. She then exclaimed, "You tell Mary we'll look forward to seeing her!" and you could tell she meant it.

While Francesca continued visiting and filling out her grocery list, I slipped away and took Babe for a stroll. I was a little nervous that someone might recognize her and felt relieved when no one did.

There was a relatively new store in town called The Sweet Shoppe. Banana splits and root beer floats were only five cents. I thought the soda jerk was dreamy. He was tall and blond. His name was Bill Tycorn, and his family owned the place.

I peered into the window to see if Bill was working, but when he spotted me and waved, I turned around and ducked out of there with Babe at my heels.

It was time to go snooping again. Mr. Mosley had mentioned he was going to visit his brother, so that's where I headed.

It was relatively cool inside the sheriff's station — they had an overhead fan that kept the air stirring smartly. At first, it didn't appear anyone was there. I was about to call out when I heard muffled voices coming from Sheriff Daniel's private office at the back of the building.

I had been warned many times not to listen in on private conversations, but I couldn't seem to help myself. Maybe the sheriff was questioning a notorious prisoner or he had caught the arsonist!

When I tiptoed to the door, I heard someone crying.

"I know how awful you feel. I wish ... Hell, it wasn't your fault." Sheriff Mosley's voice, low-pitched and soft, was offering some words of comfort.

"I can't help it. Seeing Sarah every day ... I can't seem to put it out of my mind."

To my amazement, it was Matthew Mosley. I crept closer. Did you know if you cup your ear to the surface of a wall, it improves your ability to hear noises on the other side?

"I don't think I can stay there. I don't think I should." Matthew was sobbing.

"Now, Matthew, you weren't responsible for the death of that little girl. Look at the thing objectively. What more could you have done?"

I shivered. Is that why the poor man acted so strange, especially around me?

I needed to find Francesca, so Babe and I tore out of there.

Emily told me Francesca had walked down to the dress shop, Chez Fay. What in the world Francesca would be doing in there, I couldn't imagine.

Chez Fay was owned and operated by Fay Phillips and stood next door to her beauty salon. She was fairly new in Lost Nation, having been here even fewer years than myself. Born in Des Moines, Fay was quite tall and had a large-boned elegance that was hard to ignore. She and Francesca were looking over the "summer frocks," as Fay put it.

Francesca didn't gussy up much; what purpose would there be in frilly dresses or high heels in a vegetable garden?

Today was somehow different.

"I don't know ... I just don't see anything here I really like, Fay."

"Well, what occasion are we celebrating?" Fay liked to use the word "we" instead of "you." Her mode of expression was theatrical, and when she spoke, she made full use of the scales.

"No occasion. A woman feels like dressing up once in a while. What could be more natural?" Francesca offered as if her appearance at Chez Fay was every-day ordinary. Truth be told, diamond-studded fingernails couldn't have seemed more out of place on Francesca. I could not recall the last time she'd worn a skirt. Maybe it was Cox's funeral. Yes, I can picture her navy suit and matching felt hat, complete with veil, come to think of it. And her gray raincoat, as it was perfect weather for a funeral, cool and misting.

Anyhow, the idea of Francesca putting down good money for girly clothes was odd. Very odd.

"Let me put on my thinking cap. Hmmm ... You know, I may have something in the back. A sky blue dress with short sleeves and a Peter Pan collar. We could take the lace off; maybe it wouldn't look too ... I'll just check this week's shipment."

As Faye searched for the dress, I took a chair near the door. I wanted to tell Francesca about Matthew, but at the moment, I was more intrigued with my grandmother's behavior.

I watched, astounded, as Francesca sniffed the various perfumes on the countertop in front of her. She held up some lacy handkerchiefs, tracing the delicate pattern with her fingertips. After a few moments, Fay came bustling out with the dress fairly floating across her arm.

"Yes, here it is. Isn't it wonderful?"

It certainly was. When Francesca swept out of the dressing room, she resembled a movie star. She pirouetted, looking at herself in the mirror.

"Wow!" I enthused.

Francesca never said a word. She got back into her own clothes and handed the lovely garment to Fay, along with some nylons and silky underthings. After some thought, she decided to try on a pair of heeled sandals and bought those, too. Then, she looked me up and down long and hard.

"You know, Sarah, you're growing like a weed. You haven't got a decent dress in your closet."

"A dress? So who needs one?" I asked, but it was no use — I would spend the next hour trying on clothes, shoes and hats. Hats! What would I need with a hat? I was still at an age where dungarees were more than adequate ... but Francesca's enthusiasm was hard to dismiss. And after a while, I actually found myself enjoying the moment.

Finally, we left the shop, struggling as we walked, for all the boxes and packages. Babe, who'd been sitting quietly, walked dutifully at my side.

We didn't see the Duisenberg, so we sat down on a bench in front of Fay's shop. After thirty minutes or so, Francesca checked her watch for the third time. She was tapping her foot in agitation.

"Where could he be?" she asked herself.

It was time to tell Francesca what I had heard.

When I'd finished, Francesca admonished Babe and me to stay where we were and told me to keep an eye on the packages.

She motioned through the shop window for Fay to keep watch over Babe and me and headed toward the sheriff's office.

I saw her storm through the jailhouse doors and heard most of her side of the conversation. People in the next county probably heard her. How dare Matthew keep us waiting, standing in the streets. And what was all this about a child? "What is going on?"

"You don't understand, Francesca." And that's when Grandmother heard the whole sad tale.

* * * * *

It was a bitter start to autumn in Mohawk, Michigan. Matthew was staying at an old mining town, the largest in a string of mining settlements stretching along the central spine of the Keweenaw Peninsula. He had been barnstorming around the state during the late summer, crop dusting and stunt flying by turns. He was hanging around to attend one last air show when a freak arctic storm blew in from Canada and began dumping snow. The weather forced Matthew to put a hold on his plans, a decision that would alter his life.

Twenty-seven children were on their way home from school when their bus skidded across a patch of black ice on a downgrade and crashed into a stone wall. Most of the elementary-schoolers scrambled out with bruises and fractures, but one was pinned tight. Volunteers from the local fire department worked liked demons to cut her out, and it was clear she was going to need some serious medical attention — attention they were unequipped to give in Mohawk or any of the nearby communities.

Matthew offered to fly the little girl through the zero-visibility storms to Flint, which was the closest city with the necessary doctors and facilities. The chances of Matthew getting through were slim, but he never hesitated. If he could manage to get to Flint, his precious cargo would have a slim chance of survival. Staying put, on the other hand, amounted to her death sentence.

Matthew reassured the girl's parents. But sometime during the flight, he lost radio contact. His sense of direction was impacted, and he crashed into a fallow wheat field. The little girl died and with her so did a vital piece of Matthew's peace of mind. What would he tell her parents? And why had he survived the accident? The guilt haunted and drained him as he lay in his hospital bed.

Matthew's leg was broken so badly, they had to put a pin in the bone to keep it together. His face was a crazy quilt of scars and bruises. He'd damaged his spleen and one kidney. He learned that, due to the severity of his injuries, he might never fly again ... not that he cared to.

His physical recovery took longer than doctors had anticipated. Matthew's leg didn't heal properly and had to be broken and reset. An additional surgery repaired two torn tendons.
Eventually, his body would mend. His soul, however, was a different matter.

Francesca didn't share the details of her exchange with Sheriff Daniel that morning, so I didn't learn the harrowing story until years later. Apparently, she had bawled like a baby after Daniel recounted the events.

Twenty minutes later, Babe and I waited dutifully while Francesca went to Joe's Tavern to retrieve Matthew Mosley. He wasn't drunk. He was staring into space with a cold cup of coffee sitting on the counter in front of him.

When we got home, Francesca invited Matthew to join us for some lemonade. He thanked her and sat. Daddyboys and Mommy had sent another letter. I could hardly wait to read it.

... The ship is pearly white and spanking bright. The dish fairies and the brass polishing fairies and the window washing fairies have been hard after it day and night, you can tell. We have a stateroom with a private toilet and a tiny shower and a balcony on the upper deck, with a view of the limitless ocean rolling, rolling, rolling past our window.
Every night is a new pleasure. When we sit at table to dine, a bottle of champagne nestles in its silver bucket surrounded by shaved ice, awaiting our pleasure to uncork its sweet power. All this compliments of Mr. Toynbee and World Travel.
Your mother is in bloom like the apple trees in spring and looks like a young girl. We love you and miss you and wish you were here. Hey, that's a fine title for a column, isn't it: "Wish You Were Here."
Love Daddyboys. I send kisses, Rachael.

When I finished reading, Matthew stood up and stretched, like a cat. He bobbed his head to me and moved toward the back door.
"You know," he said, "I haven't had a Saturday night on the town for an age and a half. I'd be honored to escort the two prettiest ladies in Lost Nation to dinner at the best restaurant in town."
What was this?
As if he had read my mind, he pointed outside to the Doozy. "I especially owe you two, since you were kind enough to get Lizzie there all patched up so perfectly. And I do thank you."
"You have a date," Francesca answered.
I sensed that something big was happening, but I couldn't for the life of me figure out what. I realized I would have no choice but to go along. I started to say something sarcastic, but I stopped short when I saw the soft look on Francesca's face.

Chapter 9
Hidden Treasures

Friday brought black clouds and pouring rain. It would have been silly to hire Lincoln for chores; there wasn't a whole lot a body could do surrounded by ankle deep puddles. While pursuit of our adventure list was out of the question, I did wade out to the barn in order to feed RedBird and Miss Blossom.

Babe's skinny frame was plumping up nicely, as Francesca had begun feeding her a mixture of milk, water and oatmeal. She insisted the added calcium would "make Babe's teeth so strong they would never fall out." They never did.

On the rare occasions Matthew joined us for breakfast, he hardly ate and was politely quiet as a library. At times, he reeked of alcohol from the night before. As the evening he'd been so friendly became a distant memory, it was obvious that Matthew's 10,000 demons still ran his life

Even when Francesca muttered some pointed reference to a hangover, Matthew scarcely noticed. Instead, he drifted out into the day and vanished. We never knew where he went; we simply let him be.

Since we were trapped inside and on our own, we devised new diversions.

The attic could be reached by a pull-down stairway in the back of the double linen closet in our upstairs hall. It was a spacious hidey hole of family artifacts: wooden trunks stuffed with petticoats, corsets, ascots, worn-out Levi overalls cheek-by-jowl with work boots from five different decades, a cupboard full of classic English novels that had been translated into German, suitcases packed with quilts and curtains and gloves ... at least 20 pairs of ladies' gloves.

"Shall we investigate, child? No telling what we may find up there."

"Indubitably," I replied.

I couldn't recall ever having been inside the attic before. What I knew about such places had come generally from radio shows, like "The Shadow." I hadn't quite made up my mind about ghosts at that time, but I figured an attic was a likely place to encounter a phantom. Or maybe even an arsonist in hiding. Just the day before, Sheriff Mosley had told us no arrests had been made in connection with suspicious fires that had recently flared in the area. One thing was certain ... Whoever had frightened us by the pond was still out there.

The entrance into the "mysterious chamber" was a solid oak door mounted on well-oiled springs. It opened silently and was therefore highly unsatisfactory in the squeaky/scary noise department. But the smell that came wafting out of the dark was damp and stale enough to evoke a hundred spirits.

At the top of the stairs, a long thin chain hung from the ceiling. When Francesca pulled it, a bright light flooded the space. Except for a few king-sized cobwebs hanging around, the attic looked like any ordinary room. It was a big disappointment. A fairly high ceiling sloped on one side. Some faded throw rugs covered the wooden floors, and the windows were grimy with a layer of dirt and yellowed lace curtains. If the arsonist had been lying in wait up here, he'd have died from a coughing spasm.

"These could stand a good wash," Francesca sniffed, fingering the stiff curtains.

We took them down, fanning away the dust motes. I wanted to grope through the fascinating trunks right away, but Francesca was firm: First we scrub.

So we trooped up and down between the kitchen and the attic with pails of soapy water, furniture polish, brooms and dust pans. Francesca taught me the trick of tying an old tea towel over my nose to prevent what she called seismic sneezing.

We found piles of newspapers which Cox had obviously been saving. Something of a pack rat, he resisted parting ways with something once he possessed it. He and Francesca had constant tug-of-wars. "Treasure!" he'd exclaim. "Trash!" she shouted back.

Eventually, Francesca would sneak a carton of magazines out in the dead of night. Cox never seemed to miss them.

This morning, instead of putting the publications straight onto the garbage pile, Francesca began to finger through them one by one. Cox had circled various articles of interest. There was one from a February 26, 1933 *New York Times* piece, titled "Golden Gate Breaks Ground," a piece about the official start of work on what would be the longest clear-span bridge in the world. We discovered clippings of Henry Ford and his automobile enterprise; reports of Charles Lindbergh's trans-Atlantic flight; and profiles of Ted Williams' batting records with the Boston Red Sox, some pieces dated as recently as 1943, the year Cox had passed.

When she finished looking over her husband's collection, Francesca carefully folded the clippings and placed them neatly back in the same box. That's when she spotted the yellow envelope.

It was addressed to her in my grandfather's careless handwriting. She held it gingerly, as though a rubber snake might be lurking inside. It'd be just like Grandpap to pull a prank like that so long after his own death. Finally, she undid the seal.

There were two poems inside, on separate pieces of paper. The first was labeled "Anon." She read it out loud:

> *"Do not stand at my grave and weep;*
> *I am not there, I do not sleep.*
> *I am a thousand winds that blow.*
> *I am the diamond glints on snow.*
> *I am the sunlight on ripened grain.*
> *I am the gentle autumn rain.*
> *When you awaken in the morning's hush, I am the swift uplifting rush of quiet birds in circled flight. I am the soft stars that shine at night.*
> *Do not stand at my grave and cry;*
> *I am not there. I did not die."*

We were both stunned. Then, she read the second poem. It had been written by Christina Rosetti in the 1600s and became one of Francesca's favorites. Many years later, I read it at her wake, which consisted of flowing champagne and many shared memories of what a wonderful "dame" she'd been.

The poem was titled "Remember."

"Remember me when I am gone away, gone far away into that silent land when you can no more take me by the hand and I, half turned to go, yet turning, stay.

Remember me when no more day by day, you tell me of the future that we planned. Only remember me.

You understand, it will be late to counsel then or pray. But if you should forget me for a while, and afterward remember, do not grieve.

For if the darkness and corruption leave a vestige of the thoughts that once I had, better by far you should forget and be happy than that you should remember and be sad."

Francesca sat very still. I remember how the muted light leaking through the window softened her face. She turned those pages over and over in her thin hands and dabbed them across her forehead as if they could replenish some memory etched there. She stood and walked to the window as she sighed to Cox across Untimely Death: "Why didn't you ever show me?"

The mood remained somber as we went into the kitchen for lunch. Francesca made sandwiches halfheartedly, probably more for my sake than hers. I don't think she was very hungry. The poetry hung over her like a shroud.

When we finished, she only said to me, "It's a terrible thing when you discover something truly important about someone you love only after they're gone."

The rain was coming down harder than ever, and water gushed down our driveway like a mountain river in an April flow. Matthew hadn't been back since breakfast, and frankly, we were relieved.

Francesca had recovered her vitality somewhat and was ready to tackle the trunks in the attic at last. What fabulous secrets might we find? What remnants of lives lived long ago?

The first was a steamer trunk that looked old enough to have been brought from Essen by the original Pittschticks. It was dotted with colorful dated decals. It wasn't elegantly made, but it was sturdy and snug-fitted. No doubt, some German carpenter had lovingly fashioned the thing himself as a preparation for his family's journey to the New World.

The hinges creaked slightly, making me tingle with anticipation. Francesca gave a whoop of delight when she recognized the contents.

Her mother's wedding dress, yellowed now with age, lay across the top of old photographs. A christening robe, once worn by Francesca, was folded along with a set of tiny, lacy outfits, all in various widths and lengths.

"Oh dear, my first grown-up hat," she said, awe-struck that her mother, Frieda, would have saved such a trivial thing.

It was navy blue felt, shaped like a crescent moon with a kind of veil across the front. Francesca tried it on and ran down to her bathroom mirror to see herself.

She looked so beautiful. I could easily imagine her at sixteen years old. Her skin glowed, and her eyes sparkled. I peeked around the corner, half-expecting that her childhood sweetheart had come to fetch her for a weekend date.

As soon as I blinked, the mirage disappeared. Back from my daydream, the person before me now was my sweet, regal grandmother wearing a funny-looking hat. We looked at each other and burst out laughing.

The giggles came and went as we continued opening trunks and uncovering hallmarks of the family's past: my mother's wedding dress, my baby scrapbook, wedding albums, anniversary photos, my first pair of shoes and even a tiny petticoat. All my report cards and the handmade notes I'd given my parents on holiday as well as my father's army pictures.

I found baby photos of my father. It was unsettling, seeing him as a child. He'd always seemed too capable to ever have been anything but a full-grown man.

"Oh, look. Love letters," I said, pointing to a stack of mail addressed to my mother from Daddyboys when he was in the service.

He had written unfailingly two times a week. They were wonderful letters, full of telling and observant descriptions about army life.

September 1942
"... walking around the compound can be rather trying as saluting officers and returning the salutes of any and all is mandatory. Your arm goes up and down like an oil derrick.

"And in the beginning, when the various insignia resembles hieroglyphics, it's wisest to salute everything in uniform, even the county sheriffs."

March 1943
"... I keep the various vehicles here immaculate and running perfectly. Of course I cringe down to the bottom of my insteps when I see some jackass officer with his shoes on the dashboard!

"One day, I remember seeing a particular second Louie scuffing up the insides in this way and practically lost my head. He was a nice enough guy but even more of a hick than yours truly!"

Daddyboys had another surprise for us. At the bottom of the trunk, we found a blue spiral notebook with the words "Sketches of Humanity" written across the front. Inside lay an old curriculum for the University of Iowa Correspondence Course of English and Literature. Several of the assignments had already been completed with top marks. Professor Gump had even written my father encouraging notes. Daddyboys' compositions had "... depth of soul and clarity of thought ... ," Gump wrote.

It turned out that "Sketches of Humanity" amounted to a final exam. Students were directed to choose ten names from a list of famous people and in fifty words or less illuminate the essence of that personality.

Thomas Jefferson was Daddyboys' first pick.

"A huge and evocative man with hair the color of fires blazing and leaves turning. He probed life's mysteries with his intelligence and his hands through a viewpoint broad enough to encompass all that he did not know. He was equally dedicated to the serious and the whimsical, having composed The Declaration of Independence and invented the collapsible farthingale."

In pencil, scribbled across the bottom of the page was "59! No good!"

My father's second pick was Babe Ruth.

"He was built more like a pastry chef than a baseball player." This line had been scratched out. The rest was as follows:

"Even though shaped like a dumpling, the Babe was a ball-playing machine. His homeruns and his cigars were of legendary *length and his appetite for The Game, women and food was Bunyanesque. You can shout out Cobb or Gehrig or Young but baseball is still spelled B-a-b-e-R-u-t-h."*

The penciled remark on this was "infantile!" But the handwriting didn't look like the professor's; it looked like Clay's.

Francesca began to thumb through the rest of the descriptions.

"Here's one about Roy Rogers, called 'My Hero.'"

"Through the sagebrush, tumbleweeds carom in the wind like lost souls. A coyote's lonely call echoes down rocky canyon walls in harmony with the mourning dove.

Into this American landscape comes a fair man on a golden horse. The sunrise carries the song of his soul like a joyful noise.

The idea of the West lives in the heroic block of his Stetson. And the faith and trust of children rest on his shoulders, light as air.

It was a deal he made with himself.

The King of the Cowboys ... just a man with a good heart who rides into the sunset."

My father, my funny old grease monkey Daddyboys, wrote these things?

"How many are there?" I wondered out loud.

"Seven completed and one that is half-written."

"You mean he never finished them? But they're really wonderful. Isn't there a final grade?"

"No. There's one last letter from Professor Gump, saying how disappointed he was that your father didn't finish the course." Francesca frowned. "Sarah, what's the date on that letter?"

"Let's see. It says July 10, l937"

"Oh, Hell..." Francesca started to say more but stopped.

"What is it?"

No answer.

"Francesca, what is it?"

My mother had been ill the last month before I was born, explained Francesca. "She carried you above the placenta, instead of below, and they weren't sure whether you were going to struggle into this world alive. Rachael was warned to stay flat on her back day and night, and Clay was beside himself with worry. He was so loving and sweet with your mother."

Because of me, my father had to give up a writing career. I burst into tears.

"Sarah Sue Morgan! Your father never regretted your coming one moment of his life, and you know it!" She threw her arms around me and held me tightly, though I squirmed and writhed to get away. I couldn't stop crying.

Francesca finally calmed me down by devising a plan.

"I think Mr. Toynbee might be very interested to see these 'Sketches of Humanity.'"

I was still teary, but Francesca made me happy with her idea, and I hugged her 30 seconds longer.

"Do you think Daddyboys can still get his certificate from the college?"

Francesca and I spent the evening painstakingly typing two sets of copies to send to the magazine and university. We ate casually on fried chicken and au gratin potatoes. Babe went out a few times, only to return covered with mud.

All in all, it was a grand, fine day.

Chapter 10
Dark Places

It had been nearly two weeks since we last saw Matthew Mosley. He had become more of a curiosity to me than anything else, but Francesca seemed to have set her heart on catching sight of him. I couldn't help noticing the way she sometimes perked up at the sound of the Doozy rolling up the gravel drive.

Then, one day, out of the blue, he appeared at the door.

"Good morning," he said. In his hands, he had a John Deere cap, which he turned over and over while searching for his next words.

Francesca waited. Fifteen seconds passed, then thirty.

"I was thinking we should … it was time that we have that dinner," he said slowly.

Francesca turned to me. "Sarah?"

"I guess so," I answered with an exaggerated shrug.

Matthew took a deep breath. "Good. Good."

"We can't possibly get away until Saturday evening," Francesca said.

"All right," he agreed.

They discussed eating in Lost Nation, but Matthew felt we deserved more of a splurge than our community could offer.

"After all, I have stood you up for two weeks." He looked downright sheepish.

I watched Francesca bite her tongue.

* * * * *

It was a beautiful summer evening, the sun sinking into a riotous fan of purple and orange. Francesca looked lovely and animated. Something had set back her clock. In that pale blue dress, she might have been forty-five instead of nearly sixty.

When Matthew saw her come out of the house, he hitched in his breath.

I was feeling very grown up. My dress was pale lemon, and my new black patent Mary-Janes were shiny enough to see my reflection.

Matthew looked like a movie star who'd been on a bender, handsome but raggedy-edged. He had on some soft dove gray flannel trousers that whispered hand tailoring and a white shirt that brought up his tan and the color of his eyes. His tie was red and blue and looked snazzy against his blue blazer. Matthew even smelled good, with no trace of the usual night-before rum.

We were going to Clement's Steak House near Clinton, about 40 miles east of Home Farm. Babe wasn't supposed to tag along but had obviously made up her mind to do so. She hurled herself through the flap of the dog door Matthew had built for her and leaped into the Duisenberg.

It was a pretty drive. Babe stuck her head out the window, the way dogs do, and I could imagine the honeysuckle and early summer hay tickling her nose.

We tuned in to a Duke Ellington marathon — a Saturday evening special broadcast on the local station. The Duke's music was like a delicious secret. It made me swoon.

Now that I look back, Francesca and Matt were behaving strangely. If one caught the other looking, they both quickly glanced away. At times, they spoke quietly about Home Farm and about flying. I tuned out of the conversations, opting to read my book about old Mr. Scrooge instead.

The restaurant was supposed to be situated on a road lit only by the lights in the parking lot. They would be our beacon, Matthew had been told.

But we got lost.

Matthew pored over an unhelpful map that had been printed long before the war. When the road we were following suddenly came to a dead end, we were surrounded by corn fields.

I could see Francesca was starting to get antsy. But Matthew felt sure he could find the place.

"It has to be around here somewhere," he insisted.

So he continued to drive around and around and around.

My stomach started growling. Francesca was drumming her fingers on the passenger door. And Matthew just kept driving, insisting over and over he wasn't really lost.

"Stop the car!"

Francesca's command startled me and Babe so much we practically jumped out of our skins. She got out of the car and stared into the dark.

I hope she isn't leaving me here with him. We'd be here forever! I don't like being lost in the dark, and I especially don't like him.

Francesca's voice was soothing as she read my mind. "Not to worry. Everything will be fine, Sweetchild."

She got back into the car, closed the door with a bang and ordered Matthew to turn right. "I think I saw a beam of light in the distance. Drive in that direction; I'm pretty sure there's a farmhouse."

Her tone left him little choice.

His attitude soured considerably, even though — or especially because — she'd been right on the money.

We arrived at the farmhouse within two minutes. In a flash, Francesca was back with a piece of paper in her hand. She thrust the directions at Matthew, who took off like a slingshot. The ride to the restaurant was silence personified, with tension so thick a buzz saw couldn't have sliced it.

You can imagine the remainder of the evening.

The fancy restaurant Matthew had been promised turned out to be more of a tavern with a hint of dive tossed in. He and Francesca were still giving one another the silent treatment. In fact, the only time Matthew spoke was to order a series of rum and cokes.

The food wasn't that good, either.

I had the children's portion of prime rib, which was tough enough for bootstraps. Francesca picked at a listless salad, and Matthew kept tossing back Cuba Libres, a cocktail that became popular during the war years, when scotch and bourbon were hard to get. Matthew had obviously taken to the switch with gusto.

The more he drank, the further he sank into his irritated gloom.

On our way out, Francesca and Matthew argued over who was going to drive. But my grandmother stood her ground and finally managed to snatch the keys out of his hand.

Matthew looked daggers at her but plopped himself in the passenger seat, where he was soon snoring to beat the band.

I was exhausted, unused to this kind of emotional tug-of-war. It occurred to me then that people live at different emotional settings. Some are perpetually riding a seesaw, while others glide through life on a much more even keel.

Matthew Mosley was a tilt-a-whirl. I began to equate Matthew Mosley with the eye of a hurricane. He craved experiences, every sort, good and bad. I found him fascinating in the way a mongoose is fascinated by a snake — fascinating and exhausting.

I guess I'd been asleep and dreaming about a house ablaze. The images were so real that my eyes watered from the smoke. Startled, I sat up and looked out the car window. It took me a moment to realize what I was seeing.

A fire!

"Look, it's Joshua Teems' storage shed!" I shouted.

Francesca was already slowing the car, and Matthew was out of the vehicle.

"Stay put, you two," he said as he hobbled forward to help.

What if the arsonist was back? I watched in dread as flames licked into the night sky.

Some neighbors had arrived and had begun helping the Teems men smother embers hopscotching toward the barn. By the time they formed a bucket brigade, I could hear terrified horses shrieking inside.

Francesca grabbed a blanket from the back seat. After Joshua wet it down, she wrapped it around her shoulders and covered her face with a handkerchief.

Matthew tried to stop Francesca, but she wasn't going to listen to any argument. We could hear the horses becoming frantic to escape, bucking and neighing. Matthew shrugged and followed Francesca into the conflagration. Together, they somehow managed to lead the animals to safety.

In the chaos, I could see everyone was doing something vital. I couldn't just sit there and watch, so I snuck out of the car and moved closer to the action. Babe started barking and jumped out through the car window, but instead of following me, she took off like a shot. I ran after her, yelling her name. But she vanished into the dark, and I was too scared to go after her.

As I turned back toward the flames, I heard a fire truck clanging along Thunder Ridge Road. Within minutes, the Lost Nation Volunteer Fire Brigade had arrived and gotten things under control.

Sheriff Mosley arrived on the scene and immediately began gathering evidence — through observation and by listening. While he was speaking with Francesca and Matthew, I burst into tears. It took them a moment to realize why I was crying — Babe had disappeared.

Still covered in sooty sweat, the Mosley brothers patted me awkwardly on the back. The Sheriff comforted me as best he could. Francesca drew me into her arms.

"That's one smart dog. She'll be back," Daniel assured me and turned back to Matt. He spoke firmly and quietly.

"You don't think he maybe hung around for a while to get some kicks out of it, do you? The wood was still wet from the storm. He must have used ... kerosene, by the smell of it."

Daniel turned to me and asked which way my dog had run.

I pointed toward Home Farm.

It was about a half hour more before the fire was truly out. The Sheriff officially requested we all camp at the Teems' farmhouse for the night. "This guy is crazy as a bedbug, and he could be anywhere. I'd feel a whole lot better if you were all someplace where I didn't have to worry about you."

Joshua Teems was more than happy to accommodate us.

"If it hadn't been for you coming along when you did, I hate to think what would've happened. There is always room for you at the farmhouse; you know that."

He then passed around a cool jug of hard cider, to help us "sleep."

I was missing Babe with a sharp pain right in the middle of my heart — a pain I'd never felt before. The idea that I would never see her again was bringing an entirely new kind of despair and emptiness. That's when Matthew Mosley surprised me by picking me up and holding me in his arms. I was too painfully tired to care.

Chapter 11
Unforeseen Recoveries

Instinctively, I groped for Babe and then realized she wasn't there. Through cloudy eyes and a foggy brain, I scanned the unfamiliar room.

My once-beautiful lemon yellow dress, now torn and soot-stained, lay in a wrinkled heap on the floor. Visions of the night before came flooding back — the fire and Babe's disappearance.

As I stretched, dull aches and pains invaded my arm and leg muscles as I began to take in my surroundings.

Joshua Teems' comfortable old place had once been a part of the Pittschtick holdings. It had been sold off sometime around 1900 to Joshua's father, Micah, a firm believer in the medicinal properties of apples and a literal interpretation of the Good Book.

Joshua had scoffed at his father's tenets and been a wild child in his teen years, spending some months with the state Youth Authority. The town nannygabbers even whispered he'd served a short spell in the state penitentiary.

Anyhow, after Micah was carried off by a stroke, Joshua married and settled down. Mirabella, a pious and sweet-faced Baptist, was the type of woman old man Micah would have been proud to have as a daughter-in-law.

Faced with her unwavering faith every morning and night, Joshua took over the apple orchards with vigor and begat Jacob and Isaac. Those two boys were like blue tick hound dogs — big and sweet and not too bright. Joshua's only concession to his former devilish ways was the fermenting of hard cider, which, he maintained, came from a recipe that went all the way back to the Garden of Eden. When Mirabella was taken by the influenza in 1932, Joshua was left to raise the boys by himself. He did a good job.

I found a bathroom and drank about a gallon of water straight from the tap. I then wandered my way through the big empty house and out into the yard. Ashes and charred wood littered the ground. The barn frame was still smoking. I wondered where the horses had been taken. No sign of the adults either.

The sun's rays broke me out in a sweat that trickled down my neck and chest. I was hungry, disoriented and sad. I called out several times for Francesca and Babe, but when neither responded, I simply collapsed in a heap on my knees. Then, flashbacks of an unsettling dream from the night before overran my brain. I could almost hear Babe yelping for me, sounding like she was hurt or afraid.

Without thinking, I stood up and started running in the general direction of Home Farm, screaming for Francesca.

"Oh, my God, Sarah! Here I am, Sweetchild!" my grandmother called, appearing out of nowhere.

I wrapped my arms around her and held on tightly as she whispered words of comfort in my ear.

"My poor, dear girl," Francesca said over and over. The adults had been retracing the events from the night before and were searching the area for clues. They had left me to sleep late.

"We have to help Babe; she's hurt," I finally said. "She's hurt! She needs me. She needs *us*!"

"Did she come back last night?" asked Francesca.

"No! She's ... in a place that echoes. I ... I dreamed it, but I know it's true! We have to find her, Francesca." And I took her arms and shook them. "We have to help her!"

Jefferson, Matthew, Joshua and Sheriff Mosley looked at me oddly. Francesca, however, listened with heightened attention.

The Pittschticks were not, strictly speaking, religious when it came to church-going and psalm-singing or praying out loud. For Francesca, the organized-religion idea of God was simply too narrow. Instead, Francesca believed that God was everything and everywhere. God was time, space, matter, good and evil, all rolled into one. Her opinion about suffering was that it was a part of the learning process and that it could be a blessing in disguise. Francesca put her faith in what she called the "benign character of the Great Unseen."

Francesca began asking me gentle questions about my dream. Sheriff Dan, Matthew, Lincoln, Joshua and Jefferson were following us by way of the shortcut as we ambled toward Home Farm. When we finally reached the porch, I had calmed down a little. Francesca settled me into a rocker and continued her gentle prodding. "Close your eyes and tell me what you sensed, Sarah," she said.

I took a deep breath and let the nightmare roll back over me. "I heard trickling water," I offered.

Francesca nodded her head. "Could be a well, boarded-up or dry."

"There must be fifteen in this part of the county alone," the sheriff said.

"Could be an underground spring," Lincoln chimed in.

Since Babe had last been seen running into the woods from the Teems' property, the adults decided to continue searching the area while it was daylight.

Lincoln spotted something first. He knelt down and touched it with his hand, a patch of something dark and sticky. "Blood," was all he said.

I pressed against Francesca.

"Yep," Lincoln said, pointing down.

"Babe! Babe!" I hollered.

Matthew motioned Francesca and me to wait while he and the sheriff walked ahead.

"I can hear her," I said as a faint whimpering sound made its way through the trees.

Then Matthew motioned, "Over here!" He was gesturing at a gaping black hole.

Believe it or not, it was rare to hear of someone or something being trapped in a well. The Pittschticks were too fastidious and too wrapped up in their children's welfare not to take the greatest care in covering up such potential hazards. But someone had pried the lid off.

Matthew shined his flashlight into the pit.

"There she is," Matthew said. "It's a ways down there. Jefferson, I believe we'll need your rope now."

"Please," I whispered, "can I just see her?"

"Okay. But don't excite her. If she's hurt, you don't want her to move till we can get someone down there."

On my belly, I crawled to the edge of the well and peered down. I could barely make out Babe's shape in the gloom.

"It's all right, girl," I called softly. "It's okay. Shhh. We're coming to save you."

But the mouth of the well was too narrow for any of the men to fit.

"Well, you'd better hog tie me onto that rope. I don't want that dog hurting any longer than necessary."

"Francesca, you can't be serious ... It's too dangerous," Matthew protested.

"Just do it."

Lincoln and Matthew conceded defeat and helped her fashion a harness. Her light frame was misleading. Though slimly built, she was as strong as an ox. Matthew hunkered down as much as his cast would allow and thought for a minute.

"It doesn't look like you'll have enough room at the bottom to squat beside her," he said. "You're going to have to lean down and check her out for broken bones. If her back is broken, we'll have to rethink this. If one or more of her legs are broken ..."

"Shit!" The word exploded out of my mouth unintentionally.

"Sometimes that's a very appropriate word," Francesca said to me. "Now, hold on to some really good thoughts."

I could hear Francesca's feet slipping along the casing as she tried to find a purchase.

"Stop a minute," she said and proceeded to take her shoes off one at a time and toss them up to us. "Okay, I'm ready."

Matthew worked the rope, and Jefferson held the flashlight steady until Francesca could reach the dog.

"It's okay, girl," we heard Francesca say.

A few seconds later, Babe yelped, and Francesca said softly, "No, Babe. It's okay. Easy. Easy."

"What is it?" asked Matthew.

"She snapped at me. I think she's in some real pain here."

"One of you gentlemen got a sock?" Francesca called up.

Lincoln sat down, undid his shoe, peeled off a heavy gray work sock and handed it down.

"I'll make a muzzle," Francesca called up.

Then she examined Babe again.

"Oh, my God..."

"What is it?" I asked, not wanting to know yet needing to know.

"I need something for a pressure bandage," Francesca answered. "She's got a gaping wound that looks to have lost a lot of blood."

Matthew immediately took off his shirt and ripped it up the middle. He threw it down the well to Francesca. After what seemed like a million years, they were ready to be brought up.

"Take it slow — I've got the dog in my arms."

We could hear a constant whimpering that broke my little heart. I held my breath. Francesca's head came out first. Her hair was matted against her forehead, her arms covered with blood. She held Babe close to her chest, the dog's broken leg hanging at a crazy angle. The trip into town was horrible. Babe trembled and shivered and cried. I did, too.

"It looks like someone took a knife to her," Doc Gearneart said. "She's got some serious contusions, too. But I'm confident she will make a full recovery. It'll take some time, though. Yes, sir." He turned to me and patted my shoulder. "You and Frances'll have to nurse her and keep her quiet. Make sure the wound stays clean. Give her these pills. Make sure she eats proper. Can you do that, Sarah?"

I promised we would.

I don't know what time it was when we finally got back to Home Farm. Matthew, Francesca and I sat on the front porch, numb and exhausted.

Francesca managed to find enough energy to check the mailbox, and when she got back to us she said, "I've been wondering..."

Matthew and I both looked at her as she paused before finishing her thought. "How the Hell did Babe fall into a well with a slice out of her side?"

Francesca glanced at Matthew, who shook his head.

"Is anyone here ready for some *good* news? Sarah, I think this is for you," she said, handing me an envelope.

The letter from Daddyboys couldn't have come at a better moment.

Dear Frances and Sarah,

"We've arrived in England and are ready to ferry to France ... The ship, a smaller sister to the Queen Elizabeth, looks, at first, to be roomy and comfy. But when we saw the top-deck cabin that had been engaged for us, there was just enough space inside for one overnight case and ourselves as long as we didn't try to change our minds!

The captain is a handsome fellow with an enormous handle-bar moustache and ruddy skin. He is quite friendly though a touch imperious. When he urged us to be awake at dawn the next morning in order to catch our first glimpse of France at fabled Calais, we saluted smartly and appeared at the appointed time.

I've never seen anything quite like those cliffs. They were a glorious sight, with the climbing sun pink on the horizon and the gulls and terns swooping.

Train travel is a lot more civilized in Europe, except in third class, where the French cheerfully toss the remains of their lunch out the window. We arrived in Paris later that morning and were taken to Hôtel Plaza Athénée.

The city is half in ruins from the war, although rebuilding takes place at a furious pace. It's a crying shame, seeing what must have been the most beautiful city of the modern world reduced in some places to rubble.

Our hotel rooms are too elegant for a grease monkey and a baker from Lost Nation, Iowa ... all green velvet hangings and delicate rosewood antique furniture.

We're told that international society has flocked to this hotel of enviable glamour since 1911.

The telephone at the side of the bed has three buttons on it: One with a tiny drawing of a man carrying a tray; a second one depicting a woman with a towel; and another resembling a man carrying a hanger. They represent the room service waiter, the maid and the valet for our floor. If you wish to summon any of them, you just press the appropriate button.

Posh, huh? Your old Daddyboys has decided to keep those gentlemen and ladies busy! Always wanted to patronize a French laundry ... now I'll get my chance!

Love, DB

Kisses and Kisses and Kisses, Rachael/Mommy

"Rachael is going to let some stranger do her laundry?" Francesca laughed. "No doubt she'll be glad of her new unmentionables — she'll have nothing to be ashamed of."

Matthew said, "You make her sound like a prude. After all, she is your daughter, Fran."

No one ever called my grandmother Fran. It irritated me.

Francesca also had a letter. It was from Des Moines. She rolled her eyes when she spotted Great Uncle Harry and Aunt Maude's return address.

"I'll read it later," she said and slammed the kitchen door on her way inside the house.

"Francesca and Maude aren't too close," I explained to Matthew, who was looking puzzled. "It has something to do with Harry. My great uncle used to be in love with Francesca, but no one is supposed to talk about it."

"Did she love your grandfather Cox?"

"Of course she did. He was funny and made her laugh about practically everything."

"I see," was all Matthew replied.

Chapter 12
Inklings

Sheriff Daniel was waiting for us when we picked Babe up at the animal hospital.

My poor little dog still resembled a refugee from a disaster area, with her cast, stitches and bandages, but to me she looked absolutely gorgeous.

"We were lucky we found her," Daniel said. "I just wish I had a photograph of you hanging by a rope down that narrow dark hole, gaily throwing your shoes in the air!"

Then, Babe weighed in with her own editorial. Cast and all, she squatted right there on Main Street in front of God and everybody.

"The vet says Babe was cut with a knife," the sheriff observed. "I'm thinking that means someone did it on purpose. Now, the person could have been defending themselves if the dog tried to attack them."

He turned and looked at Francesca.

"Is she the kind of dog that'd go after someone, maybe to defend herself?"

Francesca answered carefully. "Babe is not vicious by any means. She may have been provoked, or she may have thought she was protecting us."

Matthew said, "I'll bet dollars to doughnuts this was the same guy Babe chased after few days ago."

"It could even be the same person that's setting these fires," Daniel speculated.

"You think he'll be back?" Francesca asked.

"Be a fool to. But these folks don't think the way the rest of us do. If the person setting these fires is the same convict that escaped from the state facility, he's got a rap sheet long as a skunk's tail. Believe it or not, he's an educated man. Used to be a doctor, from the report I got last week. Anyhow, he supposedly escaped by hiding in a laundry hamper."

The Sheriff scratched his jaw line. "There was another fire in Dubuque last night. The head shrinkers say these fire-setters usually have some type of agenda. Maybe they want revenge. Whatever his motives, this guy is dangerous, and until we catch the S.O.B., you ladies need to be careful. Don't trust anyone you don't know, and don't take any dumb risks."

Matthew hadn't said anything, but he was looking at Francesca with concern. Without thinking, I blurted out: "We might be safer if Matthew moved in to Main House ..."

Francesca and Sheriff Mosley tried not to smile. Matthew looked embarrassed and carefully studied the ground. No one said a word, but something got decided at one point or another, because Main House did soon have a new resident.

We gave Matthew the first-floor bedroom and bath, so he wouldn't have to navigate the stairs every day.

Francesca and I helped him move his things. It was fascinating, discovering what this mysterious man considered valuable: A fist-thick book of maps; two worn leather aviator jackets; and an assortment of gloves and scarves, neatly folded by color. He also had 13 dog-eared books on aviation and craft maintenance, none with covers, as well as a stuffed cobra, with fangs rampant! It was a hideous-looking thing and scary at first. And I learned something truly weird: Once a cobra is stuffed, it's impossible to get the hood to widen out.

That was a big disappointment.

Although Matthew had some nice clothes and hairbrushes and such, he certainly traveled light. His life hadn't been substantial like the one I'd lived in Main House, surrounded by family portraits and furniture that had been with the Pittschticks for generations.

Matthew Mosley was as wild as the west Texas wind and free as that red-shouldered hawk that lorded it over Home Farm. Either one could just pick up and go ... whenever something pushed him too far and he didn't feel he could push back ... whenever he got too disappointed or someone got too close.

There was no sign of the urge to run in his behavior today. I was familiar with that particular look animals have when they're going to slaughter, so I'd have recognized that look on Matthew. On the contrary, he seemed unusually calm and relaxed.

Francesca was downright bustling cheerful — so much so that she finally shared Maude's letter with us.

"Your Uncle Harry and Aunt Maude will be paying us a visit over your birthday on July 17," she announced.

"Your birthday!" said Matthew. "Oh, we'll have to do something. Something special, won't we Fran?"

Grandmother asked me if I had anything in mind.

I licked my lips to capture a last drop of chocolate milk while I considered options.

"How about going to the Clinton County Fair? We haven't been there in a dog's age," I said.

During the summertime several counties across Iowa sponsored fairs to promote tourism and show off the skills of locals. In the past, Mommy had won a slew of blue ribbons for her pies with crusts light as angel hair. Francesca had won a prize for my birthday quilt, while Grandpap had actually won a cash prize for a three-foot-long pipe he carved all of a chunk of walnut.

The more we discussed this possibility, the more enthusiastic we became. Then, Francesca's eyes lit up, and she bolted upright in her chair. I knew what she was thinking.

"Francesca, you wouldn't."

"Wouldn't what?" asked Matthew.

"Maybe you should!" I prodded, warming up to the idea.

"Should what?" Matthew asked again.

"Race!" Francesca and I shouted in unison.

Francesca had always been notorious for having a lead foot. She could drive like nobody's business on any kind of road. Through a fluke, which grew out of a dare, she discovered she drove best on oval dirt tracks in front of thousands of screaming fanatics. Grandpap had even kept a saucy little roadster for her occasional foray onto the racecourse at the Clinton fair grounds.

But she hadn't raced since Cox's death, and the roadster had been sold long ago.

"You mean auto race?" Matthew asked, somewhat horrified.

"Yep. Francesca's been in more races than any other driver in the history of the fair!" I said, puffing my chest out proudly.

Francesca had been about to celebrate her twenty-fourth birthday in 1910 when the Clinton County Fair added car racing to its agenda. There were only four entries that first year, all of them men.

Cox and Francesca were newly married, and teasing was as much a part of their relationship as spitballs were to the World Series. As it happened, Cox was teaching Francesca to drive.

As she explained to Matthew, "We constantly fought about the power of the car. He told me over and over that I was going too fast for a woman. You can imagine how I felt about that kind of nonsense. Without telling anyone, I entered the race. Daddy and Cox only discovered my little plot a few minutes before the race started, as the officials were announcing the names of the drivers. It was too late to call me off by then ... I had already pulled onto the track."

"You should have seen her, Matthew," I broke in. "She was the cat's pajamas!"

Matthew asked how I would know, since I hadn't been born yet.

"Are you kidding? Francesca is practically a legend in these parts."

Francesca had borrowed a scarf and some goggles. She managed to scrounge up trousers and a collared shirt. She'd entered the race as Francis, with an "i," and the judges assumed she was a man. Of course, Grandpap knew differently.

"Weren't you ... nervous?" Matthew asked, unsure of what to make about this tale.

"I can still taste the swirling dust as I revved the engine. It covered me like a curtain. It was marvelous. I was excited beyond belief. It was ... the single greatest experience of my life."

Matthew's head jerked back in surprise. "You, a daredevil?"

Francesca shrugged her shoulders.

Matthew went on, "You mean to say that racing was better than getting married? Better than having Rachael? Or half-pint here?"

Then, it occurred to me that Matthew was bewildered that a woman, especially one as regal as Francesca, would dare step into such a traditionally masculine pastime — and a dangerous one to boot.

Francesca was beginning to get the drift, too.

"There's nothing that happens in a woman's life that rivals holding her own newborn in her arms," she said carefully. "My wedding to Cox was a most tiresome day. Everything that could go wrong did go wrong. As for Sarah," and she paused here to smile at me, "she'll be the best friend I ever have."

Matthew was sitting on the edge of his seat, intently looking at Francesca as if he were seeing her for the first time. Maybe this would be okay after all.

"But racing ..." she continued, "You see, it was the only thing I've ever done in my life for which I had zero expectations of myself. No woman I knew had ever done such a thing."

She looked into his eyes and finished, "It all came right from the seat of my pants. It was marvelous."

Francesca admitted her father wasn't too keen on what she had done and would have "loved to skin" her hide with a "personally picked birch branch."

"But as soon as the judges handed me the trophy, I was out of there like a shot. In fact, I didn't show my face until after nightfall," Francesca laughed and brushed the top of my head with her hand. "Hell, they didn't even realize a woman had won until much later."

Matthew sat silently, absorbing this information. With a twinkle in his eye, he asked Francesca if she was going to get out the old racing silks.

"You gotta, Francesca. You just gotta!" I screamed.

"You could use my car," Matthew chimed in.

We looked at the man in utter shock. For a moment, I even felt forgiving toward Matthew for his ... well, everything. I didn't want to like him, but he did have an awful nice car, and it was a grand gesture.

"The Duisenberg?" Francesca asked. "Hmmmm. It's a generous offer. Let me think about it."

It was strange, having a male other than my father and Grandpap in the house. Matthew was certainly different. And as the days passed, he seemed to warm up and open up.

Similarly, something closed-down in Francesca began to bloom again. She began spending more time on her appearance. She wore scent and a rather feminine shade of rose lipstick. She actually brushed her hair more than once a day.

Francesca and Matthew's friendship grew in depth and closeness. They'd spend entire evenings on the porch in lengthy conversation. They developed silly inside jokes between them, the same way my father and mother had. I think the part of her that withered when Cox passed away had finally been reawakened and invigorated. I could see it in the way Francesca would listen quietly yet intently when Matthew spoke and in the way she brushed her hand against him when it wasn't necessary.

And despite my confusion and initial misgivings, I was starting to like Matthew. To be fair, he made quite an effort to get on my good side. He secretly taught me how to play poker until I became well-acquainted with the terms and strategies: bluffing, check, raise and ante. I was on my way to becoming a card sharp.

He helped me with Babe, too. I had trouble keeping her from putting too much strain on her mending leg. Since she was still a young dog, she wanted to run around and play. Matthew created a sling on a rope with a pulley. That allowed Babe to run around with her bad leg never touching the ground.

The *Lum and Abner* radio show had just ended. We were eating spice cookies and drinking milk in the kitchen when Matthew casually asked Francesca about Maude.

When Francesca closed her eyes and stood up in a huff to leave the room, Matthew gently took her by the wrist to keep her from escaping.

"Sarah, I think it's time you got into your pajamas," he said.

"But it's early yet," I protested.

"Sarah, I'd take it as a mark of great personal favor if you'd go upstairs for a while." he said, firmly but kindly.

"Don't you dare go," said Francesca.

A rock and a hard place, that's what it was. The horns of a dilemma! I wanted to stay, and I wasn't about to take sides against my own grandmother, but I didn't want to start an argument between her and Matthew.

They both looked at me as I tossed a cookie into the air.

"Heads I go, tails I stay," I said as the cookie landed with a splat on the table. I scooped up the pieces, kissed Francesca and went halfway up the back stairs — out of sight but within earshot.

"Fran, what is this between you and Maude?"

No answer.

"One of these days, you're going to have to grab the bull by the tail and face the situation."

"It's none of your business," Francesca said tightly.

"Growling at me won't be helpful. Look, whatever happened, happened. It can't be changed. It can't be erased, and it can't be forgotten. The only aspect you can change is the way you feel about it. Isn't that what you told me that day you rescued me from the tavern?"

"You don't understand," Francesca said adamantly. "No one understands! Sarah? Are you in bed yet?"

I quickly tiptoed upstairs and yelled from my bedroom door, "Goodnight, everybody!"

I closed my bedroom door loudly from the outside and then tiptoed back down and heard Matthew say, "I could be wrong about this, but maybe you've never given anyone the chance to understand."

I heard a chair scrape across the kitchen floor followed by Matthew's voice becoming softer.

"I've lived for over a year under the shadow of something so gut-wrenching, I was afraid I might never recover. Even though I look back and tell myself I did better than anyone had a right to expect, it still hurts. How long have you been carrying your burden?"

There was a silence followed by a terrible sigh. "Over forty years," Francesca admitted. "God, I hate telling you that."

"Why?"

"It makes me sound so old."

I heard Francesca stand up and step across the floor. I ran up the stairs, fearing I would be caught. But Francesca did not come after me; she had gone to the stove for more coffee.

A tinge of guilt came over me for listening to such an intimate conversation. But it soon faded and was replaced with a new feeling: Jealousy.

Francesca Pittschtick Schneider was the most fascinating person I had ever encountered — novels included. She was my best friend, and I naturally assumed she told me about everything. Now, I was hearing her share private things with this strange man in our kitchen. He was starting to get in the way.

Matthew's voice softened.

"Fran, you'll never be old. Of course you'll age, but being old just isn't in your soul. It isn't your style. Come here. It's all right. You know that I'm crazy about you."

Then, there was silence. I couldn't hear anything. No one was talking. What were they doing? I dared to sneak to where I could see inside the kitchen.

They were kissing.

I was horrified! I couldn't bear it any longer and scuttled to my room. I was angry, but I wasn't sure why.

I pouted as I slammed dresser doors and drawers — something most of the women in our family have always done when they're upset.

In went the shoes. Bam!

Out came the nightgown. Bam!

I placed my dirty clothes into the hamper. Bam!

I realized that if Matthew and Francesca liked each other too much, she wouldn't need me as her best friend any more.

Why was this happening? Francesca *was* too old, much older than Matthew. If anyone had a right to like him, it would be me. He liked me, didn't he? He was my card partner.

Feeling lonely and despairing, I tossed and turned in my bed until Babe scratched on my door.

"Go away!"

Babe whimpered and scratched on the door again.

"Oh hell's bells," I said and let her in. Babe scuttled up onto my bed, grunting a little in pain as she settled her wounded side. She looked at me with her loving eyes and licked my arm.

I couldn't share how I felt with my grandmother, because it was about her. I was thankful to have my little red dog to hug.

Chapter 13
Passion Comes Calling

Matthew insisted Francesca start practicing for the County Fair races, which were only two weeks away. Using a tractor, he carved out an oval track in the meadow below Main House and watered the dirt down every morning to keep the dust from flying. Matthew also retrieved an old aviation watch from his gear to time Francesca's runs.

Since Francesca hadn't raced in years, she started out gun-shy of the Duisenberg's big engine. But after a few practice runs, she positively relished the power of all those horses.

"We've got to name her," Matthew said, pointing to the car. "Great ships, trains and aircraft always have names."

"How about Silver Ghost?" I blurted out. And that's how I came to name the Doozy.

Matthew and I were responsible for cleaning the Ghost after Francesca's training sessions. As we buffed and polished, Matthew spoke a little about his life as a boy, and I began to look forward to those moments alone with him.

As we chatted, we gave the chrome such a gleam, I could see Matthew's reflection. The curve of the metal elongated his nose and softened his sculpted cheekbones.

"This car is rare, isn't it? I've never seen one before, except in magazines. How'd you come to own it?"

"Let's chalk it up to a misspent youth. I was quite the gambler in my younger days," he admitted. "I could sense what kind of poker hand my opponents had or even what they were thinking by the way they bet."

"What do you mean?" I asked.

"Well," he mused, "I could always tell if someone really needed the score, for one thing."

"How?"

"I don't know ... except there was a kind of look to the eyes. A tremor in the hand. A quick breath. Maybe I smelled fear."

He began to polish again.

"You said 'man.' What about a woman?" I asked. "Can you read fear on a woman?"

He raised his eyebrows. "What a strange idea."

"Not really." I waited.

He closed his eyes for a moment, rolling the thought around in his head. Finally, he pronounced, "Because ... well ... Aren't you a little young to be asking me such tough questions?"

"Francesca says you'll never get to know things unless you ask."

"I'll just bet she does."

We worked in silence for a while, buffing in unison. "Sarah, you don't have to rub down to the metal."

I stopped and looked at Matt.

"How come you don't like tough questions?"

He shook his head. "Tough questions demand tough answers." With that, he turned on his heel and stepped back from the car. Just like that the conversation was over — which irritated me some, so I picked up the bucket of water and doused him.

"Hey!" Matt called out as he picked up the hose and sprayed me. Babe began barking, and suddenly, the three of us were chasing each other with sponges, soap and water, Matt and Babe hobbling along.

Then, Francesca yelled, "Come on in, you hooligans, and get dried off. I have some gingerbread and cherry coke ready."

Gingerbread and cherry coke! The perfect after-polishing snack!

For the next few days, we spent hours readying Francesca for the race. The evenings were reserved for light summer meals,

conversation and games. And of course, we always made time for swimming at the pond.
I continued to live in confusion. Sometimes, I loved the way Matt made Francesca feel. At other times, I wished he would move far, far away. Sometimes, I could barely abide speaking with my grandmother; at other moments, I couldn't wait for her embrace.

Of an evening, the crickets were scraping gleefully, working their legs together. Their chirping echoed throughout the property. The three of us took to sitting on the porch to listen to the riotous concerto. Francesca and Matthew would look at each other and smile. Sometimes, they would hold hands but only momentarily. I would steal glances at them both, often feeling content, wishing this summer would go on forever.

To this day, I sometimes still wish that with all my heart.

The Fourth of July was a big day in Lost Nation. Most everyone in town came out to celebrate. The parade would be starting at 11:30 a.m., followed by lunch and the three-legged race. A slew of games, including the watermelon-eating contest, fleshed out the afternoon. The evening would end with a picnic and a gorgeous array of fireworks.

We got an early start for the festivities. It was an important day, what with the wounds and sacrifices of World War II still too fresh in everyone's minds. Francesca and many of her friends would be marching to help encourage support for their ongoing Red Cross and USO fund-raising drives.

"Just because the war's over doesn't mean there aren't still plenty of service men and women in real need," she often observed.

The local school band and local musicians provided the Sousa tunes; car enthusiasts showcased their vehicles; and the farming community lined up their John Deere tractors.

Matthew, Babe and I watched from the sidelines, hollering and waving at Francesca when she and her female community activists passed.

"That was the best parade ever," said Hunny Clack, briskly brushing her long hair from one side of her body to the other.

"You always say that," Greely said.

"Well, that's because each year, it's better than the last." Hunny looked at me and winked.

The townsfolk began making their way to the park to stake a prime location in the shade of the elms. The men were busy sipping on iced cold beer and pitching pennies while the women unpacked lunch delicacies. Homemade biscuits, warm fried chicken and award-winning pies were positioned cheek-by-jowl along trestle tables set up end to end.

"Seems like I could be of some help here," offered Matthew with a courtly bow. "You ladies shouldn't have all the fun."

Hunny guffawed. "Why, Matthew, go on with you. No man ever helped at a picnic since I can remember."

"And we don't want any do-good S.O.B. making the rest of us look bad," Greely noted.

Matthew's sister-in-law wasn't all that impressed.

"You can never tell with this man," Starr said. "He's friendly one day and the next ... Well, Frances, you ought to know."

But Francesca was conveniently busy searching for the mayonnaise jar.

"It's over here, Franny," Matt said as he reached for it.

Now, he was calling her Franny? That was even worse than Fran. I looked around, wondering if anyone else had noticed. If they did, no one said anything, although Sheriff Mosley took an extra-long swig of his beer with his bushy eyebrows raised.

"Get your fingers out of that pie," warned Hunny, slapping Doc Gearneart's hand away. In response, he took a well-used deck of cards from a vest pocket and began laying out solitaire.

"Everyone knows you make the second-best boysenberry pie in the county," he said, with a strong emphasis on the word second.

"What do you mean second-best?" Hunny shrieked in mock dismay.

Conversation continued lively as we ate, and Hunny ensured everyone participated in the gab fest, even me.

"Sarah, honey, what do you hear from your folks?"

I told them about the Queen Mary and how Daddyboys said it was as big as a city. "It has dress shops, a beauty salon and a gymnasium."

"What would anyone want with a gymnasium?" Greely said with a yawn as he reached for another piece of pie.

"And they sat at the Captain's table, and Mommy is looking more sophisticated every day," I finished.

Emily Porter, in her birdlike manner, wanted details about Paris, and even Mary Purdy, who normally kept to herself, asked to hear more about their escapades.

"Daddyboys says Paris smells of rain and chestnut trees. The hotel is plush, with marble floors all over the place, and the windows have velvet curtains. Hardly anyone speaks English, but Mommy is doing her best with the French she learned in high school."

Emily tipped her head back to take in the sun.

"Imagine Clay Morgan winning a writing contest," she said, shaking her head.

Doc Gearneart looked up from his card game.

"Clay Morgan is a deeper man than you may think."

Hunny clucked her tongue. "Don't let me forget to give you the package from Paris," she said, looking at me. This set me off again, bragging about everything I'd read in Daddyboys' wonderful letters.

After a while, the discussion took a more serious tone.

"Daniel, have you heard anything about the arsonist?" Doc asked.

Suddenly, everyone got quiet.

"Yes, Daniel," said Mary, folding her arms tightly across her chest. "Did they ever arrest anyone?" She turned to look at the rest of the group. "Don't you just hate the idea of someone starting a fire? What a horrible way to die. I can't imagine dying by fire," she said and shivered.

"Well, now, that's a happy thought," said Greely.

The sheriff admitted another suspicious blaze had been reported in nearby Landers.

"If I ever catch up to that son of ..."

"Greely!" admonished Hunny.

He looked at his wife sheepishly for a moment. "Well, I'd take him with my bare hands."

Starr changed the subject, turning to Francesca and Matthew.

"You two and Sarah must come out for dinner some night soon. We've got some lovely quail in the deep freeze with your name on it."

"We'd love to," answered Matt, placing his arm around Francesca's shoulders and giving her a hug.

Several surprised looks were followed by a murmur here and a remark there.

Francesca and I didn't win any ribbons in the three-legged race, but we sure had fun. We busted a gut with laughter as we kept falling and tripping over each other. During the watermelon-eating contest, I ate until my stomach hurt. At least I didn't upchuck like Stevie Enoch!

That evening, as we cleaned up the leavings of our second picnic of the day with family and friends, Matthew dropped the bombshell.

"Franny here is driving my Silver Ghost in the races at the county fair in Clinton. I've got some money that says she'll beat the pants off of everyone else."

Who needed fireworks?

This tidbit of information drew more gasps than the idea of Francesca dating a man fifteen years her junior who also happened to be living in the same house with her and her grandchild.

When Hunny Clack slapped her thigh and said "Good for you, Francesca," I don't think she was referring to the races.

But before anyone else could offer an opinion, Matthew piled us into the car and with a jaunty salute to his audience, we drove off.

When we'd settled on the porch, Francesca set about opening the large box that had come clear across the ocean. Matthew used a pocket knife to cut through the twine.

"Quel Elegance, 23 Rue des Fraises, Passy, Paris, France," read the address on the outside of the box.

It wasn't heavy enough for books. Daddyboys thought books were one of the greatest treasures of the modern world.

There were two smaller boxes inside the larger box. Both were wrapped in gold paper. The legend on one of the items read, "Quel Elegance."

"Ah, the aroma," Francesca said, putting her nose up to the package. "Jasmine, not too strong.

Both of the boxes had white embossed name cards on them, with the recipient's name inscribed inside in hand-printed script.

I opened the one addressed to me.

"Look, a velvet dress. I love it," I said excitedly. "Feel how soft! This is a dress for a princess."

Matt picked up a card that had fallen out of our packages.

"It says to 'the two prettiest women in Lost Nation,'" he read then added, "Now isn't that the truth."

Francesca was holding up what I thought was a nightgown. It was the fanciest one I had ever seen: silvery and sheer, like running creek water. There wasn't much to it, and it was see-through, which I thought was odd.

The gown also had a robe with it that looked like butterfly wings glistening in the light.

Francesca stroked the delicate fabric. She held it up to the light then snuck a look at Matt. He almost whistled but then seemed to think better of it.

"Francesca, you can't sleep in that; you'll wreck it," I said.

Matt burst out laughing.

"What's so funny?" I wondered.

"Not a blasted thing, child," Francesca said. "You have to admit, it's the perfect costume for a boudoir."

Francesca carefully folded the nightgown and robe and placed them back inside their box. She asked me to take them upstairs and get ready for bed. I knew that meant she wanted to be alone with Matt.

"Are you going to kiss again?"

Francesca shook her head. "That's Sarah for you."

This time, I actually went to bed, where Babe and I fell fast asleep.

Chapter 14
Healing

It was time to take Babe's stitches out. Her wounds, including her broken leg, were mending well. It had a lot to do with my care, according to Doc Gearneart.

"You take after your grandmother, you know. Have you ever considered becoming a veterinarian?"

I liked Doc. He was no-nonsense when it was important and whimsical when it was important. He had mastered the gruff thing, which reminded me a little of Grandpap. And like Grandpap, he was a lot more teddy bear than grizzly.

Later that same day, we drove to Cedar Rapids, where a specialist examined Matt's leg. The doctor would decide if more surgery was required or if Matt would have to find a way to live with bones that would never heal.

I pressed my nose against the front window and looked out onto the streets.

"Babe wouldn't be alive if it weren't for you," I offered.

"But you had the dream and the courage to follow through on it," Francesca said. "In a way, we all made that miracle happen."

I turned back to the window. "Do you think Matt will ever fly again? Will his leg get healed?"

She put her arm around me and said nothing. I felt so safe in her embrace. Our love was as strong as ever, even though we were currently dragging it over rocky ground. As the clock ticked loudly, it occurred to me that some significant piece of her life was also on the line in that treatment room — that she was treading water hard between the devil and the deep blue sea. If Matt was healed, maybe he'd go back to flying and leave her behind. If he was crippled, he might be so bitter that their relationship couldn't survive the strain.

I crawled onto her lap and hugged her.

"I love you," I whispered. "I'm sorry I've been a poop. I don't mean to be, but it seems to happen anyway."

"It's alright, child. You're just growing up."

"I don't like it much."

"It's hormones. You'll soon be turning into a young woman."

"A crazy one?"

"If you're lucky."

The door opened, and Matt walked out. He was grinning from ear to ear.

"I'll have to keep using a cane for a while but no more surgeries. The bones are healing. Although, it won't ever be one hundred percent again, I will have full use of it."

Francesca didn't say a word; she seemed as tight as a bow string.

Like an accomplished mind reader, Matt walked over and took Francesca's cheeks gently into his hands.

"I won't even think about climbing into my plane unless you're there with me, Fran. I'm going to take you up in that blue yonder and keep you there until you fall in love with it." He then kissed her on the mouth, a long lingering kiss in front of God and everybody.

Chapter 15
The Trade-last

I always looked forward to birthdays. We weren't rich by any means, yet in our family, birthdays were big. The one dark cloud on an otherwise glorious horizon was the inexorable approach of Harry and Maude.

Matt and I were whipped into a cleaning frenzy by Francesca, who had assumed the charming manners of a drill sergeant. Maude was never to see Francesca's floors anything less than eat-on-them spotless. My knees ached, and my fingernails were worn to nubbins.

As Matt's leg grew stronger, his disposition positively flowered. In the face of our relentless task-mistress, he was actually cheery and took to whistling and cracking jokes. It was disgusting.

Babe and I snuck off whenever The Eye wasn't trained on us. In some ways, I guess my hours with Babe began to take the place of the ones I used to spend with Francesca. Between Matt, car racing and house-cleaning, my grandmother had little private time left for me, which hit me hard. And although I felt a piece of my life had been lost, there was little I could do about it.

Instead, Babe and I spent as many snatched minutes as we could down at the fishing pond. I wasn't to go by myself, since there was still a criminal at large, but Matt convinced Francesca it would be alright with Babe at my side. Just the same, he taught me to use a .22 caliber revolver, thereby spurring quite a debate between him and my grandmother.

Francesca wasn't opposed to firearms on principle. That would have been laughable for a woman who'd lived so many years on a farm.

And she wasn't opposed to my learning to shoot, a common practice in rural America, especially in those days. I'd hunted quail and pheasant with my dad and Grandpap a few times. Grandpap had taught me to use his lightweight .410 over-and-under when I was eight. I knew all the safety rules and put them to good use. I wasn't a great shot, but I was competent and felt perfectly comfortable carrying and loading that gun.

But shooting a pistol was a whole different kettle of fish.

"I don't know, Matt," Francesca said with a frown. They were rubbing down Miss Blossom and Redbird.

"I'd feel a hell of a lot better knowing Sarah had some real protection. It's not practical for you and me to be watching over her every second. As a matter of fact," he continued, scratching Blossom's chin, "it wouldn't be a bad idea for you to carry something, my dear."

And so Matt bought Francesca and me each a small pistol and taught us how to use them. He'd set up bottles across the top of the old split-rail fence, and we'd blast away.

"Squeeze. Don't jerk your arms like that; you'll pull right off the target. That's better. Slow and steady."

I wasn't supposed to actually shoot anyone; the gun was there primarily for show and as an alarm system. I never played with it or pointed it at anyone or anything except the practice bottles. Francesca would have skinned me alive. To tell you the truth, I'm not sure I could've fired the weapon in my own defense, but I wouldn't hesitate to protect Babe.

Babe and I lay on the bank of the pond in the shade with our faces near the water. I could see our reflections swirling. It was humid but not unbearably so. Babe had her head across the back of my legs, and I was about to feed her a piece of carrot when I heard a voice from behind. It startled me, and I sat up.

"I thought I'd find you here."

It was Francesca.

I figured she'd come to drag me back to the salt mines, but instead, she put her hand gently and firmly on my shoulder, pushing me back onto the ground. She sat down beside us and trailed her fingers in the water for a while.

"I've got a T.L. for you, Sarah." That was all she said for a while.

Where I come from, a T.L. was supposedly a cowboy term that was shorthand for trade-last. It was something of great value, a story or a secret that you held back when you were bantering with someone across a campfire or sipping coffee in the kitchen. It might be a compliment or a bit of gossip. But you held it until the end, in an effort to persuade the other person to give up something extra-special first. It was the thing you traded last.

I waited.

"I've been like this about Maude since I was sixteen years old," she began. "I ... I can't help myself. Whatever it is, it drives me." She began to dig tiny stones out of the embankment and added, "It isn't actually Maude at all, you know. It's Harry — dear, sweet, bullheaded Harry."

I wisely held back the gasp that was stuck in my throat. The subject of Francesca and Maude's falling out was never to be discussed in our house.

"It wasn't really Maude's fault, no matter how I've blamed her this long time."

She shook her head, then lay back and rested it against a log. She gazed upward, as though for help or guidance, into the kind of sky she loved more than any other, a buttermilk sky. The clouds looked fluffy and slightly curdled. Then, she closed her eyes for a long time, and just when I thought she had fallen asleep, she spoke again.

"I've been trying to sort out these confused feelings about Matthew, you know. All my life, I have acted as though I cared very little for the opinions of other people. Maybe that was all sham." She sighed. "Faced with an opportunity to practice what I preach, I'm stuck but good."

She sat up then and folded her knees gracefully into her arms. Her face was turned away from me, but her shoulders were as expressive as her eyes would have been.

"Harry and I ... God, it was so many years ago. I loved that man. Still do. Not any more than I loved Cox, I think, but differently. First love is a powerful force in a person's life."

I clapped my hand over my mouth. *Yowie-zowie!*

"But Harry and I were so unlike in some ways. He was ... still is ... much more conservative than I. He had a ... a different set of scruples."

She thought a moment before going on.

"I wanted to ... I asked if we could ... You see?" she asked, without turning her head back to me.

Not really.

Francesca let me think about this for a moment. I had lived on a farm all my life, after all, and knew a lot about animal behavior. I was familiar with terms that could be used in mixed company like "procreate" or "beget" (Grandpap's favorite). When it came to men and women, I had overheard this and that and seen my parents be affectionate with and to one another. And I could reference the movies I'd seen.

"Hmmmm," I nodded finally, "like kissing and hugging."

She seemed relieved. "Exactly like kissing and hugging. And when I told him, he was ... shocked first, then angry. He didn't speak to me for a long time after that." She hung her head. "I was crushed and heartbroken. Within a matter of weeks, he and Maude had made plans to marry."

Francesca stretched back out along the edge of the pond. One small tear fell from the corner of her right eye.

"I wasn't wrong. For myself, I mean. I know that now. Actually, I knew it then. And neither was he wrong. In fact, about a year after he and Maude were married, he apologized. Said he'd wished he hadn't been so prissy and stupid about the whole thing. That he loved me and always would. That he thought it was best if he and Maude moved to Des Moines, as their marriage might have a fighting chance away from me."

Francesca had begun to really cry. Her waterworks had been shut off at the source on this subject for over forty years. Now, they turned back on with a vengeance.

"But I never let him make peace with me," she sobbed. "Not really. Eventually, the sadness disappeared, and anger ... bitterness took its place."

She turned to face me then. "Don't think for a moment I figured this out sitting here. I'm not nearly that smart. I've been wrestling with this heaviness in my heart for most of a lifetime. Sometimes, the anger still wells up and overflows, like Old Faithful, and I do mean old."

She reached out for me and hugged me till I thought she'd break my ribs. It was wonderful and terrible and scary.

I kissed her and told her everything would be all right. I stroked her hair and told her I loved her. It was the first inkling I ever got of the grown-up and the child changing places. I felt her shivering and held her tight.

Finally, I couldn't stand it anymore and not really knowing what to say, I blurted out, "Does this mean we can stop cleaning now?"

Suddenly, Francesca began laughing her head off. She cuffed me softly on the ear and took a deep breath.

"I guess we could give it a rest," she gasped.

I had never seen her in such agony and probably didn't respond the way she had needed. But as deep as this secret had proved to be, Francesca had more.

"That wasn't the trade-last," Francesca said, surprising me and making me feel somewhat uncomfortable.

"Oh, Lord," I said.

Francesca sniffled and looked me straight in the eye. It was the most uncomfortable feeling, looking into her soul like that.

"I love Matthew Mosley."

I nodded dumbly, feeling relieved, resentful and betrayed at the same time.

"But don't you see?" she said, shaking me, "More than anyone else ever. More than Cox. More than Harry. And I'm too old! Too old!"

She crumbled against me, all the wind and pride and hope knocked out of her. I hadn't an idea in the world what to say. I knew there weren't any words in the Oxford English Dictionary that would make a difference. What if she were right? I didn't think she was that much older than Matt, but what did I really know about such things?

I wondered how Matt felt. My experience told me that Francesca wasn't one to worry unless there was something important to worry about.

Francesca went on in a rush. "What if Matthew's regained health fires up his wanderlust? He'll be gone in a flash."

Childhood doesn't prepare you for these types of moments. We were having a very adult conversation. But I loved my grandmother and wanted to help her. I figured the least I could do was listen.

I felt her pain go right through me. I wished like anything it could have been me suffering. It was maddening to feel so helpless.

Babe behaved perfectly through the storm, being comforting in a manner only dogs can manage. She licked away Francesca's tears and tried to curl up on her lap. Looking back, I wished I'd thought of something so simple and appropriate.

The sun crawled across the sky, and the day cooled down.

"I love you, Sarah. I never told anyone these things before. I had to tell someone and ... you're a part of my soul."

I kissed Francesca's hair, the way I did in the morning sometimes.

"You had to give me your trade-last, because I'm your Sweetchild!"

It was all I could think of to answer, but it filled the air between us like a train whistle blowing.

Suddenly, I sprang to my feet and ran straight into the water, with Babe right behind.

"I beat you in! I beat you!"

With that, Francesca put one hand on her hip and waggled the first finger of the other at me.

"You took advantage of my weakened condition, and I am going to get you!"

She dove into the pond with all her clothes on, including her shoes. She chased me and Babe around and around, and then she grabbed my legs and tickled my feet until I shouted, "Uncle!"

Chapter 16
Taking Chances

It was a relief to lay down the mop, the broom and the scrub brush. After our heart-to-heart at the fishing pond, Francesca's behavior veered 180 degrees. I had never thought of her as a rock; she had always seemed too elegant to be cut out of stone. But some part of her inner self had shifted and softened.

She still had a temper, didn't I know. She was still stubborn sometimes. But a steely part of her core had melted away with her tears. Francesca had finally come to a real understanding of the folly of Maude and Harry and herself and what that had meant over the last forty years. Enough was finally and truly enough. Some folks never see the top of that particular mountain, and I remember how I noted the change.

It rained the day they arrived. Maude's hair was soaked and had no curl to it, not even a bend. She closely resembled a drowned rat sporting a drenched and wilting hat. Her too-slim figure was not enhanced by the sheath dress she'd picked up in Des Moines. In short, to Francesca, she was a sight for sore eyes.

"Lord, Maude, wouldn't you know you'd bring woeful weather with you!" She hugged Maude who remained limp and unresponsive.

Francesca sailed gaily on. "Harry, Maude, you remember Matthew. Matthew, would you help Harry collect the luggage? Sarah, you rub that dog dry before you let her in the house!"

Aside from the fact that this was more words of friendly chatter in one minute than the two had shared in the previous five months, Francesca's behavior to her sister was remarkable on other counts. Besides the hug, I saw them exchange a kiss for the first time in my life.

Obviously mystified, Maude and Harry glanced back and forth at one another in an effort to figure out what the devil was going on. A new game was afoot, and our visitors hadn't quite figured out the rules.

Matthew was as taken aback as anyone. I don't know how much Francesca had confided in him. But watching him watch her, I could see him warming up to the civility of the proceedings.

"I thought I'd give you the guest suite on the western side, Maude. I know how you always loved the view. How does that sound?"

Maude nodded slowly, waiting for the pit in the cherry bowl to manifest itself.

"Here, let's go up the back stairs. I think it'll be easier, don't you? Sarah, if you think that dog is dry, you have another think coming."

Maude mumbled something about its being a lot of work to ready a room that had been closed up for so long.

"Nonsense, nonsense! If I can't spoil two of my favorite people, what's the good of living in this great hulk of a house?"

"Really, Frances," Harry broke in, "we'd be happy to take that little room on the first floor."

There it was, a lump in the seam of the conversation. That little guest room on the first floor was currently housing one Matthew Mosley, bachelor, the idea caused a silence.

No one spoke a word for a long — one might even say pregnant — moment. Then, Francesca looked Harry right in the eye, smiled and said, "Matthew is staying there."

I'm not sure Maude or Harry understood the entire significance of that admission. Maude started to say something, and Harry hurried her along with his hand in the small of her back. They were soon unpacking and putting clothes away before too much thinking was done. The first thing Harry wanted to do, before going over Daddyboys' accounts, before planning out the schedule of work we'd lined up for him, before anything, was to get his hands on the "Doozy," as I had taken to calling it. Matthew wasn't too fond of this nickname, which is why I liked it so much.

"Duisenberg. Duisenberg! It's got dignity, Sarah. It's got tradition. Dui-sen-berg!"

Harry mooned over the car like a lover. He caressed the left rear fender while he spoke.

"This is the finest example of automotive craftsmanship I've ever seen. Of course, I saw a Doozy once before," he said with a sigh to Matthew, who winced at the sound of that word, "In Paris. In the thirties, it was. A car to fit the times, I always thought. A woman owned it. I was told by a doorman that she was one of those fake countesses, or something. She'd race around the city, and gad! you could hear her coming for a mile. I always wondered if she'd poked holes in the damned muffler!"

Matthew had begun keeping the Silver Ghost in the barn on rainy days. Miss Blossom and RedBird didn't seem to mind. He'd rigged a lamp up to a battery, the better to putter.

In a thrice, Matthew had the heavy hood up and was showing Harry some of the innovations in the engine. You can't imagine how impressive it looked, like some huge sleeping python curled in upon itself. It was clean as a whistle.

"Judas Priest!" exclaimed Uncle Harry. "Look at that! Takes your breath away, doesn't it?"

Matthew basked in the ensuing stream of compliments.

"Smell this interior," Harry remarked while smacking his lips. "Prewar. You can't get leather like this anymore. And the woodworking is all hand-done ... you can see it! Say, you wouldn't mind starting her up, would you?"

"Mind? Are you kidding? Sarah?" Matthew said with a mischievous grin.

Looking very smug, I carefully opened the driver's side and slid onto the soft seat under the steering wheel. I primed the engine, ignited her, and a roar echoed through the barn, causing the horses to prance restlessly in their stalls. It was a moment of pure power, my power as much as the car's, and I could see that Uncle Harry was impressed. He didn't say a word, which was even better.

"Rev the engine now, Sarah," Matthew said.

And I did, taking care to keep the pressure slow and steady. The engine's growl was even deeper and more satisfying. Lovely!

At that moment, Francesca appeared at the barn door. Flicking her umbrella twice, she had to yell to be heard.

"If you are about finished in here, we need you at Main House for lunch."

"We'll be right there, Franny, dear," answered Matt with a grin.

Harry snuck a peek at Matthew out of the corner of his eye.

After clearing the lunch dishes away, we sat back down around the kitchen table. Francesca handed Harry a list of appointments she'd made for the folks of Lost Nation who needed car repairs.

"This seems fine, Franny."

Franny? Now, that was odd. I could tell Maude thought so, too. My grandmother didn't even blink as she responded.

"As you can see, I've left four days for the Clinton County Fair, the 16th to the 19th. That'll give us plenty of time to celebrate Sarah's birthday properly."

"It's an important one, isn't it?" chimed in Aunt Maude. "I remember when I was about to start my double-digit years. I hounded poor Mums for high-buttoned heeled shoes."

"You did?" I asked in disgust. "Why ever for?"

"I couldn't wait to be grown up, I guess," she answered. "Frances was always the tomboy. I was much more ... well ... ladylike, I guess you could say."

Suddenly, Maude's face fell. You could tell she realized she'd accidentally hurled a gauntlet down right there in the center of the table. She looked quickly at Francesca and was about to say something mollifying when Francesca only laughed heartily.

"You're still much more ladylike, Maude! That's not exactly a state secret."

You could have pushed our entire little group over with a feather.

"Now," Francesca continued, still smiling, "When we go to Clinton, I think we can all fit in the Duisenberg. At least, that is Matthew's and my plan if you have no objection."

"I, for one, can hardly wait," sighed Uncle Harry approvingly.

"I've booked rooms at the Lakeview Court."

"Oh, Frances!" said Maude, "We haven't stayed there since we were teenagers. What fun!" She clapped her hands together.

"And I've written ahead and made reservations for dinner on the 17th for the five of us at Federico's."

Oh, boy. This might turn out to be an okay birthday after all, Paris or no Paris.

Federico's! They made little bread ball things laced with garlic. And eggplant parmegiana that tasted nothing at all like eggplant. It positively melted in your mouth. They served egg creams and Dr. Brown sodas, because Papa Federico and his family had come all the way from New York. I always ordered something they called bruschetta, which consisted of triangles of thick bread covered with tomato wedges drenched in olive oil, onions, oregano, dill and garlic.

But the dessert was the best: frozen banana skins filled with whippy-soft homemade fruit-flavored sherbets.

Man oh man! The Big 10 was going to be perfect. It was going to be a perfect birthday.

"Seems to me a special present might be the order of the day, and I don't mean something practical," said Uncle Harry. "Frivolous, that's the ticket. Or something whimsical. What do you say, Franny?"

Francesca looked at Harry in a way I had never seen her look at him before. She was about to answer him when the Clack mail truck rattled into the yard.

The rain had let up momentarily, but the path to the driveway was covered with four inches of water. Matthew ran out the back screen door, which slammed firmly behind him, and over to the car where Hunny was still sorting out our loot for the day. I watched out through the window.

"At last!" she cried in triumph, "I knew I had it here somewhere."

She pushed the package toward Matt. "Sign here, please. And how is everyone today? That's Harry and Maude's car, isn't it? Thought I saw them drive through town earlier. You tell Sarah not to open this until her birthday, says so right on the wrapping. Bye, now!"

It was a huge box with wonderful French postage stamps across the right-hand top. I knew Uncle Harry collected stamps, so I graciously offered them to him.

"Great, Sarah. Love to have them."
Maude broke in, "But isn't there a letter?"
"Here it is! It was inside!" I yelled, waving the peach-colored envelope around in the air.
"Well, open it, Sweetchild." Francesca delighted me as only she could when she called me by my favorite nickname.
"Let's see ... *'Dear kind folks and gentle people'* ... that's us. *'We are, how you say, truly Frenchified as of this ecrivant.'*"
"That means 'writing,' but doesn't it sound so much better in French!" laughed Maude.

Our stay at the CINQ is nearing an end. Rachael and I could live here forever, if it weren't for the large hole in our hearts which can only be filled with your presence. We have dined at the Moulin Rouge. We've driven madly around the Arc de Triomphe, fearing for our lives. We've trailed lazily down the Seine on a barge and been extended a private tour of the Louvre.

We've seen the sun set through the fabled rose window of Notre Dame de la Cite. We've bohemed it up and down the left bank (rive gauche) and shunned umbrellas in the rain, like real Parisians.

We even attended a party at the American Consulate last night. All très grand, with liveried footmen no less! And we ran into an officer with the Allied forces here who was the principal of a high school in Clinton before the war!

I flipped the page over.

We talked about the fair there and wouldn't you know he'd heard of Frances the fearless race car driver? But our true meeting of the minds came over the subject of trout fishing. The officer said he'd rather talk trout than turkey any time.

The upshot is, it seems we're some kind of removed cousins on his wife's side and they've invited us to visit them at 'The Villa' in the South of France next week! (His money came from Daddy's Daddy, not Uncle Sam, so Harry, don't you worry about his wasting the taxpayers' do-re-mi.).

Mr. Toynbee is all for the trip and hopes to lure me into writing a little article about how small the world is getting. Imagine

me, *Clayton Louis Morgan, a paid writer! I shall have to wear flowing coats and take to calling my self C.L.*
Mr. Toynbee has some bee in his bonnet about my 'hidden talents' and is bound and determined to mine them, like gold dust from the mother lode. Well, he'll be disappointed soon enough.
We miss you all.
Harry, watch out for Tom Blackfeather's truck. I've promised him you can make the same magic I do. I can't thank you and Maude enough for everything.
Daddyboys

"The South of France," Francesca twinkled. "How many kings and harlots bathed in the sun there, I wonder?"

"Wait! There's something from Mother, too." I read from another piece of paper.

Dear Mother and sweet Sarah,
This has been the finest and best time of my life. I only wish you two could be here with me to make the experience complete. You should see the shoes I bought. Red, red, red! And I purchased a petticoat to match. Won't Lost Nation melt with envy?
Love and kisses to you and Aunt Maude and Uncle Harry.
Rachael.

"Chance of a lifetime, that's what it was," remarked Harry.

Francesca took his hand in hers and patted it. Then, she got up and kissed her sister on the cheek.

"They couldn't have gone except for your generosity. Don't forget that."

I was getting a little more used to this hugging and kissing stuff. But it still seemed odd to see Francesca act this way.

Matthew had been silent most of the afternoon, which wasn't unusual. The letter seemed to spark some life into him as he suddenly became downright chatty.

"Fran and I thought we'd cook dinner together tonight. We've been saving some quail in the freezer just for your visit. And," he said, turning to me and winking, "we thought we'd play some cards later."

"I love bridge!" said Maude enthusiastically.

"Well, actually," answered Matt, drawing out the phrase in a purely Oklahoma style, "we're kinda partial to poker."

"Haven't got enough players for a competitive game," Harry broke in.

"Oh, yes, we do, Harry, my man. Sarah makes five."

Maude's jaw dropped.

"You can't play poker with a child!"

"We only bet pennies, nickels and dimes. Most you lose is a dollar. Besides, it teaches the girl arithmetic," Matthew explained as he rooted around the hall closet for a deck of cards.

Maude snorted. "Does her mother know about this?"

"Her mother," said Francesca, "is in Paris, France wearing red shoes and red petticoats and drinking champagne from the bottle. I can't see how even Rachael could object to a friendly card game."

"How could that child afford to lose a whole dollar?" Maude couldn't think of anything else to say at the moment.

"Who says she'll lose?" asked Matt.

"But it's gambling!" said Maude.

"With the devil as dealer," said Francesca with a laugh.

After dinner, which was the best meal I ever ate at Main House cooked by a man, I ran up to my bedroom to get "the stash," which was nothing more than a piggy bank Grandpap had made me. It was huge and had four different-sized slots for coins that led down into four separate compartments. I'd saved enough money over the years to have started my very own savings account the Christmas of 1943.

Buy-in for the game was a dollar. White chips were pennies, red chips were nickels, and blues were dimes. I took out two dollars' worth of quarters and jangled them around in my pocket as I ran back down to the kitchen.

"Best quail I ever ate," said Harry, patting his stomach. "Can't imagine myself ever whipping up something that gourmet. Quite impressive, Matthew."

"They were almost sweet," added Maude, who dried each dish until the pattern was almost worn off. "What did you use, Matt?"

"Triple Sec," he answered, counting out the chips. Ten whites, six reds and six blues for each person. I could hardly breathe, I was so excited.

"I never heard of that," said Maude. "Whatever is it?"

"A liqueur, my dear," said Harry. "Matthew, what do you say to a drop of pretty good brandy? I brought some with me."

"You twisted my arm, Harry."

"Here's my money, Matt," I said.

"Good girl. Fast pay makes fast friends."

Maude started up again. "Frances, this is wrong. I just can't sit here and ... "

"Maude, shut up." That was the grandmother I knew. Still, Maude sat back in her chair with her mouth hanging open in surprise.

"You heard her, Maudie," Uncle Harry said lightly. "Shut up."

Maude had the grace to smile back. "Why are you all ganging up on me?"

"No ganging up ... Let's just leave any future disputes to the wisdom of Mr. Hoyle," Francesca said as she set a large bowl of black cherries down on the table next to Matt.

Edmond Hoyle was a writer best known for his works on the rules and play of card games and a favorite of Francesca's, who quoted him accurately and often.

Over the course of our evening, Matt and Harry began partaking of the brandy at a freer rate. The more they drank, the looser their tongues. Also, the worse they played.

"Count your money on your own time, Sarah," Matt growled the third time he bought in for more chips.

Matthew and Harry were getting along like two fraternity brothers, an alliance that seemed to provoke Francesca, who was downing hard cider.

Her cheeks grew flushed as her repartee grew pithy. The more she flung her humor around the room, the more Harry and Matt roared with delight.

Francesca was a good card player who happened to like wild games. Baseball was her favorite, with threes, sevens and nines wild and fours bringing you another down card. You had to pay a nickel for the threes and the fours, which caused a lot of moaning and shrieking around the table. You don't even think of staying in the fray with less than four of a kind.

Some of the conversation and most of the strategy seemed to bounce right over Maude's head. She'd been awfully sheltered during her life, considering she was a married woman and lived in a good-sized city. She looked like she couldn't decide what to make of the whole experience. Then, she took a couple of nips of the cider and bluffed us all out of a pot with an ace-high nothing of a hand. The more sips she took, the better her game. She even introduced us to Black Mariah.

"High spade in the hole and high hand splits the pot," Maude explained with a newfound confidence.

"Maude!" Harry bellowed. "Where the hell did you ever learn such a thing?"

"Mind your own beeswax, darling. You don't know everything about me."

We all hooted and hollered indignantly over how she'd taken us in, especially Uncle Harry. "Maude! I'd hate to think you've been sitting there all evening, taking advantage of us!"

Maude smiled wickedly ... and promptly won another pot.

I couldn't remember the last time the Main House had been so full of raucous fun. Probably before Grandpap died. He had always been the instigator of madcap. Strings of cherry bombs under the back porch awoke you on the Fourth of July; short sheets on your bed greeted you on your birthday; toothpaste sandwiches showed up in your lunch box.

He was a terror, especially when he was young. Once, as a little boy attending a red one-room school house, he'd lassoed the outhouse and dragged it clear off its mark with the teacher still inside.

By the time midnight rolled around, we were settling up.

"Everyone, count up your chips in groups of fifty cents. The odd ones go into the pot for showdown," Matt announced with authority. "Five-card, high-only, all cards face-up," he added, rifling the cards expertly.

"I wish I knew how in the hell he does that. I just spew the cards all over the floor."

"Here, here!" I sputtered. "No buttering up the dealer. Okay, now. Read 'em and weep."

Matt began laying the cards out, face-up, one at a time in rotation around the table: seven, a two, king and another king.

The dealer got an ace. He dealt another round: a six, a nine and a king.

Maude had a pair of kings and began to giggle. Matt dealt two more cards, both tens.

No one could beat my straight with a five high. I raked in the money: four dollars and sixty-seven cents.

"How are you going to spend your loot, Moneybags?" Uncle Harry asked.

"There's not a whole lot I can do with four dollars, Uncle Harry."

"What an odd child you are, Sarah," Maude broke in. "You're not like any child I've ever known. How much money is a lot of money, then?"

"Well ... five hundred thousand dollars sounds right to me," I answered, carefully gathering the cards and the poker chips and storing them in the cupboard by the fireplace.

My ill-gotten gains went straight into my piggy bank.

Chapter 17
The Scarecrow

Babe must have jostled me. It was nearly three in the morning, according to my clock. I was startled but not afraid, because she often woke up in the middle of the night. She had excellent hearing and obviously felt duty-bound to investigate every significant noise.

Babe and I made our way slowly and oh-so-quietly down the back stairs. With my exquisitely honed spying skills, I could have snuck up on a tribe of Chippewa across a field of balled-up wax paper. Still, I had to be careful, because getting caught would have meant missing the action. Ahhh, it was Francesca and Maude. After what Grandmother had shared with me about the two of them, I was salivating to hear what they were ... discussing. I use that term as a politeness , because although their voices never rose above a whisper, the sisters were having a real blowout.

"I don't think it's any of your business, dear." Francesca said, emphasizing the words "business" and "dear."

Maude came right back with "I'm making it my business. I want to know exactly what's going on in this house. And I want to know now!"

"Why, whatever could you possibly be insinuating, Maude? And don't think for a moment I owe you any explanations!"

"You know exactly ... exactly what I mean, Frances. This ... this person ... this man ..."

"Correction! You mean this fascinating and attractive man, Matthew Mosley. Let me tell you about him so as there are no unfounded perceptions. He makes his living as a pilot, a little barnstorming here, a little crop dusting there."

"You know damn well what I mean Francesca. He is living here."

"Yes," Francesca answered. "He's here because of the arsonist. You remember the arsonist, don't you? Or do you think I conjured up a crazy person — not to mention real fires — out of thin air?" I heard her snap her fingers for emphasis. "Huh! Should the arsonist ever meet with you, it's he who would need rescuing."

"What a convenient explanation for this pilot person. Now, stop beating around the bush! You know precisely what I mean." Maude took a breath and continued, "I have always hated your games. They aggravate me so."

Francesca's tone grew more sarcastic. "Maude, have you considered some mental gymnastics to loosen your mind? It seems to have gotten stuck somewhere in the Middle Ages."

"You have a single man ..." Maude let the accusation hang in the air.

"How very perceptive of you, dear. Would you rather he be married?"

"You're impossible!"

"You're a prig," Francesca hissed.

Someone slammed a glass down on the table.

"Maude," Francesca began again more calmly, "have some more cider."

"Don't you dare try to intoxicate me!" Maude snapped back.

Someone pounded the table; it was surely getting a beating through all this. Francesca must have been gathering her thoughts, because then, it was quiet for a moment.

"Maude, we can take it outside and come to shouting over this. Frankly, at the moment, there's nothing I'd like better. Or ... we can communicate like two reasonably mature adults. God knows, if we aren't mature adults by now, we never will be."

Another silence. I could picture Maude mulling over her options — her face working this way and that. Then, to my utter astonishment, she capitulated. "Oh, all right. But you must know this whole business is sordid. Sordid!"

"I'll make a note of that. Let's see s-o-r-d-i-d, sordid."

The two exchanged more pithy comments before mutually deciding a question-and-answer session might work best.

"Mature questions, that is. I will endeavor to answer in kind, or I may choose to remain silent. To protect the innocent, of course. But beware! Don't ask a question if you aren't fully prepared to hear the whole truth and nothing but the truth." Francesca cautioned.

"I'm not sure I want to know anything, much less everything," Maude broke in, "but I feel it's my duty. Well ... to protect Sarah."

"I beg your pardon?"

Uh-oh.

"I thought you said I was going to ask the questions, Frances."

"Ask away," Francesca said and slapped the table with the palm of her hand. It was a gesture I'd often seen her use to punctuate an uncomfortable moment.

There was a shuffling sound. Someone was shifting position. Literally and figuratively.

"You and Mr. Mosley have a relationship; is that right?" Maude began.

"Right as rain," Francesca shot back.

"What kind of a relationship is it exactly?"

This was the moment I should have slipped quietly back to bed.

"He's a good friend."

Maude snorted.

"Yes, he's a lovely man who brought me something precious in my dotage."

They were calmer now.

"Maude, you can't possibly know how lucky you are," Francesca said with real feeling. "I know how happy you and Harry have been. How well-suited the two of you are."

I could hear someone's fingernails tapping on the table top.

"Don't misunderstand," she continued. "Cox and I had a good life. But I see now that you and Harry had the kind of marriage you both needed. Maude, I could never have given Harry the fulfillment you have given him. Let's face it — I'm just not that kind of woman."

Silence. I wondered if Maude was feeling as uncomfortable as I was. I could hear the large German grandfather clock ticking from the parlor.

"That's ... good of you to say ..." Maude answered after a while. "No ... listen. I feel a ... a change in you after all these years. It makes me happy to feel like I have my sister back. I have you back, haven't I? It's not my imagination?"

Francesca acknowledged she had changed. "Meeting Mathew Mosley has stirred something inside of me ... I'm in love," she admitted quietly.

Harry had been Francesca's first love, there was no doubt of that, but she had felt betrayed by him. Grandpap was gone. Now, Matthew was here, and he was so vital; he cared so much.

Maude started to cry.

Francesca went on quietly. She thought she had settled for second-best by marrying Harry's brother, Cox, thinking it would ease the pain of a broken engagement.

"I realize now that you can't love your way out of pain. You have to grieve properly before you can get on. I was so young — and rash." I heard Francesca sigh. "Cox was a good man. He was fun and easygoing and so full of the devil. At the time I married him, he was the right choice for me, a sound choice. Don't forget, he allowed me to be myself. I'm not sure too many men would have done the same."

Harry would have never allowed it.

"So my loss was really my gain. I still had some wild ways in those days."

"Then ... you're over Harry? The hurt, I mean?" my aunt asked. She was still sniffling. No one spoke for so long a time I almost nodded off against the banister.

"It's time to get over him, wouldn't you agree?" Francesca said at last.

"And Matthew?" Maude asked gently.

"I'm in love with him. Wow, I can't believe I am saying that out loud. But I am fiercely, proudly and softly in love with him. I haven't felt these things in my heart for decades, if I ever felt them at all."

The conversation took a turn. Maude's voice sounded more co-conspiratorial. I could actually hear the sparkle between the two that comes when women share intimacies.

Matthew's features were explored. The women marveled about his calloused hands and how strong and graceful they were. His swashbuckling looks gave him sex appeal. But how did he feel about Francesca?

"He says he loves me. He acts as though he does care about me. But he's a gypsy, a wanderer, someone always looking for the next adventure. God knows I understand those longings. If I'd been a man, maybe I wouldn't have stayed here at Home Farm."

She said she realized that Matthew was still healing and that once he fully recovered from his plane crash injuries, he could well be leaving. "In some ways, I don't care. He's given me so much life in such a short time. Maybe that will be enough to last me the rest of my days."

More silence.

This time, Babe and I snuck back upstairs. It was weird to think of my aunt and Francesca as friends. As I snuggled against Babe, I wondered if Matthew would really leave. That meant I would have Francesca to myself again, something I thought would have made me content.

It didn't. In fact, the idea made me feel sad.

* * * * *

It was a hot and humid morning. The sun was high in a cloud-filled filled sky when I ambled down the back stairs to start a new day. No one was around, so I made my own breakfast: orange juice and oatmeal cookies. Babe carefully placed her forelegs onto my lap to kiss me and do some serious begging.

I distracted her. "Where's Francesca? Go find Francesca."

First, Babe ran around the entire house, but no grandmother. Next, she ran out the back door and within moments, ran back in again. I understood she wanted me to follow her and was about to do just that when the front doorbell rang. Babe tore into the parlor, barking wildly.

"Be quiet! Babe, stop that!"

She sat.

When I opened the door, there was a thin, grizzle-haired man standing on our front steps. He looked like a human scarecrow.

"May I help you?" I asked politely, wishing I hadn't opened the door.

Babe's growling drew the stranger's eyes to my feet, where she sat bristling, hair on end.

"That's my dog," the man rasped after a long moment.

Chapter 18
Night Terrors in the Day

My mind whirled, and my knees felt weak. I leaned my hand against the wall for support and tried to think.

It was impossible not to notice how thin he was. His face was creased with weather and worry. His clothes, whatever color they'd been when new, were gray and nearly transparent from washing and wearing. He looked like he hadn't been sleeping and smelled like bathing had not been a priority.

"I saw the notice on Thunder Ridge Road. That's my dog." He motioned a bony hand and reached for her collar. She snapped at him. Whether he was lying about Babe or not, I couldn't tell, but it was obvious the little red dog wanted nothing to do with this collection of bones.

"Whoa there, girl," he said. "She always was spirited. I've been looking for her everywhere."

"This can't be your dog."

He looked past me, through me. I shivered.

"This can't be your dog; she's never gone missing," I repeated.

"I know my own dog, miss." Now, the hairs on the back of my neck stood up.

"You can ask my dad," I lied. "He's just out back."

He smiled, but not kindly. "I may have to take this up with the sheriff."

I tried to close the door, but his hand held it open. His strength, even in his puny condition, couldn't be overtaken by a nine-year-old. He leaned down and looked me in the eyes.

"Since I can't prove my claim, I won't insist on taking her with me today." He moved his face closer to mine. "If I were you, I'd keep this visit to yourself. It will be our little secret. After all, it would be a shame if something happened to that nice-looking woman you are so attached to. A crying shame."

We were startled by voices coming from the side yard. He took a step back, put a finger to his lips and scuttled off.

My knees buckled, and I sank to the floor. I grasped Babe roughly around the neck and whispered into her ear, "I'll never give you over. Never."

I wanted to run and tell Francesca but thought better of it; he'd threatened her. His words froze me. I wished Daddyboys were here; he'd protect us. I didn't feel comfortable telling Matthew.

I took a deep, long breath to quiet my hammering heart and wandered outside to sit down under the elm. I needed to collect myself. Francesca and Maude were in the vegetable garden. I leaned back against the tree and observed the two sisters working together side by side.

I tried to put the ordeal out of my mind, losing myself in Francesca and Maude's efficient, graceful movements. It struck me that the two were almost the same age. I'd never realized that before. To me, Maude had always seemed like an old lady, while Francesca was regal and somehow ageless. She wasn't really a grandmother at all; she was a friend and confidant, an adventuresome woman. Yet she and Maude must have been born in similar years, time-wise.

The likenesses were obvious. They both had that glossy, pretty grayness that comes with dark hair if you're lucky. They were both supple. But there was an undeniable electricity about Francesca. She had "it"—whatever "it" was. Whether it was her innate character or her love of life in general that lit her face and form from within, I can't say. She certainly wasn't matronly. Never had been.

"Do you remember Albert Geiger?" I heard Maude ask my grandmother.

Francesca laughed. "Do I? Every parent in town practically locked their daughters in chastity belts while he was here. A Bible salesman, of all things!"

I wondered what a chastity belt was and if I should get one to keep the scarecrow away from our home.

"He sold more than a few Bibles to those poor women who stayed home all day, alone, with only the dirty laundry to keep them company."

"Maude!"

"Mother bought one, you know."

"Maude!"

"She did! She did! I still have it. He inscribed it to her on the title page, just underneath the copyright."

"Maude!"

For once, Francesca seemed to have a limited vocabulary.

I continued to watch them. They were weeding in rhythm but in total opposite energies.

Maude pulled slowly, gently. She looked at each weed almost regretfully when it gave up the earth and lay down in her palm. Francesca attacked those weeds like they were enemy troops, come to ruin her life's work. She ripped them out of the ground and threw them onto a trash heap and slapped her palms together with a smack, all in a kind of cadence, one women of the soil have used since the beginning of time. Maude worked at the garden purely as a pleasurable way to pass the time. Francesca was committed to the earth. She looked up then and saw me.

"Ahhh. There's my girl. You must have been burning the midnight oil."

I turned my face away to hide the blush that blossomed there.

"What's the matter, Sarah?"

"I had bad dreams last night," I answered as Francesca sat back on her haunches and brushed the surface dirt from her hands. Francesca didn't use gloves, the way Mommy and Aunt Maude did.

"Come and tell me," she said.

Guilt flooded through me; there were too many secrets. I had spied on her. I had listened to conversations that weren't any of my business. And now an awful man had come to our front door, claiming Babe as his own and threatening to do something terrible if I told.

I sat dumbly for a moment before collapsing into Francesca's embrace and burying myself in her sage smell.

"There, there, Sarah," she said.

"Sarah, dear," said Maude, reaching her hand out to me, "can't you tell us?"

I only shook my head as the stranger's face leapt into the front of my consciousness. I made a quick calculation and did what children like me always do in a situation like that. Lie.

"I had a dream," I began, "about a man, a weird man. He was skinny. He said Babe was his. But she didn't like him, and I told him to go away."

You know by now that Francesca didn't take dreams lightly. She thought they were psychic messages or spiritual lessons. So while Maude was clucking her tongue to demonstrate her empathy, Francesca raised my head and looked at me closely.

"You're sure that's all?" she asked pointedly.

I squirmed and gathered myself, and then, I lied again. "Yes. That's all."

At that moment, Babe nuzzled her nose under my right arm.

"I love her more than anything else in the world, except you, Francesca!"

My grandmother's gaze narrowed and intensified. Gad, she was powerful.

Chapter 19
Out in the Open

"**W**ell, look here... if it isn't the goddesses of the soil!" Harry called out as he and Matthew approached the garden.

"Honestly, Harry, such language." Maude was not amused. Harry waggled his lips in salute.

"You should see what we've been about. Lost Nation's conveyances have fallen into an appalling state of disrepair with Clay away. Busy as a bee is what I'll be while I'm here."

Uncle Harry boasted about how Matthew was smarter than a whip snap when it came to engines.

Maude responded predictably. "Dirty old smelly gasoline is what you two are about. I don't like the odor now any more than I ever did in the past." She sniffed for emphasis.

Daddyboys had been working on Mr. Blackfeather's vehicle before he left for the cruise. The project was more of a challenge than my father had let on.

"Rattletrap!" is how Uncle Harry described it.

Matthew smiled and remarked, "Clay has held that metal contraption together with a needle and thread and a touch of glue. It must have 80 thousand miles on it."

Francesca looked up from her weeding. She sifted the loamy dirt through her hands.

"He's on the Roll in Oklahoma," she said, speaking about Mr. Blackfeather. "Tribal oil subsidies. He has to drive back there several times a year to vote on where the money goes when it's spent."

Maude shook her head. "You don't mean to say that he's one of those rich Indians?"

"He could buy and sell us all," was Francesca's answer.

Harry was puzzled that Mr. Blackfeather would want to live in Lost Nation if he had enough money to go anywhere else. Francesca said it was because of the great spirits that were supposed to reside in the hills above the town.

"He's never seen them himself, but he heard stories about them during his childhood, all the way back in Oklahoma," Francesca said.

"You mean that all kinds of different Indians think this is a ... a holy place?" I asked.

"That's what Tom says." Francesca went back to weeding.

Matt walked over to the garden plot and squatted next to Francesca. He began weeding in her rhythm. "To take nothing away from Tom's spiritual inclinations ... I've been on a reservation," he said. "It's not a pretty place. The men are mostly drunk, when they can get liquor." His face grew thoughtful. "And they can't seem to reconcile their ancient ways of living with their income. The reservations are filled with shoddy homes and poor schooling. Sometimes, I guess the only answer is taking your money and getting out."

"How really awful," sighed Maude.

"Can't expect any better, dear," Harry pointed out. "Silliest ones think you're stealing their souls if you so much as take a photograph."

Francesca's eyebrows lifted. "Harry, you make them sound like savages," she said in a deceptively soft tone.

Harry saw what was coming and put up his hands to try and fend off the lecture. But Francesca breezed forward.

"Before a white man ever set foot on this continent, our native brothers had established a thriving culture. The so-called Five Civilized

Tribes developed reading and writing. Why, parts of our very own Constitution were lifted straight from the Cherokee nation's document. "We white folks made and broke too many treaties to count. We sequestered a sovereign people on pig sties the government called reservations. We sent them blankets filled with small pox germs and inhibited education. We made the children speak English and take European names." Francesca leaned toward Harry, who leaned back. "Yes, they have beliefs that differ from yours and mine. How very American of them ..."

Harry sighed.

I had taken a seat on the ground near Francesca and was wriggling my toes in the weeded earth. The women had watered that morning, and it was still damp and malleable. It felt gorgeously cool and crumbly on my feet. I could imagine some Indian princess doing exactly the same thing decades before on this exact spot.

"I'll bet Tom misses his kin," I said.

Francesca looked at me and smiled.

Harry stretched defensively and changed the subject. "Listen. Matt had a grand idea. Let's eat at Ernie's tonight."

Until now, the idea that Matthew Mosley and Francesca Pittschtick Schneider were an item was nothing more than gossip around town. It had been whispered about, sure. But add innumerable busybodies to the stew, all the regular kind of nosy folks in a small-town restaurant, especially bartenders and waitresses, actually seeing the set-up first hand, and only heaven could conceive of the outcome. Francesca was stunned for the moment. Her mouth gaped, and she was about to say something when Maude cut her off.

"Do you think that's the wisest idea?"

Matt was a wonder. So many times, I'd seen him skirt serious questions. But this time, he stood up to emphasize his thoughts before answering.

"It's time, you see? I may look like a fool, but I'm not one. It's just ... time."

He leaned over to Francesca, grasped her right hand and kissed it with a smack. "It's time God and the folks in this county saw for themselves what the hell is going on here. Wouldn't you agree, Harry?"

Harry was caught between a rock and a hard place. He'd made a kind of tense peace with Francesca, you see. Which meant he also realized how unique a woman he'd let slip away so many years ago. Of course, he was still a conservative-thinking man.

"Don't be an idiot!" Harry said. "I didn't mean we should all troop in there and put on a show-and-tell."

The lids on Matt's eyes lowered a fraction.

Sensing the harshness of his words, Harry softened his stance. "I didn't mean to offend. But let's face it, it is a small town. That's one of the reasons we moved away—the gossip is unceasing. Matt, you don't have to stay and live here. But Fran does. What happens to her after you go along your merry way?"

"One — who says I am going anywhere? Two — we aren't children anymore, Harry." Matt sat perfectly still.

Francesca went back to digging with a vengeance. Without looking up, she warned we'd all be ready for dinner at six thirty that evening, or she'd know the reason why.

Isaac and Lincoln would keep an eye on the place while we were out. I prayed they wouldn't run into the stranger. What if something bad happened to those nice, oafish boys, because they didn't know he was around?

Like he could hear my thoughts, Isaac arrived just then. He was long and gangly with honey-colored hair. He looked just like a giant Saint Bernard puppy. He loose-limbed his way down the drive and knocked on the kitchen door.

"Yoo hoo! Mrs. Frances. I'm here."

Francesca and I were rinsing one another's hair with rain water in the kitchen sink, a once-a-week ritual. Francesca swore it left her hair shiny and soft, and I followed along happily enough.

"Come in, Isaac. Gingerbread and cherry coke on the table."

He nodded and looked at me.

Isaac was the nicest boy. Not dull-witted by any means, he just took his own sweet time to react to life. He was unusual for a farm boy, because he loved to read poetry and was quite familiar with The Romantics and Emily Dickinson, among others.

"Here, Sarah, let me help dry."

You might have thought I would have felt embarrassed having Isaac dry my hair. But he was just this rather large boy-person who didn't have a sister of his own to torment. We'd been neighbors since long before I was born. I never thought a thing about it.

As he rubbed a towel softly across my head, he said, "Don't you worry about things here, Mrs. Frances. You know that Lincoln and I'll take care of everything while you're gone."

"I know you will, Isaac. Did you read the book of sonnets I sent along?"

"Sure did. I brought it back with me. I like the one about the moonlight on the bank. I could almost feel the night air, you know?"

Francesca asked him if he had any questions about feeding the animals. He told her I had already left special instructions pinned to the barn door. "You sure have beautiful printing, Sarah."

"Crud," I answered. Getting compliments from young men, even Isaac, was awful, simply awful.

Isaac smiled that slow smile of his and placed the book of sonnets back into its place. "What should I read next?"

Francesca offered him a volume of poems by Edna St. Vincent Millay, which he took appreciatively.

Isaac drained the soda glass, chomped on the cookies, stepped into the cool gloom at the front of the house and let himself out by the front door.

"I think he likes you, Sarah," Francesca whispered.

"Maybe like a brother."

"Yes, for now. He's a nice boy with a soft soul. Not bad-looking either."

"Stop plotting, Francesca."

"I don't know what you mean."

"Isaac is only 15-years-old, you know."

Francesca took my face in her hands and kissed my nose.

"Whatever in the world has age got to do with it?"

She had me there.

Francesca and I wore the same outfits we had the first time Matthew had taken us out. Maybe we could turn them from disaster wear into "good luck" outfits. One thing for sure, Harry and Maude were stunned by Francesca's appearance. You'd have thought she was wearing harem pants.

"My God! Frances," Maude said, wide-eyed. "What are you wearing?"

"A dress, dear, Surely you've seen a dress before?" answered Francesca with a demure smile.

"But it's so ..."

"Perfect, absolutely perfect," Harry broke in. "Why, she looks like a debutant."

Matt called from outside, "Everybody ready?"

I didn't want to leave Babe behind, in case the Scarecrow man came back. Even though the Teems were on the case, I would worry every minute we were gone.

Francesca looked at me inquisitively.

"I was just thinking about that dream I had."

"And?"

"I don't want to leave Babe here. What if something happened? Don't get a bee in your bonnet."

Francesca peered at me closely. I felt her eyes piercing into my soul, where she'd uncover the truth, so I pretended to sneeze. I was quite convincing and even rubbed my eyes lightly with my fingertips.

Francesca's gaze hadn't changed any, but she agreed.

"All right, Sarah, no bonnet bees this evening. But you are responsible for Babe."

I bear-hugged her, knowing I hadn't fooled her for an atomic second. She'd let me have my way for reasons of her own, not the least of which was her understanding that taking Babe along was important to me.

The men sat in the front seat, while the women, including Babe, sat in the back. It was still muggy, so we left the car windows down the entire drive into town. Harry and Matt spoke about Chicago and the future of international airplane flights.

The sisters didn't say much. Maude kept glancing at Francesca's outfit, and Grandmother kept pretending not to notice. I kept looking out the window but didn't catch sight of the skinny old man. Maybe we'd all enjoy a peaceful night on the town.

Ernie's was a charming, lively place and one of our favorite spots to eat. New York-born Ernie Jones had been an army cook during World War I and had opened the restaurant with his savings in 1921.

He ran the place with his sister, Selma , a war widow. They offered two different meals each night, six nights a week. Tonight, it was spaghetti and meatballs or chicken fried steak complete with home-made soup or salad, French fries or baked potatoes. Sweet corn bread with butter came with every meal.

Selma was at the door when we arrived.

"Why, Maude, what a whale of a nice surprise," she said, clamping her arms around my great aunt in a hug. Selma was very big on hugging. In fact, she was just plain big.

"Ernie," she called over her shoulder to the kitchen, "guess who's here? Maude and Harry and Fra ..." She was stunned into silence mid-sentence by Francesca's sweeping entry.

"Selma, it's so nice to see you. You remember Sarah, of course, and this is Matthew Mosley," she turned toward Matt. "This is Selma."

"Good to meet you, son." Selma had a foxy look on her face and some sarcasm in her voice. "Are you some friend of Harry's?"

"Actually, he's with me," Francesca said quietly.

We were now officially off to the races.

Matt was polite and well-behaved, his presence generating quite a buzz as people whispered to one another. You could almost see the questions hopping from table to table. He didn't kiss Francesca or even hold her hand. But everyone knew they were a couple.

Ernie snuck out of the kitchen to say hello and take a gander.

"Hear you're an airplane stuntman. Tough business, idn't it? Heard ya broke the leg. That so?"

Matthew nodded.

Ernie wasn't usually this sociable. Most of the time, he preferred dissecting business matters over small talk. But tonight, he made over Matt and Francesca like they were Fred Astaire and Ginger Rogers. My grandmother and her escort were creating quite the stir.

It appeared every person in the place had a sudden need to use the restroom, each stopping by our table for a moment or two to get an eyeful. It was as if Francesca and Matt were on exhibit.

Harry was irritated, and Francesca looked ruffled, but Matthew sat as cool as a cucumber. Maude, surprisingly, was unshaken by the entire episode and even offered Francesca encouragement throughout the meal.

"Ignore the attention; it will pass." Maude squeezed Francesca's hand.

"Dessert, anyone?" Ernie had brought gooseberry pie, remembering it was Francesca's favorite.

"Tell ya the truth, Frances, ya look like some kinda queen sittin' here," Ernie exclaimed with a nod.

At that moment, Fay Phillips from Chez Fay swept through the front door. She saw us and wriggled a hand.

"Frances, that dress looks ... elegant. So fresh," she said, walking over. "And who is this?" she asked, ogling Matt.

"Matthew Mosley, ma'am," Matthew drawled and slowly got to his feet. This gesture melted Fay's heart into a tiny pool. Her voice dropped an octave and got huskier.

"My pleasure, Mr. Mosley." Fay blinked her eyes at Matt. "And how long will you be visiting our fair city?"

Matt turned to Francesca and took her hand. "Long as she'll have me, I expect."

Fay Phillips' eyes widened as she examined the lay of the land. Then, she insinuated herself away. Maude laughed. "Did you see the look in her eyes? I enjoyed that, I must say."

"Maude," Harry remonstrated, "you sound positively gleeful."

With that, the second public showing became a resounding success.

Chapter 20
Possibilities and Uncertainties

It had been a grand night. We laughed and carried on all the way home, rehashing the display we'd put on for the locals. It was refreshing to see us all getting along swimmingly for a change.

When we got back to Home Farm, Maude suggested poker and hard cider. I, of course, would have to drink regular old juice. When my Great Auntie won just about every hand, Harry teased it was all due to the reddish concoction she'd been swigging straight from the bottle. In response, she dabbed a little cider behind each ear.

You could tell Harry was stunned and pleased by the about-face in his wife's demeanor. I watched the two nuzzle as they went arm in arm up the back stairs to their room.

The night had cleared, and a silver moon filled the sky with a pale light. I could hear the cricket choir harmonizing just outside and the bullfrogs' basso profundo calls all the way from the pond. I sat on the window seat in my room and gazed out over my kingdom.

A skinny shadow swaying near the big elm tree startled me. I squinted to get a better look. As my heartbeat flipped into double time, I stared into the night and imagined the shadow scuttling closer. I shut my eyes tight and rubbed them hard. After a moment or two, I looked again and saw nothing. Was I imagining things? With my heart still relentlessly in drum-solo mode, I went downstairs to the kitchen to see if Francesca and Matt were still awake.

Matthew was puttering around the kitchen. He turned his head when he heard me.

"Couldn't sleep, Sarah?"

I had to protect Francesca, so I lied and said I was hungry.

Peanut butter and sweet pickles have the power to lighten any mood. Matt liked the idea, too, and made a sandwich for each of us.

"I think we're gonna need some milk, here," he observed as I tried de-buttering the roof of my mouth with my tongue.

We sat quietly, munching. To this day, I can't tell you why, but after a while I simply blurted out, "Are you going to marry Francesca?" Opened the mouth, out the words tumbled.

Mr. Strong and Silent didn't respond right away. Instead, he finished his glass of milk and peered at me intently. It's hard to eat comfortably when someone's staring at you. I put what was left back on my plate.

"You are fond of hard questions aren't you, Sarah?" he asked finally. "I'm not sure the topic is any of your business. Are you?"

"Francesca says it's rude to answer a question with a question." I countered.

"Does she, now?"

"You did it again. You answered a question with a question."

Matthew nodded and said nothing.

We sat in a kind of lip-zipped mental stand-off for another moment until I got up to get a cookie from the tin box on top of the refrigerator. I had to stand on a chair.

"Here, let me help," Matt offered. "I don't want Francesca's Sweetchild to fall and hurt herself." He also grabbed a bottle of something from the cupboard. He poured himself a glass, took only one sip and set the glass on the table.

"Well," he finally admitted, "I'm not planning on any ceremony tomorrow, or anything, and neither is she. But marrying Fran isn't the farthest thing from my mind, either. I do skirt around the idea once in a while." I heard the tip of his shoe tapping the kitchen floor. "She's as nervy as I am, you know. Who can predict how things would be between us? Oops ... that's another question, isn't it? And again!"

"What about me?"

Matt cocked his head and raised an eyebrow. "What about you?"

He threw up his hands then and started over. I watched him choose his words carefully.

"That would be up to your grandmother. It'd be tough for her here. You saw how the locals treated her ... us tonight. It's a small town with small-town thinking. That can be a good thing in some cases, of course." He dragged his hands tiredly through his thick hair. "On the other hand, I can't picture her except in this place." He opened his hands to Home Farm. "Her rose garden and her vegetables ... her whole history ... this house. Apart from you or me or Rachael or anyone else, Fran has a connection to this plot of ground. It's fertile because of her. It's alive. She makes it that way."

So why would you want to take her away?

I knew better than to ask, but I wondered if he would consider leaving without her.

"Francesca said you might take off one day because of your flying."

I immediately regretted betraying a confidence, but since it was too late to withdraw the observation, I pressed with another.

"She said you wouldn't be content here."

There was a long pause. "She could be right about that." He tossed back the remainder of the dark gold liquid.

"Do you love her?"

He answered almost eagerly, "There's something grand about her, something fine," he said. It sounded like he'd discovered that fact for the first time. Then he turned and looked at me again. "I think we've had enough hard questions for one evening, young lady. It's time for you to go to bed and for me to sip a bit more."

As Babe and I snuggled together, I held her protectively and tried not to think of what or who might've been lurking outside my window. I also had a knot in my stomach, thinking that Francesca could leave me ... could leave Home Farm. In the same breath, I realized I'd hate it if Matt left her behind. She'd always and forever be thinking of him, missing him.

"Every way out of this is lousy," I whispered into Babe's ear.

Chapter 21
Changes on the Horizon

Finally the Big Event loomed around the corner, the one Francesca had been training for and most everyone in town was chattering about — the County Fair car races. Mastering a powerful machine like the Doozy took hair-trigger reactions, muscle and a "feel" for clutching the up and down shifts. So many decisions had to be made in a tenth of a second: How much brake was too much? Which drivers got rattled when you passed on the inside? How much intestinal fortitude could a person muster?

Matthew had balanced the ideal amounts of patience and encouragement with Francesca. You could practically see her confidence growing with each spin around the makeshift track. She was ready.

As we were stowing our suitcases in the trunk, Francesca reminded me to grab my fishing pole and some hot dogs. Matthew looked at us questioningly. "Fishing?" he asked.

"Sarah here has a reputation to uphold," Francesca said. "I'm not the only celebrity in Lost Nation."

"Well, this I've got to hear," Matt looked at me with real interest.

The year before, Daddyboys, Mother, Francesca and I went on a fishing trip together. It was the first extended outing without Grandpap, who had passed in 1943. Gasoline was still difficult to find, not to mention expensive, so we cashiered our first destination, Traverse City, Michigan, in favor of the more reachable Montpelier on the Mississippi.

It was a sweet little burg surrounded by lush countryside dotted with grape vines and cherry trees. The region had nearly 181 miles of Lake Michigan shoreline and 149 miles of additional deep blue-colored lakes. Because you could angle for game fish like trout, salmon, blue gills, even steelhead, it was a Mecca for rod and reel aficionados from all over the country.

Our trip took place over the July Fourth weekend, which coincided with an annual trout tournament. My dad, with his wizard-like hands, was an expert at tying lures. But I didn't like those furry things, nor could I stand the way worms continued to wiggle long after they were pierced. Instead, I used hot dog slivers for bait.

We all registered to be eligible for cash prizes in the categories of First Catch, Biggest Fish and Most Caught.

We all certainly missed my grandfather. But since he was a bit of a purist when it came to fishing, he probably wouldn't have enjoyed the free-for-all as much as we imagined he would. Instead, he would have been playing practical jokes off the water. Forget the fish; it was the fishermen Cox would have been after.

But it would have been sensational for him to have seen me win my prize. I caught the first fish of the day, reeling in my little trout four minutes and 17 seconds before the next official catch was tagged. I also won ten dollars and attracted a lot of media attention from a group of sports writers.

I was asked how I could be such an expert fisherman at such a young age. They smiled as I told them about all my training in our pond and how I had the best coach in the world. I pointed toward Francesca, and she curtsied as the writers swarmed in her direction. She made a totally believable pretense toward embarrassment with each photographer's flash as she and I posed together.

What type of bait did I use? When I told the reporters it was hot dog slivers — slivers, not pieces — they roared with laughter. Several newspapers ran the story the next day, many making reference to my hot dog bait in their headlines.

Daddyboys began referring to me as his little genius. Francesca cut out all the articles and purchased additional copies of the papers that ran our photo.

Back in our driveway, my next-door neighbor, Isaac, who was lurking at the edge of the story circle, had heard this tale so many times he now knew it by heart. But like always, he just grinned and nodded his head.

"Wow," Matt offered when I finished. "I am duly impressed." Then, he snapped his fingers. "Wait a minute. Isn't it your birthday? Sometime soon, I mean? If there's a celebration coming, I want to know all about it."

Francesca looked smug. "We're full of surprises, Mr. Mosley. Depending on how the wind blows or the stars are aligned, you just don't know what little Sarah and I might conjure up." Francesca twirled across the porch and winked at me.

Isaac was holding a package.

"I brung you ... er brought, I mean, I brought you this," he handed me a package wrapped in the funny papers from the *Daily Pulse*.

Suddenly, all fishing stories were on hold. What was this weird boy doing?

"What is it?" I asked, already starting to rip into the twine bow.

"Not now! You gotta save it for your birthday." He raised his voice but didn't shout. Then, he quick-stepped his way in the direction of the garage.

How weird ... Isaac Teems giving me a present. I carefully put the package into my suitcase.

The luggage and fishing gear were neatly stowed, and Harry and Maude were ready to go. Francesca, of course, was attending to last-minute business. She always had a checklist to go through prior to traveling.

While we waited, we got a visit from Hunny Clack, who had more mail from the South of France. "How exciting," she said and drove off. "Oh and have a grand time, Frances. Beat their overalls off …" Her voice trailed as she rattled into a cloud of dust.

Matthew offered to let Harry drive, which thrilled my uncle down to his toes. As we pulled away from Home Farm, I realized that when I returned, I would no longer be nine. I was practically all grown up, going into double digits now.

Francesca came across a letter from Des Moines and decided to open it first.

"It's from Professor Gump, Sarah. He responded about your dad," Francesca said.

When Maude asked what we were talking about, we told her about finding Daddyboys' essays and poems in the attic.

"He had a dream but didn't pursue it. He had to quit, because Rachael was having a hard time with her pregnancy," Francesca explained. She turned to me and said, "But look what we were blessed with."

Professor Gump had included an enrollment packet for the journalism and English programs at the university in the fall. He also encouraged my father to complete his previous writing assignments and submit them for full credit.

"Hard to imagine a man in my family being a real writer," sniffed Maude. She looked up at Harry, who was driving and humming to himself. "That's quite an achievement, wouldn't you say, dear?" she asked pointedly.

He continued humming, a steady drone. It would be a soft undercurrent to the trip.

Maude turned to Francesca. "I swear he's becoming hard-of-hearing in his dotage."

Francesca smiled. "More than likely a case of selective audio difficulty."

Maude's face took on the closed-down look it retreated to when some concept sounded too much like Greek for her to get. Francesca leaned over and whispered into her ear, "You know, Maude, they only hear what they want to hear."

It was easy to see why Harry had drawn away from the rest of us like that. Though he was a joiner-in for the most part, opinionated and quick about it, he was undoubtedly thrilled with the pleasure of driving that amazing machine. The purr of the Duisenberg engine was like a Chris-Craft outboard. It welled up from deep inside the car's workings, oozing through the burlwood paneling and into the tenor of the conversation, coloring it ever-so slightly with ... dignity? For a car lover like Harry, that elegant rumble claimed his full attention, and he was ecstatic to attend.

"Sarah, why don't you read us your daddy's letter?" Matt suggested.

"Won't she get carsick?" asked Maude.

I lifted my nose into the air and sniffed every bit as haughtily as Maude sometimes did.

"It's okay; I read in the Duisenberg all the time."

Hail and hearty hello to family and friends.

My bride and I have been in Cannes for three gorgeous days and nights. The sunlight is soft and sweet. We noticed a golden glow that appears to color everything—the sand and the town and the people.

The villa, or shall I be wicked and say our villa, comes with a butler and a maid, a chauffeur and three gardeners!

It boasts a clay tennis court and a pool and a private lagoon. I swoon to describe your mother in her brief bathing costume, tanned and full of youthful exuberance.

I glanced up at Matt before reading the next part, then at Francesca. And plowed ahead.

Frances, you must tell us more about that pilot fellow. Why haven't you mentioned him before? Got something up your sleeve? Your daughter and I might never have known about Matthew, if Maude hadn't written to tell us

Uncle Harry swerved to the left and bobbled over the dividing line in the road. Matt cleared his throat and examined the crease in his trousers. Maude looked horrified. Francesca didn't say anything, but she glared at her sister, who chose to flick her eyes in the direction of the window.

Francesca pursed her lips and paused a moment then said, "Well, read on, child."

And what about this arsonist fellow that Sheriff Mosley wired us about? If he hadn't told us, we would have never known about him either. Dan assures me that he and his brother have everything in hand and there's not a whole heckuva lot I can do from here. Still, it makes a person wonder if maybe there isn't more excitement in Lost Nation this summer than on the South coast of France!
You take care. You're both more precious to us than gold doubloons. And I don't mean maybe!

Francesca was still looking daggers at Maude.
"Well ... someone had to tell them!"
Francesca cocked her chin. "Are you entirely sure it was any of your business?"
Matthew continued to study his pant leg with keen attention. Harry kept glancing into the rearview mirror, fearing the sisters could rip into each other's throats.
I kept reading.
Sarah, darling baby girl, your mother and I think of you here, on the beaches and in the parks and we've decided to come back to France for your thirteenth birthday! With you, of course, else it wouldn't be much of a celebration. By that time, France won't be all that far away. I'll bet you're all wondering what that means.

I looked up at Francesca and then around the car. Even Harry was paying attention now.

Your mother says I shouldn't mention it yet, as the details need ironing out and business-wise, I'm not much of a presser! BUT ... Mr. Toynbee has offered your old pops a job on his lovely magazine! That means I will be a full-time paid writer. The salary is good and I will get to TRAVEL, TRAVEL, TRAVEL!

Maude gasped and clapped her hands! "Isn't that just swell?"
Everyone else seemed to agree except Francesca. I could see the wheels in her mind turning.
"Read on, child," she said quietly.
In my excitement, I had ruffled up the page and had to smooth it over before I could find my place.

One small thing, sweet child, a very small thing, really, there will be some changes in how and where we live. You see, we might have to move to New York. Wouldn't that be the cat's pajamas?

It sounded wonderful at first. It was exciting, mysterious and frightening all at the same time.

"New York," I said loudly. The name rang through the silent car like a great bell. But in that same moment, I looked at Francesca. She would be moving, too, wouldn't she? Or did this mean I would live in New York, and she would live in Iowa? What would happen to us? I couldn't be split from myself like an atom, and that's how I would feel if I had to leave Francesca.

Then, I wondered again about Matt's plans. I had dwelled on Matthew taking Francesca away, never thinking I would be the one to leave. I plowed through the rest of the letter with haste.

We wouldn't move right away as we'd have to settle things in Lost Nation and we still need to find a place to live in New York. Everyone will have to help us including Frances, Maude and Harry. We'll talk more about it when we get home.

Lovies, lovies,
Mommy and Daddyboys

Francesca didn't speak the rest of the trip.

Chapter 22
Written in the Sky

Clinton was bustling and hustling. As we passed a parade of fair banners snapping in the breeze, I couldn't get over the swirling energy in the town or the promise in the air. All the motor courts we passed had "No Vacancy" signs, making us thankful we had made reservations.

Francesca directed Harry to the Lakeview Lodge, which hadn't changed at all since our last visit when Grandpap was still alive. It had never actually overlooked a lake; the fishing competition would take place a few miles outside of town.

Francesca and Maude registered while Harry and Matt went to make arrangements about a fishing boat. It was important, having exactly the right conveyance: not too big, with a small, quiet engine so we could sneak up on those fish.

The kitchenette cabin suites were brightly painted and smelled of Bon-Ami cleanser. The Lakeview also took dogs, always had, which made it perfect for us. Maude, Francesca, Babe and I were going to share one room, with Matt and Harry next door.

Francesca arranged for a roll-away bed for Babe and me. Then, she and Maude began unpacking while Babe and I took an exploratory walk before lunch.

The motel stood on a quiet tree-lined street. In those days, business establishments and private homes were built side by side, unlike the strict zoning regulations today. There was a wading pool on the property that looked promising. Maybe later that night, I'd sneak

Babe back there for a swim and totally ignore the bold sign warning, "No Dogs Allowed."

As Babe and I explored together, I mulled over Daddyboys' news. Imagine living in New York! Imagine eating in glamorous restaurants and mixing with "literati." I did know a little about the Algonquin Round Table — a group of infamous intellectuals/writers who met regularly, mainly to trade naughty stories and throw clever insights about society or religion or the woeful state of theater back and forth. Daddyboys was always sharing magazine articles about the feuds between Zelda Fitzgerald (author F. Scott's wife) and newspaper critic Dorothy Parker as well as the peccadilloes of that notorious group of undisciplined yet fascinating folks. At that age, of course, I didn't have a firm idea of what "peccadilloes" were.

I wondered how much I'd miss my friends and if they could come to visit. I'd seen New York in the movies, of course. It seemed a seamless collection of traffic jams and crowds of people. Could horses be kept in New York? If not, whatever would we do with Miss Blossom and RedBird?

But by far the most troubling thought to me was the possibility of leaving Francesca behind. I understood that she might not be open to leaving Home Farm, but my life without her was unthinkable. I literally shuddered at the thought.

Babe was enjoying our walk, nosing out new smells. Together, we soaked in the day's sun, sights and sounds. Although I had no reason to feel anything but delight, at times a tiny frisson of fear tiptoed over my skin. There was a prickle on the back of my neck that said something wasn't as it should be.

As we walked along the trail to the top of the hill behind Lakeview Lodge, I kept glancing over my shoulder. Nobody was following us, but I felt as though we were being watched.

"C'mon, Babe," I called as I skedaddled back to the motor court.

"Sarah, dear, there you are," called Maude.

"Just in time," Harry chimed in. "Thought we'd go down to the fairgrounds and take some lunch. Try some of those lovely fried chicken recipes." He touched my cheek. "I'll bet there isn't a decent piece of fried chicken in all of Manhattan."

"We brought lovely food from home," Francesca said.

Harry rubbed his hands together with relish. "Even better."

"Wait till you see the boat, Sarah," Matt said in a jovial way that was unusual for him. "If you can't catch a fish from this baby, you can't catch a fish."

Harry was skeptical. "Be lucky not to sink the moment we untie from the dock. Still think we should have taken that little Chris-Craft. What a keen specimen."

Being the county seat, Clinton was good-sized as cities went in the midwest, and it always struck me how noisy it was. As soon as you stepped out of the car, the sounds washed over you from all sides. It probably didn't hold a candle to New York, but it was exiting just the same.

Very few people are aware that Clinton was actually once named New York, so designated in 1836 by its original settler, Joseph Bartlett. The newly borne community was one of several clustered in those days on the west bank of the Mississippi River.

Continuous development and the introduction of a rail system adjacent to the settlement spurred its sale to land speculators. When the Iowa Land Company bought Bartlett's tract, they renamed it Clinton, in honor of Dewitt Clinton, who was the governor of New York State. Talk about coincidence …

There's nothing like a state fair! Ferris wheels, merry-go-rounds, tilt-a-whirls and all sorts of games awaited us, not to mention all the mouth-watering food. There would be cotton candy and popcorn, canned fruits, fried dishes and a variety of homemade sweets. There were also plenty of contests like car racing, bake-offs and livestock competitions.

I loved saying how-do to the farm animals. Rows of different-sized covered pens housed hand-raised lambs, cows, horses, rabbits and even chickens. Some of the animals would go to the butchers, true, but the best of the best would be breeders. As long as I didn't dwell on the fate of the animals, I was eager to enjoy their company.

The newborns were the cutest: piglets squealing, baby chicks chirping and ducklings waddling. Plenty of wonderful scents, too, like the smell of fresh straw and sweet feed, a mixture that boasted molasses as its not-so-secret ingredient. It was supposed to give calf yearlings a thick, glossy coat.

It was going to be my best birthday ever.

A roar shook the buildings. The animals hollered in agitation and stirred in their enclosures. We all ran out to see what was causing the commotion. Matt instinctively seemed to know where the noise was coming from and what it was. He stood with his head tilted upward and his eyes closed, savoring the sound as if it were music. It was the first airplane I'd ever seen close-up. The pilot and his craft must have been no more than 100 feet above the roof lines. The craft swooped gracefully, its metal wings flashing in the sunlight as the engines thundered above our heads. To me, it was another spectacular sight, one more memory to mark my time at the fair. But when Francesca saw her enemy, a crop-dusting biplane, her face fell.

Matthew, on the other hand, looked more spirited than ever, like a three-year-old at his own birthday party. He gave a couple of giant hand swings to the sky, and the plane waggled its wings in response. It bore down over us once more, close enough to raise the hair on our heads, before coming to rest in a grassy field some few hundred yards beyond the fairgrounds.

The plane thumped as it hit the ground. Her pilot hit the air brakes and steered it in a straight line toward a stand of live oaks. Before the plane stopped, Matthew had taken off in a trot, his recovering leg preventing him from taking full strides.

What could we do but follow?

The dust had just begun to settle when a tall man jumped off the wing and started running toward Matt. The two stood there embracing and back-patting like long-lost brothers. The pilot was huge, hearty with red hair and a craggy face. He walked in a good-natured swagger and winked at us before he let go of his friend.

We all stood in silence, trying to understand.

"You old sonuva moose! I heard a rumor you might be over this way. Say, you look fine, just fine!" The pilot's words had a lot of pronounced "ay's" embedded in an accent I'd never heard before.

Matt beamed. "Everyone, this is my oldest and most bullheaded associate, the dearest friend I have in the world, Ian Emerson. Watch out; he's a rascally chap from Vancouver."

"Canada?" I gasped. "You mean you're from the top of the world?"

The men laughed as Ian shook hands with the family and even said hello to Babe.

Matt's friend was very unlike him — so hail-fellow-well-met it would be difficult not to immediately take to him. He had a dash of the devil, no doubt, but he was talkative and cheerful where Matt was cool and wry. We soon learned that Ian had another talent: He could drink more beer than anyone we had ever met, a skill he proudly demonstrated from almost the moment he stood on terra firma.

Ian joined us for lunch, oohing and aahing over the picnic Francesca and Maude had created for all of us. We sat under a live oak tree.

"We need some brew and lots of it," Ian reminded Matt and Harry, who had gone to unload beverages from the car.

Ian then proceeded to charm Maude right out of her shoes. "Even before I arrived in America, I'd heard about the beauty of its women, and I can't say I've been disappointed, not in the least," he explained.

Maude blushed.

I noticed that Ian seemed to include Francesca in the conversation but not to address her.

"And the way you ladies cook. I'm a big man with an appetite to match," he said, slapping his rock-hard mid-section, "and the American midwest is heaven to me."

"Why are you here?" Francesca said with a piercing look.

"Have to make a living."

"And it was this particular fair that attracted you, because of its profit-making potential?"

"I've never been here before, and that's as good a reason as any, you can wager. Say, Sarah, what else can Babe do? This is one intelligent dog; wouldn't you say so, Maude, sweet?"

"I certainly would," answered Maude, preening.

Matt and Harry had returned, a welcome diversion. "Well, folks," said Ian, his mouth stuffed with a drumstick, "I'm off to check on my baby. I'll be strutting my stuff tomorrow and Thursday." He opened his palms to Matt. "Say, why don't you join me now for a test run? Get your feet wet. She's a sweet little piece, Matt, my boy." He downed the last gulp of his beer.

"Well ...," Matt began, sliding a guilty look at Francesca out of the corners of his eyes, "... we sort of have plans for this afternoon. You know."

Ian took in Francesca and Matt and nodded his head sagely. "Yes, I see. Well, what say we take a spin later? In fact, I'll be happy to take everyone up. Mrs. Pittschtick," he said, bowing grandly, "you can go up first ... after Matt, of course."

He looked straight into Francesca's eyes. He was challenging her, and she knew it. Never one to pass on a bald-faced dare, she stood up and straightened her back. Then she lifted her chin and purred, "Why, Mr. Emerson, that would be lovely, thank you."

"Right, then, I'll be looking for you here about six." He took Matt's hand and shook it as though it might disappear from his grasp. "It's good to see you, my friend. Good to see you."

With a furtive glance at Francesca, Ian sauntered away

Ian seemed to know a lot about ... things. Had Matt written him? Francesca was attuned to all these nuances, I'm sure.

* * * *

The boat was everything Matt and Harry had promised. On the one hand, it was quiet and easy to maneuver. On the other hand, its paint job was peeling rapidly, and you could see where it had been patched below the water line.

"Are you sure it's quite safe, Harry?" asked Maude, gingerly setting her foot into the unstable-looking craft.

"It's safe enough. But it'll never win a beauty contest."

Francesca laughed. "I just hope it doesn't scare the fish the way it's scared Maude."

I liked to fish. It was something I'd grown up with, spending lazy mornings putting along with Grandpap and Daddyboys. But that day, my mind wasn't on fish, boats or paint jobs. Who cared about fishing when I had an airplane looming on my immediate horizon?

It was two and a half hours before sundown when we gathered around the landing field. Ian was there, proudly showing off his craft, which he explained was a de Havilland Tiger Moth named *The Lady Victoria*.

She was bright yellow with red stripes down the side and over the nose. Matt touched her the way he sometimes touched Francesca, with a kind of still wonder. It was eerie.

"Why do planes have female names?" I asked.

"Tradition," muttered Uncle Harry as he inspected the propeller blades. "Sailing ships have always been considered she's."

Francesca stood apart from us, arms across her chest to ward off the evil spirit that lay anchored by a mooring rope in front of her. "Those that don't like women," she said, "say it's because while women may be beautiful, they are also unpredictable and hard to handle."

Matt offered, "I think it's because ... because they glisten in the sunlight. They're of the air, not of the earth. Airplanes take us up beyond where we could go by ourselves."

Maude reached out her hand as if the plane might be on fire.

"Well, Matt's up first. And then, who?" Ian asked, too casually.

"I'll go," said Francesca. "It's time, past time, to know what there is to be known about all this," she said purposefully, with a queenly wave of her hand.

Matt's body tensed up as he settled his bad leg properly into the cockpit. Was it anxiety or pain we saw in Matt's eyes as he prepared for takeoff? Then, at a thumbs-up sign from Ian, along with an "all clear," the engines roared into life. Matt immediately closed his eyes and leant his head back. You could see the tension in his body give way.

Whatever reservations Matt may have had were not evident as he and Ian looped the sky, leaving circles of smoke high above our heads. They flew upside-down, twisting and turning in perfect rhythm with the hum of the engine. With his ear flaps waving and his eye gear pressed against his face, Matthew looked perfectly natural. The flight may have not taken more than ten minutes, but it transformed Matthew's attitude. When he jumped gingerly from the cockpit to the ground, his face was filled with quiet joy. He held his hand to his chest and grinned like a child. His leg was hurting, or so it seemed, because he was limping more than he had been, but he didn't complain about it. Frances explained to me some years later that a deeper healing had taken place.

Francesca was next. Matt held his hand out, and my grandmother took it without hesitation. She was wearing her leather racing cap and a scarf Matt had given her.

"God, you look dashing," Matt couldn't contain his thoughts.
Ian gave Francesca some instructions and assured her he had control of the aircraft. She just shrugged her shoulders as if it didn't matter either way. Ian smiled and gave his thumbs-up sign. He started the engines and taxied to the end of the field. I don't know why, but I started running after them with Babe at my heels.

Aunt Maude and Uncle Harry were running behind me. Matthew yelled something as I ran beyond the "No Trespassing," sign leading to the airstrip but I couldn't hear their voices above the sound of the powerful engine or the beat of my leaping heart. Had I heard them, I would not have listened. Francesca was taking to the clouds, and I couldn't let her leave without me.

A crowd gathered along the field's fence to watch this drama unfold. I was unaware of anything except catching Francesca. But it was too late; she and Ian had taken to the air. I sat down and began to cry. Babe tried to lick away my tears, but I was heartbroken. Then, something unexpected happened; the airplane was circling and coming back for a landing.

Matt had now caught up with me and walked me nearer to the fence out of harm's way. We watched as Ian flew in. He shut the engine down and vaulted out of the cockpit. I hid behind Matt, afraid of what would happen to me. But instead of being angry, Ian was amused. He smiled as he swept me into his broad arms and carried me to the *Lady Victoria*. Babe followed close behind.

Ian climbed up the wing of the airplane with me still in hand and then set me down on Francesca's seat. He bent down and picked Babe up and placed her inside the craft, too. Once we were all safe and secure, he prepared for another takeoff.

"My, she's full of the devil's spirit," Ian said, winking at my grandmother.

"Sweetchild, wherever do you get such fire?" Francesca asked, as if surprised by my behavior.

"Looks like we have an audience for this show," Ian waved to the crowd, who were now applauding the stunt pilot's latest shenanigans.

The engine's noise was deafening as we climbed into the sky. At first, the ride was bumpy as the plane hit wind turbulence, bouncing like a boat chopping across the water. The force of the wind pushed me back against Francesca's chest. I felt her body tensing behind me as we climbed higher and higher. Her knuckles were pale as she gripped the seat belt, clinging for her life. I peeked through the glass and saw everything below us getting smaller. Once we reached altitude, I could barely make out the people below. Babe had no interest in anything except hiding on top of Francesca's feet.

As the wind blew across my face, I realized it felt good. My tears were all dry now, and sitting there with Francesca, I regained my equilibrium. Francesca and I had never been in an airplane before. Ian must have sensed how nervous we were, because he reached back and squeezed my grandmother's hand. Perkily, she gave her own the thumbs-up sign.

Ian didn't take any loops or spins. Instead, he flew over the Mississippi River and the picturesque countryside. It was breathtaking. We flew over maple, hickory, elm and oak trees and swung over ferry boats that were crossing the Big Muddy.

Francesca took one deep breath after another. And then, the picture postcard tour claimed her. She flung her arms wide to embrace it all, then clasped her airy elements — the sky, clouds and birds, into her chest. She was hooked.

All too soon, our journey came to an end. As we drifted lower and lower, I pushed back into Francesca's chest. I could feel her heart beating, wild as mine. We skidded slightly across the grass before coming to a stop.

Matt looked expectantly into Francesca's face as Ian helped us down.

"I've got to learn how to fly," whooped Francesca. She touched Matt's nose with a fingertip. In a softer tone, she told Matt, "You're just the person to show me how to do that."

Ian kindly ferried Maude and Harry up in the *Lady Victoria* for their turns as Matt, Francesca, Babe and I plopped down on our picnic site. Matt and Francesca didn't say much, but I noticed they were more affectionate toward each other than they had ever been before in public. As we watched Maude and Harry's flight, my grandmother and Matt held hands and occasionally kissed one another.

Chapter 23
Taking the Bait

Both Francesca and I were brushing our teeth, and Maude was rustling under her covers. It was still dark outside when someone started banging on our cabin door. Babe began to bark.

"It's a trans-Atlantic telephone call. They're a waitin' on ya," said the deepest woman's voice I have ever heard to this very day. "Came in on the telegraph operator's phone line. He drove over to get ya."

It took Francesca a moment to coordinate her robe, her slippers and the common room sofa. She opened the door to Madge, a robust woman whose hair was wrapped tightly in curlers of various sizes and colors. Madge was the night manager—and the day manager, too.

"I don't think I understand ... There's a long-distance call down at the telegraph office?" Francesca asked.

"Now you know exactly as much as I do," the woman responded. "The car's waiting."

"Sarah, hurry up and get your slippers and robe on."

Our driver was also the telegraph operator. When we got to his office, he handed us the receiver. He never uttered a single word.

"Hello? Hello? Daddyboys is that you? It's Daddy!" I shouted to Francesca and then said loudly back into the phone, "I can hear you, Daddyboys!"

I held out the receiver, so Francesca and I could share.

"How's my precious birthday girl?"

"Oh, we're having the loveliest time, and we all miss you and ..." I wanted to keep speaking but Daddyboys cut me off.

"Whoa, missy, hold on there," Daddyboys said, laughing. "First of all, your mother and I are going to sing you 'Happy Birthday' from halfway around the world."

After my parents sang to me, they asked if I had received their letter about moving to New York.

"What do you think about your old dad?"

"I think you're the cat's pajamas, but ..."

"Sarah, are you there?" His voice suddenly sounded faint and scratchy.

Francesca shook the phone. It helped a little, though I can't think why.

"Clay? My, this is a terrible connection, isn't it? Clay? Is that you?"

"Can you hear me now, Francesca?"

My grandmother told her son-in-law how delighted she was for him and his new position in New York. "We're all very proud of you, Clay, and Rachael ... she must be over the moon!"

"I'll let her tell you herself." Francesca put the phone back between us, so I could speak with my mother. Rachael was babbling enthusiastically about their trip and our move to New York.

"Mommy I can't wait to open my presents. Just think, they came all the way from Paris. No one else in Lost Nation can brag about that."

"Bragging is unbecoming, Sarah."

"I know, Mommy."

"Well ... maybe just this once, we'll make an exception. Oh, it's so beautiful here. It even smells different. You should see the flower beds and the orange trees. There's a town called Grasse near where we're staying, and most of the flowers they use in perfume across this globe are grown there. You should see it, field after field of fragrant, pastel blossoms."

"I love you, Mommy."

"I love you, too. You both behave yourselves while we're away."

Francesca and I burst out laughing.

We heard some more static before Daddyboys said, "Sarah, this New York business ... It's a big opportunity for me. You do understand?"

Francesca had retreated to a chair, so I took the opportunity to share my reservations.

"But what if we don't want to leave Iowa?" I asked softly

"Nonsense, nonsense. Once you all see the kind of life your old dad is in for, even Francesca will be raring to go. Your grandmother, after all, is at heart an adventuress."

I started to protest, but he cut me off and insisted everything would be fine. "You'll see, darling; it will be splendiferous for all of us."

He gave his farewells and then he was gone.

After I hung up, Francesca and I couldn't help but smile at one another. After all, it wasn't every day a person received a telephone call from another continent. Of course, I also felt sad, because I missed my parents terribly. Francesca read my mind.

"No fretting today, child. It's your special once-a-year wingding. Let's keep it that way. Remember, each thing in its own time. Right?"

"Right," I answered as unenthusiastically as possible.

In order to whisk any hint of gloom away, I decided to open all of my gifts before breakfast. Maude and Harry gave me books, which was lovely. Lots of Dickens and a new author for me—Agatha Christie—whose intricately plotted tales of improbable detectives solving murders in quaint ivy-swathed towns started my lifelong love affair with mystery stories.

From Matt, I received an ah-ooga truck horn he'd picked up at the fair. It was shiny brass with a convoluted neck and resembled a sea horse in a nightmare. It was beautiful.

My parents sent me two Paris outfits. One was for play, pants that fell to just below the knee. At first I thought they looked odd, but within a month or two I realized I was just ahead of the rest of the country. Thanks to the Frenchies and their on-the-edge style sense, I was the first in my town (or state, in all probability) to own pedal pushers. The other outfit was for dress, all lace and fine embroidered cotton in coral pink, like clouds at dawn.

I'd saved two gifts for last: Francesca's and Isaac's. His came in a small box, long and thin.

"What the heck is this?" I said, peering down into the wrapping.

Matt took the box and picked up the thing gingerly. "Looks a little like a fishing lure. I never saw anything tied like that before."

"It'll probably scare the fish away," I humphed.

Harry scratched his head. "I think if I were a trout, I just might go for this." He took the lure from Matt and waved it around in the air. "See how it wafts? Wafting is very important to any fish that knows a good dinner from a bad one."

Uncle Harry's evaluation of my lure improved my opinion of it.

Francesca's gift was wrapped in a small silken sack. It had a name on the outside that had worn away with age. It looked like it read "TI F NY & C ., EW Y RK."

Inside the sleek-feeling pouch was a black box. It was heavy and had a tiny latch. I was already excited, because it looked like the perfect box in which to hide a treasure. It turned out to be a bigger prize than even I could have imagined. Nestled inside on a black velvet cushion was Francesca's wedding ring. It was the one Grandpap had bought for her all those years ago in New York City on their honeymoon.

I was stunned and struck dumb. No one else said anything, either.

Francesca picked up the ring and threaded it onto the chain she'd worn around her neck since Grandpap's passing. She slipped the chain over my head and kissed me on the cheek. "For my Sweetchild," she whispered, "to keep her safe and us woven together in spirit, no matter how near or far we may be."

"I can't take this," I moaned, "It was yours and Grandpap's."

"Sarah, it's time; don't you see? It is past time."

No, I didn't see.

Matt took my chin in his strong hands. He lifted it. "A woman can only wear one wedding ring at a time. Maybe she's making room."

Matt's explanation surprised me. I looked at Francesca and was about to speak, but she stopped me with a wave of her pointer finger. She stood up and began to act business-like.

"Let's not jump to any hasty conclusions, ladies and gentlemen." She gave Matt a swift, sharp look. "Besides," she went on, holding her hand over her left ear, "I swear I can hear the fish calling my name. What say we eat a rapid breakfast, settle ourselves in a quiet spot on the water and win that angler contest?"

Though she surely had a way of stopping conversations, she couldn't have stopped the wave of emotion that washed over me as I fingered her gift. It hung down, appropriately enough, right to the level of my heart.

"Damn," observed Harry after suffering through his second consecutive nibble-less half hour.

The fish were not biting. Never mind that we had set out on the boat before sun-up, straight after breakfast; no one had caught anything at all, much less anything substantial. The lake was overflowing with disappointed fishermen.

"Double damn," agreed Maude. She was a sight to behold, sitting in the shade of a tremendous straw hat festooned with three different scarves. A great one for protecting her skin from sun damage, she looked like an innocent version of Bathsheba in the Dance of the Seven Veils.

"It's your damn paraphernalia," groused Harry. "All that claptrap on your head, I swear, you're scaring the fish."

"Says you. At least I've had some bites," Maude retorted.

Francesca rolled her eyes. "Will you two stop it? Please?" she whispered sharply.

Matt didn't say a word. He leaned back against the picnic hamper, eyes closed, face shaded by the brim of his Stetson. When I squinted at him, I fancied the hat had a Roy Rogers block to it. But maybe I was making things up to keep my mind from leaking out of my ear sockets in sheer boredom. I yawned big.

"Why don't you try your new lure?" asked Harry with a playful poke at my ribs. "Some gentleman caller went to an awful lot of time and trouble."

I sighed and dug the ugly thing out of our community tackle box.

"I wouldn't use this if I wasn't so desperate to catch something," I sniffed as I tossed my line out with Isaac's homemade lure into the water.

It had barely sunk into the lake when I got a hit. I stood up so rapidly, the boat tipped precariously, water lapping over the sides.

"It's a whale," I yelled.

Babe was yelping and lunging toward the water. Francesca had to hold her so she wouldn't leap overboard.

Matt peeked out from under his hat brim.

"It's a big one. Don't panic, Sarah. Let him run." Matt encouraged me, talking me through techniques. "Let out some line. That's right. Now, reel some in. Feel it?"

I pulled my rod smoothly back as hard as I could. It bowed almost in half before I felt the fish solidly hooked on the line.

"I got him! I got him!" I shouted.

Francesca shook her head. "I think he's got you, child."

Matt leaned toward me, ready to assist. But even with Matt's encouragement, I wasn't sure we could win this battle. It seemed like an eternity since the fish had hit my line, and it had only been 10 minutes according to Matt. My arms ached. My fingers and palms grew raw, but I couldn't give up. This would be the prize fish of the day, I was sure of it.

Francesca must have sensed my weariness.

"He's tired too, Sarah. You stay in there. Just relax your hands for a moment, not your arms, just your hands. Wait for a lull on the line ... good. See, he's changing direction from the way he started out ... Okay, now, hold on with your hands, and let your arms go just a little ... take a deep breath ... and another. You're doing it, Sweetchild. You can do it."

Matt stood behind me to make sure I didn't slip. We had been battling with this monster for twenty minutes by then, and the fight started to draw some attention. A flotilla of small boats floated our direction to get a closer look.

My body ached, but the crowd's cheers hiked my adrenalin, reinvigorating me.

Suddenly, the fish broke the surface. He was brownish with long fins on his back and a mouth like a trout. He seemed to be looking in several directions at once.

"That sumbich is one large wall-eyed pike," Matt said. "Twenty pounds, I'll wager. Sarah, you pay close attention. This could be the granddaddy of these parts."

Finally, the fish let go. All at once, he just stopped trying, and the absence of weight on the line sent me sprawling practically into the brink. Shaking like a leaf, I managed to get him up into the boat, but I didn't have the strength to net him, so Matt did it for me.

All the other fishermen began to applaud.

"We could have Federico's cook him up for us tonight," Uncle Harry teased.

"NOOOOO!" I shrieked. "Can't we just weigh him and let him go?"

Matt put his arms around me, and I collapsed into his embrace. I was totally exhausted and completely unaware of everything on our trip back to the dock except that fish, which we kept alive in a bucket of water. I watched him closely the whole time to make sure he was all right.

A string of boats followed us to the weigh station to see how my pike would be recorded. It was a big one, noted the official. "That's 19 pounds and seven ounces ... a mighty fine catch, young lady." The weight master tossed the fish back into the bucket of water, and we pushed the boat back into the lake. A few moments later, the pike was swimming madly back to the depths from whence it had come.

By the time we returned to shore, I was practically asleep sitting up. Matt scooped me into his arms again, and with Francesca's comforting hand soothing my fevered forehead, I began to doze.

It was the applause that stirred me. I cracked my eyes open a quarter inch and saw all these strange people gathered at the shoreline. They were looking at me and clapping. I felt a buzz in my head.

That's when I saw the Scarecrow. He was dressed in the same grayish, raggedy cast-offs he had worn at Home Farm.

I screamed and tried to struggle out of Matt's arms.

Babe saw the Scarecrow too. Growling to beat the band, she wiggled out of Francesca's grasp and took after the skinny male figure in the distance.

"Oh, shit," Matthew whispered under his breath. He carefully set me down, then jogged after Babe as best he could.

"What's going on?" asked Maude frantically.

That's when I could have sworn I saw Sheriff Dan. What the blazes was happening? Tired and confused, I could only shake my head and iron my forehead with my hands.

After what seemed like an eon, the gravity of the situation sank in. "We have to find Babe," I sobbed, Then, I grabbed Francesca with all my might. "We have to find her!"

Chapter 24
In the Clouds

When I came to, I was lying on my roll-away. For a moment, I didn't know where I was.

"Aahh, that's better," Francesca said, touching my forehead softly. "You simply wore yourself out catching that fish. And then Babe took off, and you had a fit. That's right, isn't it?" She leaned over and kissed my cheek. "There isn't something else going on that I should know about, is there?" My grandmother was looking at me with her particular probing expression.

"Babe," I exclaimed as my dog jumped onto my bed. She was thumping her tail as she rested her head across my lap.

"Where did you find her?"

"She found us."

"You mean all by herself?"

"I do."

I reached out to hug my clever and intelligent dog and was immediately ambushed by aching muscles. "Whoa."

"You'll be sore a few days," Francesca sat next to me and lightly massaged my arms. She stroked my hair and whispered in my ear how much she loved me and how proud she was of my fishing. Was she still looking at me to see if I was hiding anything from her?

You bet she was.

"Sarah, did you see anything unusual today?"

"I thought Sheriff Dan was at the fairgrounds. I thought I saw him when Babe ran." It was almost true.

"Sheriff Dan in Clinton?" Francesca cocked her head. "I wouldn't think so, child. Why would he be here?"

"I don't know ... but I know I saw him."

Just then, I heard the unmistakable roar of the Doozy in front of our unit. Within seconds, there was a crisp knock on the bedroom door, which quickly popped open, revealing the rest of my family.

"Ah, there's our girl," Uncle Harry smiled.

"And there's that damned dog," Matthew grunted. Chasing after Babe had sent Matt to the doctor's office. He would now be forced to use his cane for a few more days, as the jogging had been too much for his still-healing leg.

"If you keep it elevated and apply some ice, it won't be so bad," Francesca offered.

Apparently, everyone else had kept busy while I slept. While Matt visited the local doc, my uncle and aunt continued searching for the dog. After nearly an hour, when they were on the verge of giving up, Babe had apparently strolled onto the motor court grounds.

"Well, now that everyone is accounted for and still in one piece, shall we go to the airfield?" Uncle Harry asked. "Ian invited us all especially."

"Yes, let's," Maude said with real enthusiasm. "Alright, Sarah, get your things on and join us double time."

They left the bedroom door slightly ajar — just enough for a professional spy like me to make out a conversation.

Francesca took Matt to the side. "Would your brother Dan be in town for any reason?" she whispered.

"Why would he?" Matt whispered back.

"It's impolite to answer a question with a question."

Francesca and Matt both turned and looked in my direction. I darted to the birthday boxes and whipped out my new Capri pants.

"Next stop, the airfield." Now that he, too, had conquered the skies, Harry was looking forward to the air show more than ever. The actual races weren't scheduled until the following day. In the meantime, pilots were flying in from all over to register for the event. Ian thought we'd enjoy meeting the sky jockeys and seeing the unusual assortment of aircraft up close ... like a backstage pass at a Broadway musical, only heaps better.

Since Matt knew everyone and everyone knew him, he introduced us around. He explained that this was the first major air show since the end of the war, which was why it had gathered many of the greatest pilots still living. "I hear that the collection of flyboys at this fair will be over twice the expected number."

We were plain struck dumb in the presence of all those wild hawks, their life stories lurking behind their eyes, their souls so obviously cut from a different bolt of cloth than the rest of us poor mortals.

Some had fought against Rickthoven's Flying Circus in the First World War, others against the Luftwaffe and the Imperial Japanese Air force in the Second. More than a few had since sunk to the lowly rank of crop duster — and loved every minute of it. There were barnstormers, like Matt, more than a few now-civilian instructors and even a few who'd flown in the moving pictures. It was a small, tight club consisting mostly of men, although there were two women in the group.

The pilots all seemed to have their own language, using an aero-jargon shorthand that couldn't be deciphered by outsiders. A couple of the boys asked Matt's advice about one thing and another: fuel mix, drag, flap tension. He was in hog heaven. The rest of us gawked like star-struck fools. Except Francesca. She was quiet and somewhat shy with the larger-than-life men and women clothed in the shining armor of survival and past bravery. But she didn't look at them as celebrities. She saw them as young people, some young enough to be her grandchildren.

Terrible things happen in war, and many of these fliers had seen the worst of it. Their courage helped make our world safer, but at what cost? Up close, you could tell that some had been scraped emotionally bare by their experiences. While they might boast about hundreds of rubber band-stopped landings on aircraft carriers or flights through firestorms of shrapnel, how had those events reconstructed their souls? Some bore visible physical scars, but I began to realize that the worst wounds were most likely internal.

Their common pain and glory combined to form a shared and cherished gossamer bond. A deep-rooted understanding was evident, and their humble sense of duty and love for their country was manifest. Even a small girl like me was stirred by their presence.

Francesca felt it, too. She stood among them, graceful and quiet, and listened. Her sense of connection to all things and faith in her place in the world opened their society to her.

In their turn, the pilots were drawn to my grandmother and treated her like a peer. As if reuniting with an old acquaintance, each stranger discovered her steady presence, her honest interest. She shook a hand or nodded with heightened awareness to a tone or a nuance of phrase.

When Matt mentioned her upcoming car race, the otherworldly crowd drew closer. One of the female pilots whispered something in Francesca's ear and threw a thumbs-up in Matt's direction. Francesca smiled and shook her head. When a flask magically appeared, Francesca drank deeply from it without being asked.

I saw my grandmother perform various amazing feats of living magic throughout her lifetime. But I never saw her more incandescent, yet more substantial, than on that afternoon. She had tapped into a well-spring of grace that no movie star ever boasted, that monarchs achieve only in fairy tales.

Everyone wanted to take Francesca for a spin in the wild blue. Matt looked around at the good-natured sparring, gave a little huff, grabbed Francesca by the hand and went to Ian's *Lady Victoria*.

"What in Heaven's name are we doing?" she asked with a delighted grin.

Matt told Francesca to hop in.

"But what about your leg?"

"You can coddle me back to health later, Nurse," Matt answered.

"Look at those two acting like school children. Harry, do something!" Maude gasped as we stood in the distance watching Matt whisk Francesca into the air.

I couldn't believe they just left me like that. I swallowed hard.

"Now look what they've done," Maude said, mashing my hair to my forehead. She had picked up on my disappointment. "Don't fret, Sarah. They've probably had too much ... apple juice."

"I wouldn't mind some of that ... juice myself," Harry said with real warmth and a touch of envy.

As Matt and Francesca zoomed overhead, he waggled *Victoria*'s wings in salute.

Within moments, the other pilots ran to their planes. They took off one by one and settled into formations of four and five, trailing after Matt and Francesca. It was lovely, seeing them all bank and spiral like that.

It didn't take long for this activity to energize the interest of other fair-goers. A crowd swarmed out of the barns and the outdoor arenas onto the airfield. Hundreds of people came out from under shade trees, and some even stopped their cars along the highway to gaze at the spectacle.

Seeing an audience, Matt felt the need to put on a show. He brought the plane low to the ground — so low, the wheels practically touched. *The Lady Victoria* floated gently up, then down, up again and down again. Suddenly, Matt waved his hands around his ears. They were close enough to us now to see he wasn't handling the controls. Leaning across Matt, it was Francesca that landed the plane. Not well and not gently. But she landed straight, and Matt brought the craft to a halt without any difficulty.

"What a dame!" screamed someone from the crowd.

I started clapping and jumping up and down. Maude and Harry both looked like they had been struck by lightning. That's when Maude fell back weakly against her husband. "Give her some air," Harry said, waving off no one in particular.

Matt handed Francesca down from the cockpit as the other planes began landing. When the crowd burst into spontaneous applause, she took a bow. "Hope no one saw my vomit act," I heard Francesca whisper to Matt.

"Happens to the best of us," he whispered back. "You held your cookies longer than most. Consider it your baptism."

Francesca and the other pilots walked back to a different type of commotion.

"Aunt Maude fainted," I said, running into Francesca's open arms. My grandmother glanced down at her sister with the merest wisp of a grin. "She'll be fine. Look, she's opened her eyes."

As we made our way to the Doozy, Francesca gave one last V-sign to the still-cheering crowd then wiped a remaining glob of spittle from the corner of her mouth. Maude still looked pasty-faced and wobbled along on Harry's arm. Matt was limping and leaning hard on Francesca's shoulder.

"What a sorry bunch we are!" Francesca observed. Then, she shook her head and roared with laughter.

Chapter 25
And There They Go!

Race day dawned gray and windswept. While Uncle Harry complained about his aching joints, Aunt Maude worried over her hairdo, which hung like a limp rag. Finally, she gave up and wrapped a salmon-colored scarf around her head.

Matt spent the morning giving the Ghost a final tune-up while Francesca hovered over him, inspecting every inch of the car. Although the dirt track was damp by the time the pit crews began to assemble, it looked as if the weather would not sour enough to cancel the race.

I could tell Francesca was nervous, the way her breath came in little fits and starts. At times, she had to forcefully push the air out of her lungs. The infield was reserved for mechanics and family, so I was surprised to catch sight of a number of pilots milling around near the far turn. Ian, with his great height and booming voice, was unmistakable.

Uncle Harry hurried to Francesca's pit area, waving the registration receipt in his right hand. "There are precisely twenty-one cars in the field. Take care not to get trapped too far back," he advised.

While Matt and Francesca walked the track one last time, Babe and I trailed along, drinking in the exciting sights and sounds. Conveniently, the wind was coming out of the west and blew their voices back to us. I saw Matt gesture to the registration form. "Know any of these drivers?" he asked.

"Actually, no. So many of them are complete strangers! I guess I'm a lot older than the last time I raced."

"And a lot smarter," Matt said. "Believe me, no one has a car that can touch the Ghost on the straightaway, and no one will handle the curves better than you." He tapped her right shoulder three times before he continued, "Remember, the down-shift coming into this next turn is crucial."

The track was an oval-shaped mile. The dirt appeared to be in good condition, hard-packed, well-raked and just slightly damp from the humidity. That would make for excellent visibility during the race.

"The course bed seems bumpy here," Francesca mused, as she bent down and touched the offending area with her fingertips. "I'll try to remember not to pass in this area."

She looked almost boyish and rather dashing in her driving get-up: jodhpurs, a leather jacket, a helmet, and that lovely white scarf that billowed out behind her as she strode beside Matt, matching him step for step.

I looked behind us and discovered several other drivers studying the course. "Don't talk too loud, Matt," I warned. "We're being followed."

Matt glanced over his shoulder and said, "So we are ... so we are. Obviously, they know who their real opposition is." He continued in lower tones. "Don't worry about cutting it close in the pack. Sarah and I can always rub out any scratches with a little elbow grease."

"Don't *you* worry," Francesca said to us both, sticking her chin up and out, "I'm not afraid to mix it up."

Matt clucked his tongue in a roguish manner and kissed Francesca on the forehead in exactly the same spot I had kissed her nearly every morning of my life. "You go out there and win that silver trophy," he said. It made my toes tingle.

There were two scheduled feature races that day: a pro race, with real racing cars and experienced drivers later in the afternoon; and the one that was only open to non-professional residents of the state, which was the one my grandmother had won in the past. Every make of automobile imaginable was represented in the pit area, but nothing could compare to the sheer glory of the Gray Ghost.

There was a cheer from the crowd as the announcer's voice crackled out over the public address system. "Ladies and gentlemen, we are proud to announce the twenty-seventh running of the Clinton

County Fair 150. In a moment, our drivers will be starting their engines. For your safety, we ask that you remain behind the fences and barricades set up for your protection. The race will consist of one hundred and fifty one-mile laps. There will be one pace lap followed immediately by a green flag, which will signal the official start of the race. There will be no passing during yellow caution flags. The drivers have been assigned positions by lot. Let's wish these brave folks the best of luck with a big round of applause."

The crowd roared its approval.

"Drivers, start your engines."

There was a rumbling loud enough to make the ground tremble, as one by one, the racers revved their engines and rolled up to their assigned positions. At the wave of a checkered flag by Honorary Chief Starter Brandon Cooney, Clinton Mayor Abel Walleran drove the pace car, a brand-new 1946 Dodge, onto the track,. I only knew it was Mayor Walleran because the banner draped across the hood said so.

"There they go!" shouted the announcer.

Francesca had lucked into a so-so placement, in the third row on the inside. You weren't supposed to jockey for position during the pace lap, but everyone did ... including her. As I trotted along the infield fence, I wasn't surprised to see how many of the other drivers glanced in her direction. She was already testing them, seeing how close she could get without their flinching. Francesca knew one thing for certain ... there was a lot more to winning this kind of a race than just having the fastest car.

Halfway around the oval, the pace car began picking up speed, and by the time it left the track, the field was up to three-quarter velocity. Francesca sat low in her seat, leaning slightly over the steering wheel. Her arms looked relaxed, but I knew her grip on the wheel was iron. It was hard work, wrestling with the big elegant machine. The deep-throated roar of the Doozy was an unmistakable underpinning of the shouting crowd, the noise of the other engines, the screams of delighted patrons riding the Ferris wheel across the way, the buzz of airplanes overhead, and the bleating of animals.

Within a matter of ten or eleven laps, Francesca had passed several cars and was coasting for the moment in ninth place, looking for an opening. Suddenly, Car 14, a souped-up fire-engine-red hot-rod, was moving along in third position when its rear left tire exploded, causing hundreds of large and small bits of rubber to fly into the air. As it skidded out of control, it was hit hard by the black Ford directly behind it. Francesca, who was pinned on the inside at this point, couldn't possibly get around them. She was going to crash.

Although it must have all happened in seconds, the incident seemed to unfold in slow motion. I remember Babe and I taking off toward the far turn. I remember hearing Ian yell something at Francesca as she flew past him. I remember the red hot-rod and the Ford in their sickening dance. I saw Francesca's crash before I heard it. But wait! My amazing and resilient grandmother had somehow down-shifted, deliberately putting the Doozy into a fish-tail spin, a jaw-gawping maneuver that allowed her to slide by the wreckage with inches to spare. She brought the Ghost to an abrupt stop just shy of the center rail at the moment the yellow flag went up.

Even with his bum leg, Matt was in front of me as we scrambled over the infield rail and onto the track. Thank God, Francesca looked dazed but unhurt. When she noticed us bearing down on her, she set her chin and waved us off rather imperiously. And with a glance behind her and a roar of the Doozy's inner workings, she was back in the race. From that second onward, Francesca was formidable. Unstoppable. Magnificent. With her eyes narrowed in concentration, she brazened her way through one hole after another and breezed into the lead with thirty-one laps to spare.

Admittedly, I was miffed that my record catch was going to play twenty-ninth fiddle to Francesca's triumph. But after all, a fight with the biggest pike ever caught in a small midwestern lake will never be in the same ballpark, newsprint-wise, as winning a crash-filled automobile race.

My farm-bred grandmother weirdly resembled the sophisticated French novelist and feminist George Sand, standing so straight and full of herself on the winner's dais. She graciously acknowledged her fellow drivers and her pit crew and even blushed prettily when the Mayor bussed her on both cheeks. It was practically sickening.

At the much more fun unofficial winner's ceremony, Ian and some of the other pilots serenaded her by popping bottles of New York champagne, spraying us all in the process. He put his ham hock arm around Francesca in a brotherly hug and said cozily, "That was putting it to them, my dear. Brilliantly done — piece of cake, as you Yanks say, ... well, except for that slight graze with the south wall." He turned to Matt and continued with zest, "A woman like this is one in a million. She's going to go boodles over the flying business; you wait and see."

First, the universe stopped on a dime and then a look came over Ian's face, as if he realized he'd said something he shouldn't have. Francesca flashed a wondering look at Matt, who avoided her eyes. There was a horribly uncomfortable pause before Ian plowed onward. "Well, we're up then, lads. Let's get a move on." He turned back to Matt and slapped his friend hard across the back. "It'll be good to have you back in the sky."

Chapter 26
Of Heart and Man

Matt, never the sparkling conversationalist, was doubly reluctant to speak of this thing he had done, whatever it was, especially in front of Harry and Maude and myself.

Francesca had been silent throughout the repacking and checking-out process. There was a closed-off, pinched look about her, like she was struggling to hold in bile. She folded clothes and paced the floor — folded and paced, folded and paced, methodically. The suitcases were the only thing in the world.

It wasn't until we were all settled in the Doozy that Francesca spoke, and when she did, her words were neutral-sounding — with an underlying sting.

"I want to know what this is all about, this flying business," she said.

Harry tried to deter her from pursuing this path. "Franny, this definitely isn't the time or place ...," he began, but my grandmother cut him off at the knees. Politely, though ... ever so politely.

"Don't worry, Harry, your turn will come."

She gazed out the window, tapping her right hand with her left thumb. "Well, Matt? Exactly what business was Ian talking about? The one you haven't bothered mentioning to me?"

And like a broken tooth extraction, the tale was painfully dragged out of him.

Ian and Matt had renewed an important friendship during the fair. They had spent much of their time together reminiscing about their flying days.

"Naturally," whispered Francesca.

Matthew swallowed and continued, "He has a flying school in Indianapolis. It's ... well ... he hasn't ... he's struggling. He needs a partner to help him get back on track; that's all."

"You volunteered?" she asked.

"It's not that simple."

"You volunteered?" she asked again, more acid in her tone.

"Well, hell, Fran, he's been through a rough time."

"What a good friend you are," she said, gone suddenly still.

The remainder of the tale was that Matt was leaving immediately for Indianapolis, and Francesca would be staying at Home Farm. Matt's reasoning was feeble at best: that it was going to be hard work, getting the school on solid financial ground. He hedged and hesitated. You could tell he felt embarrassed revealing his lame litany in front of us. When Francesca mercilessly pressed him, he went doggedly on. He mentioned 18-hour days ... who knew? ... which meant there wouldn't be any time at all for a relationship.

I don't know about anyone else, but I felt like I'd been punched in the gut. Back at Home Farm, Francesca watched him gather his belongings, although why she deliberately made herself suffer like that I couldn't say. It didn't take Matt long to load the Duisenberg. He tried to say goodbye to Babe and me, but I wouldn't even speak to him.

Francesca was standing over the kitchen sink, violently hacking at carrots and broccoli. I squatted halfway up the back stairs and listened.

"I have to do this," he said.

No response.

"I'll be back."

No response.

"I love you."

I heard her turn to him then.

"If you don't leave my house this instant, I will be forced to go and get Cox's .410 over-and-under. As you know, it's in a gun case off the fireplace."

The last thing he did was hand her the big silver trophy. She took it out of his hands and smashed it on the kitchen floor. The back door slammed. I could hear Babe bark as she ran after him. The Duisenberg roared to life, and then for the last time, I heard the lovely, deep growl of the engine disappear into the distance.

He was gone.

Francesca stood on the front porch, watching the Doozy until long after its trail of dust had settled back to earth.

Harry and Maude stayed out of the fray. There was plenty of work for Harry at Daddyboys' garage, and, unbelievably, Maude spent those first couple of days helping him by handing him tools, going over paperwork.

That left a lot of silence to roam around in.

I was feeling Francesca's anguish, her disbelief, the chill on her heart. It seemed to me that the lovely spark in her soul had been snuffed out. She seemed smaller and older.

The pain I felt came in waves, like an incoming tide. It washed over every other emotion and thought. How could he? How could he?

Right then, I hated Matthew Mosley with all my heart. I hated his weakness; his lack of backbone. How could I have been so taken in by his charm?

Francesca held herself together while Maude and Harry were still with us. But the silence at the dinner table was almost frightening. No one could think of anything safe to talk about. Every time Maude made a few halfhearted stabs at conversation, it was obvious how badly she felt for her sister. But Francesca wasn't in a mood for pity, either.

When at last Maude and Harry were packed and ready to go, Maude grabbed Francesca and hugged her hard, so hard I heard Francesca gasp.

"There is absolutely nothing I can say that will help," Maude started out, still holding on to Francesca with all her skinny might, "but ... I love you with all my heart."

She kissed Francesca on the forehead, me on the cheek, took Harry by the hand, stepped into a steady rain and got into Abraham's cab. They waved and waved as the car bumped down the drive and onto Thunder Ridge Road. Francesca didn't wave back.

Without a word, she took off toward the paddock, never bothering to get a raincoat or even a scarf. As I watched from the back porch stoop, she hauled herself up onto the top rail of the fence. She sat there, dangling her legs for a long, long time. Then, she whistled up RedBird, who came a-galloping. The woman and the horse nuzzled one another for a quarter hour. At last, Francesca grabbed RedBird's mane and eased herself on to that silken back. Francesca looked back at me, shook her head, then clucked RedBird into a canter.

The horse gathered speed as they neared the far fence. What was she doing? My eyes were like saucers as I watched Francesca steer that little mare over the five-foot-high gate. The rain had slowed to a drizzle, but the ground was still mushy. As RedBird landed, she kicked up a shower of muddy water.

Francesca was gone for hours. I was frantic with worry. At one point, I considered catching up Miss Blossom and going after them. But Francesca was someone who rode like she raced a car. Considering the state of mind she was in, she might very well have been all the way to Clinton County.

It was way after suppertime when I heard the faint rhythm of hooves on the gravel drive. Babe and I slipped out the back door and trotted over toward the barn to wait. The rain poured down my face and body like a sheet. The only light came from the back porch and out through the kitchen window.

Both Francesca and RedBird were soaking and covered with mud. RedBird was panting as if she'd run for her life. Francesca's body was draped exhaustedly across RedBird's neck, her hands cramped in a death grip around a piece of that lush mane. By fits and starts, Francesca slid onto the ground, barely able to stand. When I went to help her, she pushed me away and managed to stumble into the house.

"I'll take care of everything," I called through the gloom.

RedBird was shivering as I led her to her stall. Miss Blossom nickered a greeting, but the little roan mare was too spent to respond. I dried her and massaged her legs and curried her till she sighed and snorted with pleasure. I watered her and fed her an extra serving of oats. And as I worked, I started getting mad at my grandmother.

How dare she behave this way? Maybe I had no business being angry with her, but I couldn't help myself. What if something terrible had happened? What if she'd been thrown? And killed? I threw myself on the stack of hay near Miss Blossom's stall and began to cry, great moaning sobs of pity. Some of it was for Francesca, but the larger portion, I'm ashamed to say, was for myself. Babe sat down in front of me and licked the tears off my cheeks. I felt exactly like some lost orphan caught in a storm and wished with all my might that Mommy and Daddyboys were here. They'd know what to do.

After a while, exhausted and with Babe serving as my blanket and my comforter, I fell deeply asleep.

I dreamed about Francesca and RedBird flying over the gate and Matt standing beside me clapping and whooping.

Chapter 27
Eye of the Storm

It was Miss Blossom nickering that awakened me. I hadn't a clue what time it might've been, and I was stiff as a board. The hay down my back itched. Although it should have been pitch black outside, I could make out a faint glow from the back porch light. I called softly for Babe, but she wasn't in the barn. I struggled to my feet and stumbled through the big wooden doors out into the night.

There was a deathly stillness in the air. Even the crickets were silent. I felt some unformed apprehension. My feet made squishing noises in the mud. The back door was still unlocked, which struck me as odd. Carefully, I opened it and peeked into the kitchen.

Francesca was sprawled across the floor. Stunned and shocked, I was only able to process the scene slowly, one detail at a time. I felt frozen. I was unable to cry out. After what seemed like a year, I noticed Babe lay next to Francesca.

Next, I picked up on the shallow rise and fall of Francesca's chest. Thank heaven! I tiptoed over and touched her face, but she didn't respond. Her breath reeked of whiskey, an odor I recognized from Matt's early days with us.

To say I was scared was the great understatement of my life up to that point. I felt helpless and vulnerable and shattered.

"Francesca! Francesca! Wake up!"

My grandmother groaned but didn't move or open her eyes.

Suddenly, I heard the wind start to pick up, like some gigantic fan had been cranked into motion. I was able to raise Francesca's head but could only hold it steady for a moment. I tried to lift her and drag her to the couch, but I wasn't nearly strong enough. Running into the storm for help would be futile, and I couldn't leave her alone.

I decided to stay in the kitchen until she woke up.

I rooted in the linen closet for a woolen throw and a large pillow. I covered Francesca, tucking the edge of the blanket around her legs and feet, then slid the pillow under her head. She still didn't stir, but at least she looked comfortable. While I prayed aloud twenty times she would be alright by morning, I retrieved another blanket for myself and Babe, and I slept fitfully beside Francesca on the kitchen floor.

Even in my dreams, I could hear the sound of the wind growing louder and louder. Eventually, a rasping of branches against the house alerted me. The storm was frenzied now. Just above the din, I thought I could hear RedBird whinnying in terror.

Francesca was still out cold. I looked outside the window and saw the air was filled with leaves and dust and twigs and bits of trash. The barn door started slapping back and forth, the hinges crying out. I realized this was perfect tornado weather and that Francesca and the animals and I were in terrible danger. Somehow, I had to get us all into the basement storm cellar. Dug out beneath Main House almost two hundred years ago, it was a more than ample safe haven.

After warning Babe to stay with Francesca, I grabbed a rain slick, barred the doggie door and pushed my way out into the maelstrom.

The wind was so strong I had to walk at an angle as I fought my way to the chicken coop. I opened their pen, so they could move around freely and if need be hide somewhere safe. I also hooked the small shutters on the outside of their shelter.

Next, I ran to the barn and haltered Miss Blossom. She was older than RedBird and of a calmer nature, and I figured I could handle her well enough. I tied a handkerchief over her eyes and led her out into the yard, where the rain was pouring down in torrents. Blossom shied a bit, but I whispered into her ear and blew into her nose to keep her quiet. When we'd made it safely to the cellar, she stood obediently while I unbolted the big storm doors. It took forever to drag them open. I lit an oil lamp I remembered was hanging on my right before leading Miss Blossom down the wooden ramp my father had crafted exactly for this occasion.

It was amazingly quiet there, under the earth. The dimly lit root cellar smelled of apples and potatoes and dampness. I was breathing hard by this time and sweating with exertion. My throat was dry. I uncorked a large jug of water by the apple bins and took a long swallow. It comforted me, somehow, maybe because I'd seen Grandpap do that very thing so many times in the past.

It was much cooler down below than I'd expected, and I made sure there was a supply of extra blankets in the trunk near four folded cots.

I was on my way back to get RedBird when lightning darted across the sky, followed immediately by a booming clap of thunder. I heard a crackling sound somewhere over my head and smelled smoke. I stood still for a second, trying to get my bearings in the chaos swirling around me. But I could barely stand up as the wind pushed against me, and I couldn't see a thing. I held my hands in front of my face to protect my eyes from flying debris. That's when I heard an even louder CRACK that sounded like a cannon shot.

I never saw it coming. An eight-foot branch from our elm tree split from the trunk, falling with a crash on top of me. It knocked me flat, forcing the air out of my chest. For a moment, I wasn't sure what had happened. Then, I panicked. I'd heard that people could suffocate or black out after that kind of injury. Finally, my lungs burst back to life with a tremendous gasp. I inhaled and exhaled as slowly as I could. I tried to get up then, but I was pinned solid.

The sound of the wind ticked up a notch. In the barn, RedBird snorted and pawed her feed bin in agitation. The thunder rolled over me like a blanket. It came in waves and echoed back through itself and off the foothills.

I struggled under that old branch. I swore and squirmed and twisted and kicked. I wasn't seriously hurt, but I could no more have gotten out from underneath that weight than I could have flown to the moon. I screamed, but it was no use; there was no one to hear me in that deafening din.

I don't know how long I lay there before I started to cry. I realized it was possible I would not make it through the night. At some point, I went in and out of consciousness from sheer exhaustion. Reality and dreams became blurred. My mind was deceiving me. Or was it? I thought I heard voices.

"Francesca! Babe!" I called over and over to the voices that might have been inside my head. "Save them; they're in the kitchen! And RedBird! Don't forget RedBird!" Although my eyes were blurry from rain and dust, I thought I saw the shadows of giants standing over me, dressed in flowing cloaks, their faces covered, the brims of their dark hats streaming rain. From somewhere, a pinpoint of weak light glowed.

"I'm okay. I'm not hurt. Please help us," I whispered again and again. One of the giants squatted beside me as the other two forms lifted the branch off me. "Let's get her inside." Then, they carried me to the cellar and lay me down on a cot. After a careful searching touch of my limbs, I was covered with blankets. As the blood in my fingers and toes began to circulate again, I became slightly more alert. But I was still weak and felt dizzy. When I could make out RedBird's unmistakable snorting nearby, I knew we'd been saved.

I saw that one of the giants was carrying my grandmother in his arms. But he didn't put her on the other cot right away. His face was still hidden, but I could tell he was staring at her face. At last, as gently as he might have handled a new-born babe, he lowered her inert body onto the cot and covered her.

Babe came running in and jumped on top of me. She nudged her nose under the blanket and laid her head on my stomach. I was too disoriented to respond.

The giant glanced back at us once from the door. With a shake of his head, he disappeared into the night. The wind still roared above us, but in the storm cellar, it was quiet and dry. I closed my eyes and faded into oblivion.

Chapter 28
The Calm after the Winds

It was uncanny how, during that summer, the weather so often mirrored the emotions washing over Home Farm. When I opened my eyes the next morning, I had never seen such a day. It felt as if all the evil in the world had been scoured away. The sun played hide-and-seek behind fat, puffy clouds. A gentle, northerly breeze softened the air.

Coming out of the storm cellar, I was blinded by the sun. The garden was a shambles, true, but all the dead leaves and most of the branches had disappeared. I scratched my belly and heard it gurgle in response, informing me it was at least noon. When I discovered that Miss Blossom and RedBird had already been returned to the barn, I realized Francesca was not only up but at it.

I was supremely interested to observe what kind of shape she was in.

"Don't slam that screen door, Sarah" were the first words out of her mouth. She was certainly in A State. It reminded me of what Matt often referred to as "The Rasps." He'd explained it as a condition that showed up after "a night of bourbon and bad dreams." Francesca definitely exhibited a colossal case of "The Rasps."

She laid her forearm across her forehead. She massaged her temples gently for a moment before running her tongue around the inside of her mouth. Her body was never quite still, as one tic jerkily followed another. She reminded me of one of Grandpap's favorite homespun phrases — fidgety as a bug on a cat's paw.

She glanced at me, then away. Her eyes flickered and darted across the gap that lay between us. "I ..." She didn't finish her sentence, stopping to lick her lips. She sighed then tried again. "I can't ..." was followed by another sigh. She shook her head stridently enough to loosen some cobwebs and looked me right in the eyes. "I pray I will never behave in this self-pitying, self-indulgent way again. I owe you the most profound apology." The words were forceful, the voice barely above a whisper.

She stood more erect. "I pray I don't have to straighten this place out all by myself." She didn't give me a chance to respond. "The barn is a shambles. Part of the roof of the Bridal Cottage blew clear to Michigan, and that dog of yours has been barking her fool head off."

Francesca gasped for breath and rubbed her temples again. She cocked her head. "Did ... Was there ... What happened last night?"

"Here?" I asked stupidly.

"Don't answer a question with a question," she said and took a huge swig of water right out of the glass pitcher.

To me, the night's events were simply a blur, and whether I had dreamed, imagined or experienced any or all of the goings-on was far beyond my comprehension.

"I thought I heard ... voices?" Francesca probed.

I shrugged my shoulders.

Francesca walked to the sink and dipped her face under the running faucet.

"Are you sure nothing unusual happened last night?" Apparently, Francesca didn't have a clue about "last night." Thankfully, except for the hangover, she didn't seem any the worse for wear.

I had battled terror the night before and yet had somehow got us all to safety. I was quite proud of myself, and under different circumstances, I might have crowed a little. However, my tale would have had to include that ugly episode with her and the bottle. Somehow, I was sure she'd die of shame if she knew that I knew.

Come to think of it, there was the possibility that a posse of strangers also knew ... Hang it, once in a great while, the truth is the last thing that needs to be told! Period, exclamation point!

Francesca turned to face me. "How did you manage to ... get us all into the storm cellar?"

I was about to consider which prevarication to give over when the phone rang. Thank heavens. Francesca massaged her forehead with renewed vigor while I answered it.

It was Aunt Maude, calling to check on us. The line crackled, snapped and popped so that every other word was almost unintelligible. As I gave her an account of the storm damage to Home

Farm seven different times, she oohed and aahed and uttered "Really? No!" about every 26 seconds.

"Is my sister around?" Maude asked, dropping her voice to a conspiratorial level, as though my grandmother could somehow hear her over the receiver.

"Francesca?" I repeated while my grandmother was frantically shaking her hands, no. "Why, she's outside, cleaning up the vegetable garden. Insisted she didn't wish to be disturbed. You know how she is about those dumb cucumbers. Will you be home later, Aunt Maude?"

"Yes. You have her call me."

"I will ... I promise. Love to Uncle Harry."

"Kiss kiss," she said and hung up.

"My cucumbers are not dumb," said Francesca, massaging one hand with the other. "You must have been ... very brave last night. I know I ... we ... couldn't have survived without your ... thoughtful command of the dire situation." She was starting to sound a little more like herself.

When she took a deep breath, I could tell she was going to steer the conversation around a corner. "It's such a beautiful morning. I haven't seen one like it in the summer for years and years."

"Maybe I should go into town," I ventured. "We'll need the stuff for the roof, and we could use some veggies, now that the garden's demolished. I could hitch Miss Blossom to the pony cart."

Francesca grunted.

"I could call Abraham to come in the taxicab," I offered.

Francesca went to the ice box and poured herself a tall glass of orange juice.

"Yes," she said, "you could do that. But we should go together; there will be people needing our help."

There are no secrets in a small town, where all things are known and most of them are dissected at great length with relish. Small-town intimacy assumes advice is welcome, even when not solicited. There was no way anyone knew about Francesca's toot the night before. How could they? However, the fact of Matt having left was a whole 'nother enchilada.

Her relationship with Matt had been common knowledge. And as far as she was concerned, whatever judgment they'd encountered face-to-face as a couple was infinitely preferable to sneaking around. She usually made the bold choice and accepted all the consequences.

I was more than relieved that Francesca had apparently decided to wade back into life. A little like me at the pond, she was ready to waggle in the shallows. Fine; I would waggle with her.

It wasn't going to be easy with so many treacherous traces of Matt hiding innocently around and about. A perfect example was the floogle horn on the driver's side of the pickup. Francesca and I stared at it as she started the engine, and she brushed her fingers tentatively across its base twice. Her face took on a sad, faraway look.

Then, she whistled, and Babe came running, vaulting into the cab of the old truck like there were coiled springs in her legs.

"Good girl," whispered Francesca, kissing the dog's silky ear.

Babe responded with a wet kiss to Francesca's nose.

Francesca cleared her throat and sounded the floogle once, twice.

* * * * *

Lost Nation had been hit hard by the storm. Shop windows had imploded along Main Street. A hundred-year-old elm in the park had been upended. There was an army of people cleaning up everything from broken glass to underclothes still in their plastic packaging to rusted oil cans escaped from the town dump.

Francesca cruised around for a few minutes before stopping in front of Abraham's place, a small, two-story frame house with a stoop in the front. One of the pillars that held up the overhang was bent practically double.

Abraham's eldest son, Jefferson, was a huge and chiseled young man who dwarfed his father and brother. He was mightily strong and tough as nails, and he had an almost eerie knack when it came to building things. When he drew up plans for additions to houses, he already knew where support beams had to go and how large the windows could be without weakening the structure. Weirdly, he'd never had any formal education beyond high school, where he'd been a math whiz.

He'd already taken measurements of the damage and come up with a plan to brace the bowed pillar until it could be replaced.

We found Abraham in the front room and pitched in to help him clean up the broken dishes, torn sheets, wayward tools of all descriptions and half a piano bench.

"Good to have you back among the living," were his only words to Francesca.

This rather cryptic comment startled my grandmother, but she said nothing. For once, I was smart enough to keep my lips zipped. But the thought struck me ... Could Jefferson have been one of the mysterious visitors?

We spent the rest of the morning making sure our friends and neighbors had adequate food and water. We lugged supplies alongside the Porters, the Tycorns, the Blackfeathers and assisted Doc Gearneart with plaster casts and stitches. At lunchtime, we made trays of sandwiches and passed them out along Main Street. By afternoon, Francesca'd been accepted back into the fold — like the prodigal son returned. Some couldn't hold back an I-told-you-so-tinged remark, but most people cared more about righting the storm damage and seeing to their kith and kin than they did about Francesca's love life. The winds that ripped through Lost Nation in the middle of the night were actually a blessing for us — they focused the town's energy on a new set of mind-boggling circumstances. My grandmother had always been an ally of Mother Nature, and in turn, Nature had taken care of her.

One man's curse is indeed another woman's blessing.

On the way out of town, Francesca pulled up in front of the jailhouse. She just sat and stared out the windshield for a long time. Then, after looking carefully up and down the street, she entered the office. Through the window, I could see her address Sheriff Dan, but I couldn't hear anything.

He started to speak, and she held up her hands to stop him. She turned away from him and picked up a magazine, waving it around her head like a Samurai sword. Then, she turned toward him and said something that must have been a question, because he responded with a shake of his head. She said something else then, something that made Dan Mosley shut his eyes tight and exhale deeply. He took her shoulders and shook them ever so gently, talking calmly. She nodded once. Then, he kissed her forehead, and she turned to come back out to the car. And although Francesca never revealed the gist of that conversation to me, I knew they'd spoken of Matt.

When she sat down beside Babe and me, she only said, "I know you were watching us, Sarah. And I appreciate your concern. But you must learn that some things in life are private."

With that, she started up the engine and roared out of Lost Nation.

Chapter 29
The Ties that Bind

The next few days were just like all the other summer days I'd ever spent on Home Farm. Yet they were so very different. There was a tension in the house, a division, as though the silver thread that attached me to my grandmother had been stretched almost to the breaking point.

She worked like a dog in the garden, at her roses, in the orchards. She telephoned Maude and Harry to assure them yet again that we'd gotten through the storm and that everything was hunky-dory. She even repaired the roof of the Bridal Cottage with no one to help except Babe and me. She cooked and canned and cleaned like a woman possessed. But she never whistled any more. She smiled fleetingly once in a great while, but there was vacant space behind her eyes where the joy of living used to well up and overflow. The mere fact of being alive had ceased to invigorate her way of being in the world.

She read the newspaper from cover to cover and spent hours poring over the aviation news. She spent time alone in her room. And although she never mentioned it one way or another, she was relieved that I'd stopped knocking at her boudoir door in the morning. I knew somehow that I wasn't welcome there, that Francesca needed time alone with her grief, time to heal. That was the most awful part, I think—our morning ritual had disappeared from our lives. How I longed to take her café au lait and kiss her forehead. But I never mentioned it, and neither did she.

She continued to drink in the evenings but never got drunk again. She rarely listened to the radio and never offered to play cards. She'd lost interest in the swimming hole. Or at least if she did go, she didn't include me.

It was like living with a stranger.

My dog and I got to acting jumpy, especially at night. Babe would prowl around or worse, suddenly take off through the house, barking to beat the band. I began to notice how the timbers of Home Farm creaked in the wind and had a bad habit of settling into new positions only after midnight.

The only person Francesca could bear to be around for more than a few minutes was Dan Mosley. I don't believe they ever spoke of Matthew. In fact, they never discussed anything important at all, to my knowledge. He'd tell her how pretty she looked, and she pretended to believe him. She gave him recipes for Starr and made him fresh lemonade. He revealed the latest news about the arsonist: Someone resembling him had been spotted in South Dakota and/or Indiana, which meant he was probably out of the area. Weirdly, his mother's name had been Sarah, so just in case ... Dan was adamant we should have some male protection. Francesca dismissed such "trivialities" with a wave of her hand and led him outside to see her rose garden.

It wounded me to see her loneliness so obvious and aggravated. I was lonely, too, but at least I had Babe to comfort me. Francesca had just closed herself off, shut herself down, as though the mere idea of contact with another human being, even me, was enough to scrape away the thin scab that was attempting to form on her smithereened heart.

My grandmother rode flat out almost every day. RedBird was always soaked with sweat by the time they got back to Main House from God knows where. Francesca whispered in RedBird's ears whatever terrible and sad things were struggling for the upper ground in her soul. I realize now she was in the grip of a grand depression, and I was absolutely powerless to ease her suffering.

We got a letter from Daddyboys and Mommy on August 6; it provided a bit of relief to our dour household. It was full of glad tidings and excitement, and I was tickled by his funny, grand style. Felt guilty about it too.

We're hopping over to London on the aero plane, my dears. Too trala for words. After another two weeks seeing the sights, we'll be cruising back to New York in early September. Gad! It'll be merveilleux to see Lady Liberty and have a real old-fashioned hamburger!

We've been advised that school in Manhattan begins second week of September. Sarah can enroll there and attend for a week or two before finishing out the term in Lost Nation as we discussed. And there'll be so much shopping! All my lovely women will have to find us a pied-a-terre tout-de-suite and furnish same forthwith! We can't wait to see the two of you! You'd better plan to rendez-vous on or near September 5. Mr. Toynbee's booked us all in at the Waldorf Astoria. Ha! Won't we be the toasts of Manhattan!

Your mother and I have grown expansive with our travels (mostly around the midsections) but there will be time enough for watching our weight when we're living on the income of a starving writer. That's me, my dears.

I had a whale of an idea just yesterday. I should pen a how-to manual on fixing cars, complete with diagrams and lots of stories about Lost Nation's eccentric automobile Armada. Mr. Toynbee jumped at the idea and is searching, even now, for a book publisher.

You know, I worked hard my whole life and always felt dissatisfied with the lot I'd made for us all. I felt that I was remarkable, that we all were remarkable and that we should be leading remarkable lives.

Frances, dear, you were always OUT THERE somewhere fine, marching to the beat of an ancient and mythic orchestra few others knew existed, let alone heard. In a way, you were the reason I never quite gave up the ship. I am going to buy you the most expensive dinner and the largest bottle of champagne in NYC.

I can't tell you what it means to me to finally be able to do ... everything. I feel like a kid again. It fills me with pride (I might to have resize my hat). So, I offer you, my dearest loved ones, the sun and the moon. I'm working on the stars!

Lovelovelove,
Daddyboys

Francesca broke into tears and ran outside, slamming the screen door hard in the process. I didn't follow, but I did watch her anxiously (and surreptitiously) for the rest of the afternoon.

What a tribute Daddyboys had written to his mother-in-law! And they were so true, the things he'd poured out from his heart to hers. I wondered if her pain had been eased.

Later, I discovered it hadn't.

"We'll have to get you packed." She started in on me with an attitude.

"Don't you mean 'us?' We'll both have to get packed?" I asked meekly.

"No. I said exactly what I meant, a habit more human beings should cultivate."

"You're thinking of not going to New York." It was an accusation, not a question.

"I never considered going in the first place," she said, thrusting that jaw out.

That wasn't true, of course. And it made me mad.

"Well, if you're not going, I'm not going!" I stamped my foot for emphasis.

"Don't be ridiculous, Sarah," she warned. "Of course you're going. And I'm staying. And that's that! There'll be no more argument about it, as I find the process too unpleasant to belabor."

We were in the kitchen, drying lunch dishes. Babe stood up from the cool floor and cocked her head at our raised voices.

"You're running away from me again. I don't understand why," I hurled at her retreating back.

We really got into it then.

Francesca whirled back around. "It's none of your damn business, Sarah. You are a child, and I am an adult. I have recently experienced something rather humiliating, and I think it's best we don't share ..." she dragged that last word out. She was oozing sarcasm by now. "... My most intimate feelings. It isn't appropriate. And God knows, I've indulged in enough inappropriate behavior recently to last me the rest of my life."

My voice rose a couple of octaves as I blurted out a response.

"Don't say that! It isn't true. You said love was never inappropriate."

She opened the ice box and grabbed a bottle of hard cider. I had come to recognize the terrible wounded look that came into her eyes. Her voice dropped almost to a whisper.

"I have spent my life living in a certain way. I believed that I ... knew what was right for me. What was right for all of us. I considered life to be my friend, not my enemy."

She stopped and took a swig straight from the bottle.

"I gave up on all-consuming love while still in my teens. I'd read about that kind of passion often enough. But I was never going to experience it. And so, I poured my passion into life."

Francesca recapped the bottle and replaced it in the ice box, all the while gulping down some huge emotion.

"Life let me down. I'm not about to stagger off to New York, dragging my woe behind me, and rain on everyone's parade. I couldn't bear to see the pity in my family's eyes. I'm not sure I could survive it."

Hot tears welled up in my eyes.

"You're selfish," I cried out. "You're sad, and I don't know how to help you. We used to share everything together. Now, you only make me feel awful ... like you don't love me anymore."

She raised her face to say something, but I screamed her down.

"*No!* Don't say anything!" I felt like sobbing now, but I managed to strangle the words out. "You lectured me all my life, and I believed in you. I trusted you! But you're just like everybody else. You don't mean what you say. You're a fake. And Matt was, too." My grief was wild now. My arms gestured madly, and my body shivered. "But even so, I'll always love you, even if you don't love me."

With one last raging howl, I ran up the back stairs and slammed myself inside my room. I cried so hard, my stomach hurt.

I don't have any idea how long it took for my personal storm to begin ebbing. My gasping sobs had been reduced to hiccups when I heard a hesitant knocking at my door. I didn't have the strength to tell her to go away.

Francesca came in carrying a tray of iced coffee and homemade cookies. She set the tray down at the end of the bed and without a word, she sat beside me, gathered me up in her arms and held me. That was all. She didn't say anything or try to explain or make excuses. She just held me.

Chapter 30
A Hint of Old Times

The blow-up between Francesca and me only served to prove for the umpteen-millionth time how strong our love for each other was. However, after all that had happened, even we couldn't heal overnight. We communicated a bit more, and she didn't waste as much energy avoiding me, but we both still felt uneasy.

Then, a thunderstorm moved into Lost Nation. You could see the Great Wall of threatening clouds and squiggles of lightning stretching for miles across the horizon.

Francesca adored thunderstorms.

I was currying Miss Blossom. She had a habit of rolling her head and snorting in pure pleasure whenever I rubbed a particularly delicious spot on her belly. Babe had climbed up on a stack of canvas bags, and Miss Blossom nuzzled her occasionally while I worked. I couldn't remember the last time I'd felt so peaceful.

When Francesca stuck her head through the double doors of the barn, she asked the obvious. "Do you hear that delicious rumbling?"

"Yep," I answered. "It sounds like a big blow. Is there a tornado watch?"

"No and none expected. Just a lovely, lovely thunder and lightning extravaganza! You hungry, child?"

But of course.

Over chicken salad sandwiches crispy with diced celery and apple pieces, Francesca said, "You know, this was supposed to be a summer full of adventure."

"And?" I asked expectantly.

"Summer isn't over yet."

I looked into her face then and saw the glimmer of a twinkle. "What's up?" I asked.

"I think we should venture out into the gale and try to find the dancing tribe of Lost Nation up on Thunder Ridge."

"There's a storm brewing. Besides, we don't even know where Thunder Ridge is."

"Where's your adventurous spirit? This is the perfect day to do some archaeological sleuthing."

She was right as rain.

We were careful to take flashlights and slickers, a bag of cookies, a thermos of water, a jug of cider and a rope. Francesca actually considered a shotgun but decided it would probably only get in the way of our exploration. She did pack her pistol, which she tucked in the pocket of her trousers. With Babe on the bench seat of the truck between us, we drove off toward the foothills east of Lost Nation.

It was a gorgeous drive. The day was chiaroscuro, alternating between sunshine and shadow — the clouds billowing closer and then retreating. We followed Thunder Ridge Road south for forty-odd minutes and eventually came to a bend in the pavement with a dirt access forking off to the right.

"I seem to recall this road," Francesca said, gesturing. "I think Grandpap and I explored it once a long time ago. There was a deserted farmhouse." She paused and frowned. "No. How could I forget? It was such a tragedy. The little girl died of a burst appendix, and a short while later, the family was burned out of their home. I think it was some type of cooking accident. That's right. Eisly, Eisner ... something like that. They disappeared after that. Hadn't they been to Indiana and come back?"

I could feel a tickling sensation at the back of my mind.

Francesca rolled her neck from side to side, loosening the tension that always seemed to hover there these days. "They homesteaded this place, a man and wife and a ten-year-old girl." She looked at me then. "Well, still game?"

The dash of fear in my stomach felt spooky but fun, like the sensations you get from riding on a tilt-a-whirl or watching a Dracula movie.

"You bet. This'll be swell."

It was a good thing Daddyboys was such a whiz-bang mechanic, because our old truck got quite a bruising on that dirt road.

It was little more than a cow path in some places. You could tell where the floods had swept whole sections away.

There were several other forks in the "road," and we made a series of turns that dead-ended. The storm was still looming in the east, and the soft echo of thunder came in waves. Each time we turned left or right, she reminded me, "You'd best mark down that last turn, Sarah."

Francesca was organized. It wasn't something she waved in your face, though. Unless you knew what to look for, you might not even notice it. She didn't have a neurosis about neatness and iron the sheets or anything. But her soul was on the tidy side, and she was good at planning ahead. For example, she'd insisted we bring along pencil and paper with the rest of our survival gear. I was supposed to use them to draw a rough map so that we could find our way out of the maze of dirt roads we'd be negotiating. She had instructed me to a line and mark the mileage to the first turn. Then, I had to write out which way we went and whether or not we came to a dead end.

When she had first brought this wacky scheme up, I'd shaken my head and said, "I can't do this." How I had sat and stared at the spiral notebook paper on my lap!

"Don't be ridiculous, child. Your ancestors navigated oceans, scaled mountains and cleared trails out of dense forest to get to Iowa. I feel confident you'll be able to help me navigate from Home Farm to Thunder Ridge and back."

There's a much longer ancestral speech Francesca could have chosen to make. She could have mentioned raging flash floods, snow drifts seven feet high, hostile natives and unbearable loneliness. When she trotted out the edited version, I took it as a signal that our relationship was truly on the mend.

"Right," I muttered and bit my lip in concentration.

The terrain changed as the path underneath us began to slope upward. The trees grew closer together, and you could hear the wind hissing through tightly bunched branches.

We negotiated another right turn, and the roadbed leveled out.

"I don't think this is the way," I ventured, carefully marking "right turn." I could feel a new tickle of worry in the pit of my stomach.

"There's a pond around here somewhere," Francesca said. "At least, there used to be. Keep a lookout on your side."

We never did come to that pond, but we did stumble across the burned-out shack. It had once been a three-roomer, made of rough-hewn mismatched wood. The foundation had shifted with time, and the blackened south wall, which was all that still stood, aside from the rock chimney, had a definite tilt to it.

There was something about that place that made the skin crawl up the back of my legs. It gave me a feeling of dread mixed with a sense of loss. It may have been because you could see right through the few boards left intact or the way they creaked as they swayed back and forth or the sight of Babe's hackles rising along her neck — but all of a sudden, I didn't want to be there.

"Maybe we shouldn't investigate too closely," I said hopefully.

Francesca looked hypnotized. She put her hand to her temple as if trying to push some idea forward.

"What is it?" I asked.

"There is something ..." she began.

Now, my neck was tingling.

"... something here. No. Someone."

"Who is it?" I whispered.

Her hand slipped to the place where her throat met her chest. "There's a flood of painful memories washing over me," she said, squinting with concentration.

"Do you think there are ghosts?"

That's when we heard a clicking noise from somewhere behind us. As I whipped my head around, my heart leapt into my throat. But it was only a ground squirrel chattering curses at us from a nearby tree.

Francesca started to laugh. She couldn't stop laughing, and that made me laugh. Soon, we had a case of the giggles. Our stomachs hurt from so much laughing that all of a sudden I had to pee.

"I have to whiz," I said between gasps of air.

Francesca reached into the pocket of her windbreaker and fished out a few pieces of tissue. She advised, "Try the Sunoco filling station over there. I hear it's air-conditioned," which of course set us off again.

A good spell of howling laughter will go a long way to ease even the most nerve-wracked mood. By the time I was back in the truck and we were on our way, our visit to the burned-out homestead was fading fast.

As for Francesca and me, it felt just like old times.

Chapter 31
The Past Uncovered

In the distance, the storm again began inching in our direction. As the wind shifted, that tempest so full of threat and light made its way across the sky, while underneath us, the winding roadway narrowed and inclined ever more steeply.

Babe lay dozing with her head in my lap. Francesca's fingertips tapped the steering wheel in time to the radio offerings of one of the Dorsey brothers. I could never tell those two bands apart, even as an adult. The melody was softly swinging in that elegant way the big bands had in those years. I began to nod my head in the same rhythm.

After innumerable wrong turns, we finally came to the end of the road. The view was breathtaking, with the expanse of Iowa farmland beneath us washed in misty grayness. To the west, hints of sunshine shone down through the curtain of clouds, as though the hand of God was reaching out from the heavens. There was some odd power in the day.

Francesca's mood had shifted dramatically. At first, there had been mischief in her eyes … a sliver of wicked curiosity. Now, there was only that same pensive watchfulness I had come to recognize in her behavior of late. Her eyes flickered across the horizon; then, she slowed the truck down and pointed.

"Do you see something there?" she asked.

I noticed a dark space secluded behind a strand of strangled scrub. She parked and set the emergency brake.

Spread out below, the buildings of Lost Nation were already lit against the early gloom. I could just identify Main Street and the grade school.

Babe broke the somber mood by vaulting out of the car and squatting. Then, she stood and waited for the first set of orders.

We walked to the natural opening in the rock wall, which proved to be the mouth of a cave. At that exact moment, the rain started to fall in teasing spurts. The storm was just over our shoulders now, and the thunderclaps grew louder every minute.

Francesca had checked both flashlights' batteries before leaving the house, and their beams sprang to life at our touch. I was slight enough to wiggle my way through the tightly spaced bushes guarding the entrance and enter the darkness without stopping or stooping. Francesca, at five-foot-seven, had to bend down and wriggle her way inside, squatting like catcher Yogi Berra.

Francesca observed, "You'd think these bushes were placed here on purpose. They're like a wall. For keeping someone out? Or keeping someone or something in?"

God, it had never occurred to me before that moment; something might be IN THERE! I stopped dead.

"What is it?" Francesca asked, blowing a spider web out of her face. I was glad I hadn't disturbed it ... I hate spiders.

"Do you really think there's something in here?"

"We'll never know if we don't push on."

She pushed on, and I had no choice but to follow, though my heart was pounding in my ears.

Even with our Eveready battery torches, it took a while for our eyes to adjust. Thankfully, Babe was not in a wandering mood. In fact, she was so close to my side, I could feel her breath through my pant-legs.

When we finally got our bearings, we had arrived in a kind of rounded rock chamber smelling of long-dead-animal bones. I'd smelled some not-so-ancient ones on the farm, and I could tell. In a weird way, the familiarity of that nose-wrinkling odor was comforting.

In the distance, the sound of dripping water echoed so that it was difficult to tell from which direction it came. We made our way down one side of the rock face, which was crusty with mineral deposits and bat droppings.

A possum walked over my grave.

Babe and I followed my grandmother into the deepening gloom relieved only by our two small points of light. We could now barely detect the thunder that churned outside. It sounded like ghostly drums, muted by time.

There was a thick layer of dust over everything. The spider webs were huge, intricate and menacing, glistening obscenely in the light from our lamps. It was a scene straight from a nightmare.

The pathway narrowed gradually until we were both making forward progress on our hands and knees. There was still plenty of room to maneuver, which was comforting, because the mere idea of becoming wedged in that place was terrifying. I was not claustrophobic before that afternoon. But since then, I've never entered a room after nightfall or even reached into an unlit closet without experiencing a nanosecond of the unforgettable sensation ... something untoward was closing in on me.

Former baseball pitching great Satchel Paige once set down a number of rules for living. Among them was this: "Don't look back. Something may be gaining on you."

"Oh, my God ..." whispered Francesca.

She was crawling directly in front of me. By craning my head to the right, I could see she'd got to an area of the passageway that broadened again. She waved her light around in the darkness in front of her for a moment, then stood upright.

We'd come to a second cavern, this one the size of a high school auditorium. The plink of water drops was much more distinct.

"Aaaagggh!" I screamed.

A figure sprang up to our left. Babe started to howl. Francesca gasped.

"Wait!" she cried, holding my arm firmly.

She passed her light across what looked to be an ancient mural carved into the wall. It was a cave painting — immense, full of savage grace, primitive and luminous.

"Holy cow," I breathed out.

We carefully made our way around the perimeter of the rock wall until we stood at the center of the drawing. Its majesty was unimaginable in that dark place. It appeared out of nowhere, like a miracle, totally captivating us.

I turned to Francesca and asked if she had known these images were here.

A muffled thunderclap answered before she did.

"No," she responded. There was wonder in her voice as she delicately traced her fingertips along the carvings. "I have read every newspaper and magazine article I could get my hands on regarding the history of Lost Nation, and I never ever heard tell of such a thing."

The intricate etchings told the story of a victory in heated battle by one tribe over another. The engagement took place over an entire day, and many were lost on both sides. Some of the figures were prostrate with grieving. Some were on horseback in the thick of the fray. The children from the surviving tribe, it seemed, had been hidden away in this very cave.

The shapes were crude, but there was a power about them, an energy.

"It looks like an entire people disappeared from the face of the earth in this battle."

"Maybe that's why they call it 'Lost Nation.'"

Francesca was struck by the idea.

"History says that our forefathers took their anglicized name for this town straight from an Indian term. I wonder ... if this has something to do with Tom Blackfeather's mythology about this area."

It was about that time that I noticed something on the cave floor. I trained my light on it, but I still couldn't make out what it was. I moved closer and squatted. I poked the flashlight around and made a terrible discovery: a pair of trousers, one shirt, two thin blankets. Someone was living in this place.

Suddenly, Babe began to growl. Within the space of a heartbeat, four things happened.

"Francesca! Someone has been here!"

We heard a noise like a footfall. Francesca doused her light at the same moment she put her hand carefully about the dog's muzzle.

"Ssshh."

In a second, we were in total blackness, with only the sounds of distant thunder and dripping water for company. Francesca knelt and again blew softly on Babe's nose.

"Ssshh," she cautioned, more softly this time.

We heard another footfall. It was louder, unmistakable, thanks to the acoustics of the stone.
I could feel Babe trembling with some terrible emotion. Was it fear? Or loathing?
"I know you two are in there."
It was a dry, hoarse voice. I had only heard it once before, and I wasn't about to forget it. It belonged to the Scarecrow.
Francesca placed one finger across my mouth in a plea for silence, something she didn't have to do twice. I was sure the frightening intruder could hear my heart pounding against my ribs. I placed my hand against my chest in a vain attempt to quiet down the throbbing there.
The Scarecrow's voice had drifted in to us from somewhere near the mouth of the cave. He hadn't yet come to the crawlspace. I wondered how familiar he was with the layout.
"You can't hide from me in there forever," he menaced. "In a way," he went on, "having you stumble across my little refuge makes my life a lot easier. You will never leave this place."
A thousand questions flew through my mind in the space of five seconds. Before I could form any of them, Francesca bent down and whispered gently and slowly into my ear.
In answer, I shook my head firmly, NO.
She gripped my wrist with her fingers and twisted my arm around to my back, pushing my body away from hers in the process. I cupped my hands around Francesca's ear. "I will not leave you," I breathed.
It was little more than a sigh.
Her grip grew stronger ... became vise-like. She was hurting me. I bit my lip to keep from crying out.
"You can't get away from me, you know," called the raspy voice with maddening reasonableness. "I've been watching you. Waiting for you. I never dreamed you'd come to me. You belong to me now."
We heard a sandpaper cough. Nearer, nearer.
"Since you can connect me to this place ... I'll have to take some action. I find the idea somewhat intriguing. Perhaps that will be some consolation."
Nearer, nearer.

Francesca grabbed me by the ears and whirled my head around. She whispered, urgently and oh-so-softly, that I would have to go for help. Then, in an instant, she had Babe's bandanna off the dog's neck and tied it loosely around her snout. "No growling. Stay. Stay, girl," she whispered.

As Francesca inched her way around the edge of the rock wall behind us, she reached into her pocket for her pistol. I heard a soft click as she opened it.

"Damn. No bullets," she sighed, just audibly.

I stood there for a moment and screwed up my courage. I realized that I was going to have to slip by him somehow. My legs felt like jelly, and I prayed for the strength and courage to do as my grandmother asked.

It was up to me now, whether we lived or died.

Chapter 32
Facing Fear

I dropped to my knees, then down onto my belly. I began to snake around the cave, staying as close to the rock walls as possible. As I neared the space where I hoped to God the small opening was situated, I could hear the Scarecrow's faint stirrings as he crawled toward me.

When I felt the wall give way to my right, I backed up about 10 feet and stopped dead, easing my breath carefully in and out. I kept the rest of my body still as stone. With my breath coming back at me from the ground, I felt the tickle of something delicate brush across the tip of my nose and stifled a scream.

The Scarecrow, although a bag of bones, was taller than either Francesca or me, so it took him some time to navigate the second passageway. After what seemed like forever and a day, I could tell he had reached the mouth of the great cavern. I prayed that Francesca's timing was as perfect as always.

My heart began to pound. My mouth went dry. I inhaled and exhaled in slow, quiet whispers, my nose covered by my right hand. He stood up, brushing the dust from his clothes. I think I was actually behind him by then, and slightly to the right.

In the pitch dark, I felt as though I was in a vacuum. He turned first in my direction and then away from me in an effort to get his bearings. I heard the sound of a match being struck on the cave wall and saw the small leap of a flicker of flame. As he brought the match close to a nub of candle, Francesca hurled her flashlight. Thank God for her dead-eye aim! Both the match and the candle fell from his grasp, and the Eveready shattered to pieces at his feet. He cursed.

"You bitch."

He bent down and began to brush the jagged bits away from his body. To do this, it was necessary to move slightly farther away from the opening. He was still muttering to himself, and when I felt his total concentration on the task at hand, I slithered by.

There were some small shards of metal and glass in my way. I felt them dig into my hands and knees as I crawled gingerly and soundlessly over them. They stung like crazy, but I persevered.

Behind me, the Scarecrow's voice started up again. It echoed all around me.

"I can find you in the dark, old woman. And when I do ..." His voice faded out.

That stretch of cold, hard rock was the single longest and most difficult distance I have ever traveled. I felt whispery, creepy things coming into dreadful contact with my skin. Because my nose pressed almost into the stone, the pungent odor of animal droppings was more powerful than ever. I felt the tickle of blood dripping from the cuts on my hands and knees. But my soul was still back in that dark place with Francesca. What was the Scarecrow doing to her now? Was she all right? Was she alive? How in blue blazes would I be able to get help in time?

After what seemed like hours, I was able to stand up. I switched on my Eveready and dashed outside into the downpour. Thank heavens the truck was still there! Mud oozed up and sucked at my shoes as I ran across the open field. It suddenly occurred to me that I was going to have to drive in the rain and in the dark. I took a deep breath and hurled myself into the cab. Oh, God—he'd taken the keys with him! Now what? Think ... Think ...

I remembered Matt had insisted we keep a spare key under the floor mat. I ripped up the rubber and felt frantically around. YES!

I switched on the ignition and ... nothing.
Stay calm. Stay calm ... Don't flood it. Step by step.
I recalled everything Francesca and Matt had taught me. *Prime her up, put her into neutral, turn the key, ease the gas down* ... The roar of that engine was as welcome as Sunday company.
I held down the clutch and found what I thought was first gear. I stepped on the gas hard enough to create a rooster tail of water—but I was in reverse! I rammed the brake to the floor and stopped about ten feet from the south edge of the plateau. My face was dripping, a combination of cold sweat and rain. Tears were coming, too, which would make my misery complete.
No! No! Get a hold of yourself! Think! Breathe! Drive with your heart the way Francesca would.
Suddenly, the driver's door opened, and I felt a hand grabbing for my shoulder. The Scarecrow had come after me. I recoiled and screamed in horror and somehow managed to struggle out of his grip. I pushed in the clutch and threw the gearshift into first. I snaked my body back and forth, using my free foot to kick at my attacker. The tires spun for a moment, then caught traction. The truck lunged forward, and I left the Scarecrow behind in a spray of mud.
I began to honk the floogle horn as I started back down the mountain. I hadn't got more than a few hundred yards when I was met at the first fork in the road by Greely Clack in his rattle-trap. He threw himself out of his cab and waved his arms frantically for me to stop. With a shudder and a last skid, I brought the truck to a halt.
I was sobbing now, uncontrollably.
"HE'S GOT HER! YOU'VE GOT TO DO SOMETHING!"
Greely opened my door, shoved me aside, and sat beside me. He threw the truck into reverse and started driving back toward the cave. He was yelling something at me, but with his head out the window, and in the roar of the storm, it was impossible to make out.
"The Scarecrow's got Francesca!" I yelled again.
When we got to the cave, there were several men there. Abraham, Doc Gearneart and others were standing at the foot of the entrance. Greely Clack picked me up and handed me gently out. I had stopped crying, in my confusion.
With the downpour, it was hard to see who had lifted me in his arms. But his smell was familiar. When I looked into his eyes, I saw that it was Matthew Mosley. I didn't understand or know what to say.

He stroked my hair and whispered that everything would be fine.

"We got him. Francesca is safe, too." Matt said.

I nodded numbly.

I looked frantically around for Francesca but instead saw Sheriff Dan walking the handcuffed Mr. Scarecrow to the police car.

"Mr. Eisenstaedt here is the arsonist, and he's been hiding in the caves for some time," Sheriff Dan explained. "We've been watching for him, and when he went after you, we nabbed him."

I shivered with fear. Imagine what he could have done to all of us.

Matt misunderstood. "You're hurt, child," he said, taking one of my still-bleeding hands in his.

"I need to see her," I said.

"But you're bleeding."

"I need to see her!" I said again.

That's when Francesca eased her way through the scrub at the mouth of the cave, followed closely by Doc Gearneart and Babe.

I struggled out of Matt's arms and ran to her. I threw myself around her and hugged her with all my might. In a second, we were joined by Babe, who leaped and barked with joy. I can imagine the tableau we made, standing there in the torrential rain, soaked to the skin, thunder roaring and lightning flashing.

When I was quieted enough to stand on my own, Francesca gently turned me around so that we were both facing Matt and Abraham, Doc Gearneart, the Teems, Greely and the rest. She told Babe to sit, and Babe sat. Then she put her arm firmly around my shoulder.

By this time, Otto Eisenstaedt was secured in the back of Dan's car.

I felt Francesca shore up her backbone. She trembled with emotion. I recognized all the signs of a powerful rage.

"What in the hell did you stupid sons of bitches think you were doing?" she began.

No one said a word.

"Don't you think I realize," she went on in a booming voice, "that you made Sarah and I pawns in this?"

Sheriff Dan started to speak, but Francesca mowed him down.

"Don't you say a word! When I realize the danger you put us in ... If anything had happened to Sarah, I would have killed you."
She meant every word.

"And you," she said, turning on Matt, "I see your fine hand in all this. Your leaving was a charade, wasn't it? You put me through hell."

The men had begun to look at one another uneasily. I saw her take pleasure in their discomfort. "All of you! All of you put me through hell! What kind of people are you? How could you have been so cruel, so unfeeling?"

She shook her head and began leading me to the truck. Babe walked along at my heels, subdued now. The men were frozen in their positions, totally unable to respond. Francesca opened the door and handed me gently up onto the bench seat. Babe jumped lightly over me and sat in the middle.

Francesca walked around to the driver's side. She looked magnificent, terrible, like some Amazon warrior in the midst of battle, holding up her righteous fury like a shield.

She turned to Matt one last time. "I wonder if I'll ever be able to forgive you?" she asked.

With flinty dignity, she swung herself into the truck, started the engine, and drove slowly back down the mountain. When we were out of sight, she slumped exhaustedly against the back of her seat.

"That'll teach the bastards."

I could hear the quiet satisfaction ringing in her voice.

Chapter 33
Extra! Extra! Read All About It!

Early the next morning, the phone rang. I resented the clanging intrusion as I was nestled safely in the curve of Francesca's body in her big bed. Babe sat quietly, an expectant look on her face.

Francesca stirred. The phone rang on and on.

"What the hell ..." Francesca mumbled. She blinked her eyes and sat up.

"I'll answer it," I said.

Still groggy, I stumbled out of bed and cut short a stretch when I discovered a brand-new set of aches and pains stored in my body. Neat bandages covered the cuts on my knees and hands. I walked carefully up the small rise of stairs and down the hall to my parents' bedroom. The phone sat on the bedside table nearest the door. I picked up the receiver.

"Hello?" I managed to say in a hoarse voice.

"Is this the Morgan residence?" It was a voice I'd never heard before.

"Yes," I answered.

"Is there a Miss Sarah Morgan or Mrs. Frances Schneider?"

I rubbed my eyes and tried to focus my mind. "Yes," I said again.

"Hello. Humboldt Johnson here. I'm a reporter with United Press International. Am I speaking to Sarah Morgan, then?"

"Yes."

"I'm telephoning to verify reports of the capture of Otto Eisenstaedt, escaped arsonist. Miss Morgan, how does it feel to be a heroine? Will you and Mrs. Schneider split the reward money?"

By this time, Francesca had wandered into the bedroom. She motioned to the phone questioningly. I shrugged my shoulders and held the receiver out to her. She stood next to me, so we could both listen.

"Hello? Hello? Are you there?" asked the voice.

"Who is this?" asked Francesca.

"Humboldt Johnson, reporter, United Press International. Would this be Mrs. Schneider?"

"Yes," said Francesca impatiently. "What's this all about?"

"Don't be modest, Mrs. Schneider. It's not every day that an ordinary citizen nabs an escaped felon. Did you know Eisenstaedt was on Iowa's Ten Most Wanted list?"

Little by little, with Johnson's help, we managed to piece together the ensuing events from the night before. Sheriff Mosley had taken the now-raving criminal to the Lost Nation jail and telephoned the federal authorities. Apparently chastened by Francesca's diatribe, he had given most of the credit for Eisenstaedt's capture to us. He had referred to Francesca and me, with a total disregard for the truth, as "willing participants in the elaborate scheme that was hatched to catch a killer." Apparently getting caught up in his edited version of the events, he had discussed our "heroic actions" in such detail, we would soon be famous across the midwest.

Francesca began to purr as she soaked in this marvelous piece of irony, once again victorious on the field of battle. She then described the scene of the capture in the most dramatic terms and was careful to praise both Babe and me for our bravery.

"If Sarah hadn't been able to slip past Eisenstaedt, her knees and hands bleeding all the while, I might not have lived to tell this story. And our marvelous dog, Babe, well, her defense of me against the man was ferocious. We managed to knock him around and injure his face before he scrambled back out of the cave."

She was ever so gracious to Mr. Johnson, who warmed to his task more and more by the mild flirtation he was undoubtedly feeling right through the phone.

"Listen," he said, "this is wonderful. I think we should have pictures. Would you object to my coming out there with my photographer?"

"Not at all," Francesca said.

"Let's see ..." He was silent a moment before continuing. We heard the rustle of papers. "You're at Home Farm; is that right? Outside of Lost Nation?"

"Yes," Francesca said, still purring.

"I could get there this afternoon. Would that be convenient?"

"Perfectly convenient."

"Great! Great! I'll be there by two. Wait a minute ..."

"Yes?" Francesca asked.

"I could arrange for a nice chunk of change if you agree to let us have the story exclusively."

Francesca thought this over. "I couldn't give you exclusive rights to the story. But we won't let anyone else take pictures. How does that grab you?"

"That grabs me a-okay, lady. You sound like a pistol. Can't wait to meet you." Johnson rang off.

Francesca and I burst out laughing while Babe barked and ran around excitedly, caught up in our exuberance.

"Let's have ice cream for breakfast," I shouted.

"With chocolate and walnuts!" Francesca shouted back.

She grabbed my arm, and we began to skip down the hallway singing, "We're off to see the wizard ..."

As the phone rang off the hook the rest of the day, Francesca and I took turns telling the story until we had our respective parts down perfectly. Interestingly, none of the "cretinous posse," as Francesca now called the rescuing party, telephoned or stopped by. They had obviously decided to lie low until the dust settled. It was a prudent decision.

True to his word, Humboldt Johnson arrived shortly after two. His companion, a wizened little man named Mooch with a nervous tic in his right eye, bustled around unpacking camera equipment.

We were in our glory.

Johnson conjured up a picture of Babe and Francesca and me, with Francesca holding her pistol menacingly. He and Mooch took some shots of Home Farm, paying particular attention to the old truck. That afternoon, Francesca drove us all back up the mountain, explaining the events of the day before. Johnson took copious notes and only interrupted Francesca's insightful monologue to clarify a point here and there.

Mooch was overcome by the cave painting. I could see him tremble with excitement as he set about photographing it properly. He kept saying, "Jeepers," over and over, softly, reverently.

The newspaper men finally left Home Farm just before suppertime. They were both effusively grateful and promised tear sheets and photographs from papers across the region.

"Mr. Mooch," Francesca said when they were ready to drive away in their big Ford.

Mooch's eyes widened, because, I'm sure, no one had addressed him as "Mr." in a month of Sundays.

"What is it, ma'am?"

"I've been thinking about the cave painting."

"So have I, ma'am."

Francesca smiled and continued. "I have a feeling that coming upon it is rather a ... find. I have a contact or two at the state university, in the history and art departments. What would you say to not publishing any pictures of it until I see what's what?"

Mooch thought about this.

Francesca watched him think for a moment. "We have no contract, to be sure, Mr. Mooch. I appeal to you as a supporter of the arts and as a fellow discoverer." She looked closely at him to see if he got the point.

He did.

"Sounds like a fair arrangement to me, ma'am."

They shook hands on the deal, and the two men were down the drive and out on Thunder Ridge Road within seconds.

Francesca put an arm around my shoulders. "Men are strange, Sarah, Sweetchild. They are magnificent, confused and utterly driven. Respect them when you can. If they can feel that, their depths will open up to you."

I didn't understand but nodded in agreement anyway, knowing better than to question Francesca when she was making a philosophical observation.

I looked up into her face, her perfect face, and steered the conversation around a corner. "Why don't we talk to Tom Blackfeather about the cave? Maybe his family knows something important."

"Now that is one marvelous idea, my girl. Are you hungry, 'Little Stomach'?"

"Ravenous!"

After dinner, Francesca telephoned Tom Blackfeather and explained about the petroglyphs we'd discovered on Thunder Ridge. I imagined Tom's eyebrows furling in concentration. "You need to make a drawing. Show me the form and color, and make a drawing, you understand?" Tom told Francesca.

"Better yet, Tom, I'll show the actual work to you. I'd love to know what you feel when you first see it."

"What my soul thinks."

"Exactly."

They settled on an afternoon later in the week.

He was silent for a moment and then admitted, "It's a rough trail up Thunder Ridge. Maybe I should ride my horse and leave my truck here."

Two evenings later, Francesca and Babe and I were lazing, sprawled really, on the front porch furniture. It was exactly seven-thirty. I remember the time for two reasons: the old German-made clock in the front hallway was chiming the half-hour; and the sun was kissing the western horizon.

Francesca was staring outward and upward, into the graying sky as one point of light after another leapt into life. She seemed to be truly at peace for the first time in weeks, easy inside her own skin. She swung slowly back and forth in the old cane rocker, one leg tucked beneath her. The other leg dangled loosely, its foot swinging rhythmically back and forth, back and forth.

It was a soft night, dreamy and sweet. A gentle southeastern breeze tickled our noses with the sweet smells of ripening hay and night-blooming jasmine. Even the crickets sounded content.

I lay at Francesca's feet across several cushions I'd gathered from the various outdoor chairs. Babe, in turn, snored softly at my feet.

I was also feeling drowsy, almost relaxed enough to doze off, when I noticed Babe raise her head and prick up her ears. She cocked her head in the direction of Thunder Ridge Road and seemed to listen intently for a moment. Then, she stretched and stood up, wagging her tail.

Francesca and I looked at one another and seemed to hear the sound almost simultaneously: The Clack truck was making its way down Thunder Ridge.

Francesca sat up, and I brought my feet around underneath me.

"Hunny, isn't it?" I asked.

"Yes."

"Why would she be coming here at this hour?"

"Yes," said Francesca once again.

Rattle-a tap, rattle-a-tap. The truck turned off of Thunder Ridge into our gravel drive. The sound of high-pitched voices laughing and talking wafted over the soft air.

"She sure has the radio turned up," I mused out loud.

Francesca, Babe and I walked over to meet Hunny's truck, expecting some last-minute communication from Daddyboys about our meeting him in New York.

"Frances," called Hunny, "The heroine of Lost Nation."

We hadn't bothered to turn on our outdoor lights, and the parking area under the elm was darkening rapidly. It was impossible to make out anything except the circles lit by the truck lamps. So what came next was a complete surprise.

"For she's a jolly good fellow! For she's a jolly good fellow! For she's a jolly good fe-e-llow ... which nobody can deny!"

The truck rattled to a stop, and the ladies of Lost Nation poured out from the cab and the rear bed: Fay Phillips, Emily Purdy, Starr Mosley, Wilma Tycorn and even the reclusive Mary Porter. They surrounded Francesca and me with a gentle wave of happy tidings. Each one carried some treasure: strawberry wine, lemon pound cake, cheese, saltine crackers, salted almonds. With more laughing and singing, they led us up the back porch steps and into the kitchen of Main House.

"Isn't this exciting?" chirped Emily Purdy. "Francesca has made yet another outstanding mark on the state of Iowa."

Hunny Clack's contribution to the celebration was a sheaf of newspaper articles culled from the various weeklies and dailies available in our county. She handed them around and then set about serving up our odd feast.

"Sarah. Let's not forget Sarah," sang out Fay Phillips in her usual musical style. "See. Here's your picture, plain as day. I only wish you'd both been wearing those dresses you bought at the shop. What fantastic publicity that would have been."

Mary stood slightly apart from the rest, in her usual manner. She'd hovered at the edges of life as long as I'd known her, because, I think, she often found it too terrifying to take part. She looked like a quivering doe, ready to bolt. The fact that she was here at all was gift enough to Francesca, who walked right over to Mary and gave her a hug. Mary was even able to hug back a little.

I wasn't well-acquainted with Wilma Tycorn. She was Bill's mom, which made her a personage of extreme interest to me. She worked in the Soda Shoppe once in a while, but her days were more often spent in doing good works for the Red Cross.

She was a bit prim-looking, and therefore, I was stunned to hear her say, "Let's open that wine, shall we? This might be the perfect occasion to tie a little one on."

That certainly livened things up a bit. The questions came at Francesca and me like a hail of bullets.

"What were you thinking, to put yourselves at such risk?" asked Fay Phillips.

"I like the way she showed those men what was what. I wish I'd a been there," said Hunny.

"But weren't you terrified?" asked Mary.

"Frances was never afraid of anything, not in all the years we grew up together," explained Emily matter-of-factly. "Why, she rode astride, in pants, before the turn of the century. It was the most delicious scandal."

"Sarah," said Wilma, "you haven't been in the shop lately, so Bill tells me. We'd like to reward your bravery with a free banana split. Well, actually, it was Bill's idea. Bill, junior, that is. He's dying to hear the real story."

After a while, someone, it may have even been me, brought up the idea of a poker game.

"Poker? Oh, I don't think I could," said Mary.

"Nonsense," said Francesca, finally managing to get a word in, edgewise. "If Maude can play, anyone can play. To be perfectly honest, she actually won. I admit I was miffed."

Then, of course, we had to relate the story of Maude, hard cider and Black Mariah.

Hunny Clack hooted in delight. "I can just picture little feminine Maude suckering you all in mercilessly."

This sent a general gale of laughter around the table.

"Sarah," Francesca commanded with mock severity, "get the cards."

The wine bottles were emptied one by one. Emily filled them each with different amounts of water and proceeded to favor us with an unusual rendition of "How Dry I Am," by striking them with serving spoons. Babe seemed to enjoy this particularly and tore around the room, barking encouragement.

Fay Phillips didn't play cards well. She would wager and lose and then bemoan her lost pennies as though they were dollars. She always complained that people weren't dealing games she understood.

"Why can't you play a normal game, something I know? Something like stud."

This, of course, sent everyone into renewed gales of laughter.

Mary didn't say much. She won some and lost some. Actually, she had just bluffed her way through two hi-lo split half-pots in a row when the unmistakable sound of a Duisenberg engine pulled to a stop outside.

The room suddenly hushed. Within seconds, the ladies of Lost Nation had tidied up the plates and glasses and gathered up their belongings. With heartfelt but hurried protestations of undying love, they flitted rapidly out the back door, piled into the Clack truck, and disappeared into the night.

Francesca seemed totally unaware of Babe and me as she stood outside the back door, her body taut with anticipation.

Chapter 34
Embers in the Ashes

Babe ran to the car, wagging her tail in rapid-fire circles to display her joyful recognition of Matthew Mosley. She stood up on her hind legs and stuck her nose inside the open window on the driver's side. I saw a hand scratch the top of her head. I looked up at Francesca, who still hadn't moved.

Matt opened the car door gently. "You get down now, Babe. Good girl. Evening, Sarah," he said to me, his eyes riveted on Francesca.

"Evening, Matt," I said, my voice a whisper.

"You passing fine, young lady?" I could make out the glint of teeth when he smiled. It was a most beautiful smile.

"Passing fine, Matt."

Francesca's hand, which had been hanging stiff by her side, fluttered, as much of a communication as she was able to make.

Matt looked up at the moon, which was midway between wax and wane. "Only half a man up there tonight." He dropped his gaze to Francesca's face. "I believe I know exactly how that feels."

I snapped my fingers for Babe. "Let's go, girl," I said softly.

I walked into the kitchen, and with Babe at my heels, took up my customary spying post on the back stairway. Matt and Francesca didn't come inside, but there was a window that overlooked the back yard, giving me all the access I needed. I peeked out from behind chintz curtains.

"Fran ..." Matt's voice was low and packed with feeling. "I can't say I know exactly how you felt through all this. But I do know about pain, and I can imagine the size of yours, if ..." he straggled his hands through his hair, "... it was even a tenth of mine."

I couldn't see Francesca too well, so I got up on my tiptoes and craned my neck.

I could almost feel her body quivering. She looked electrified. They stood there like that, love and despair and hate and need and pain and joy crackling back and forth between them like lightening. When she opened her mouth to speak, no words came out. Matt took a small step in her direction.

"You saved my life. You scraped me up off the floor and blew feeling back into my heart, like some magnificent human bellows. And when I could finally stand on my own two feet again, you let me."

He took a step closer.

"I'd take it all back, the misery I caused you. I guess I was trying to open the door, let you go if you wanted." He thought for a moment before continuing. "I was afraid you were going anyhow, and I wanted to make it easier for me to take. I can't believe your greatness. I'm not sure I'm worthy of your greatness. But I'd like to try and learn."

Francesca found her voice at last. "I've always known where the door was. I wasn't looking to use it then. I'm not looking to use it now."

Matt started to move toward her again, but she held up her hand to stop him.

"Not yet. There are things I've never told you, things you have a right to know. I couldn't say them if you got one step closer."

Francesca shrugged her shoulders and waggled her neck back and forth three times. She braided her fingers together and pushed her arms in front of her. She was limbering up.

"I feel something so ... compelling when I think of you." She cocked her head to the side, choosing her words like Satchmo chooses a note. "A melody that sounds familiar to me. An echo that reaches out to my soul from my own antiquity."

She placed her hand across her heart.

"I have waited and listened for this concerto all my life. The music I hear generated by your soul and my own composition have so many notes in common."

She closed her eyes and bent her head.

"I will never again miss you the way I did these past few weeks. Whatever happens, I will not. Our ... whatever it is ... conquers distance and separation. Because after all that went on ... we are still here together. Don't you find that strange?

"I want you in my life, because ... because us together is simply more interesting, more fun, more fulfilling, more curious, more complicated, more ... real ... than us apart."

She stood very still then. Her eyes remained closed, and her head remained bent. She waited.

Matt gathered her up in a huge bear-like hug and swung her slowly around. I heard him start to cry. Then he said one last thing.

"Marry me."

He drew Francesca close, and they sank together to the porch floor, nestling amongst the pillows. She began to cry, and he stroked her hair. I went to my room.

The slivers left of that eventful summer sped by in a blur. Matt moved back into Main House. The next day, he and Francesca and Babe and I drove over to Clinton to Lenz Jewelers, because there wasn't a proper jewelry store in Lost Nation at that time.

Lenz's wasn't exactly Tiffany's. The little shop didn't boast alarm buttons or steel grillwork across the windows. But John Lenz, the proprietor and master designer, was innovative and had a reasonable selection of merchandise to choose from.

My grandmother had never worn, or owned, an engagement ring. Matt had never given one. They were like two kids with a whole dollar to spend at the five-and-dime.

"Diamonds are always a good investment," said Mr. Lenz, by way of getting things started.

Francesca waved her hand.

"Oh, no. Too traditional, I think." She turned to Matt and drank in his face. "What do you think?"

"Definitely too traditional," he answered with a grin.
They looked PERFECT together. She was prettier than ever and maybe a touch softer. And so vibrant, the glory that poured out from her soul was practically blinding. She'd obviously reclaimed her life.

Matt had finally forgiven himself for the death of that little girl. His demeanor seemed less wary. Around Home Farm, he reached out for Francesca, for me, even for Babe, constantly. He'd scoop us up in his arms and give a great hug.

"As you can see, Mr. Lenz, we're not a traditional couple," Matt went on. "Have you got something ... unique?"

Mr. Lenz rolled this request over in his mind for a moment. I watched him start to shake his head, no. Then start to move. Then hesitate. Then disappear into his storeroom. He was gone for a good ten minutes. When he returned, he had in his hands a small box, covered with black velvet. Lenz set the box carefully down on the counter.

"Open it," he said to Matt.

When Matt hesitated, Francesca snapped up the box and opened it. Her eyes popped.

"What is it?" I asked.

"A sapphire," Francesca whispered, her smile glowing.

I didn't know much about gems at that time. What I saw was a round stone, deep blue in color, which was about the size of the fingernail on my thumb.

Mr. Lenz instructed us about the unusual properties of the stone. "It's a chameleon sapphire. That means it changes colors. It's a one-in-a-million genuine collector's item. Look," he said and held the stone up to the sunlight that streamed through the window next to the counter. "Blue. Blue as blue can be."

Next, he pulled the window shade down and held the stone up to the overhead lamp. "See?" he said. "Purple. Isn't that something? I've read about these off and on over my lifetime, but this is the first one I ever saw. I found it at an estate sale in Chicago more than twenty years ago."

Francesca turned the marvel over in her hands. She kept raising and lowering the window shade to compare the coloring. She was mesmerized.

"Mr. Lenz, I think this is the stone for us," Matt said.

The tall, pale man looked at Francesca and Matt for a long moment. "When I bought that," he said, gazing at the sapphire with an emotion akin to love, "I bought it for me, because it was beautiful. I had no intention of ever letting it go."

He took the stone from Francesca and began to polish it reverently. "But seeing you two ... the way you are ... I believe I just changed my mind."

Chapter 35
New Journeys

"What's the weather like in New York this time of year?" I whined. "I don't have any idea what to pack."

I was sitting on the floor of my bedroom. My clothes were draped across every square inch of displayable space. I'd started to pack sixteen different times in the past three days. Francesca often peeked in and offered to help, but I stubbornly refused.

"I want to take what I want to take," I shouted and slammed the door. Of course, it wasn't my clothes I was worrying about.

On the eve of our departure, hopelessly confused and frustrated, I swung the door back and howled down the hallway. "Francesca! HEEELLLP!"

Eventually, we got everything sorted out. Well, almost everything. I couldn't understand why Matt kept insisting on my taking the smallest possible suitcase. It didn't seem to me that it mattered how much luggage a person dragged along on a train. But by that time, I'd beaten the fight out of myself and was tired enough to do as I was asked.

The night before we were to leave, Joshua Teems and Lincoln dropped by for some last-minute instructions. Something had been gnawing at me, and it was getting to the time when I had to say something about it or hold my peace forever.

But how could I put it into words? I was moving away from Home Farm, my perfect bedroom, the swimming pond — everything

I'd cherished my entire young life was about to disappear. What about Babe? I couldn't leave her behind.

I watched the grown-ups, with their lists and notebooks and pieces of paper spread like a cloth across the entire length of the kitchen table. Everyone seemed to be making copious notes about everything. Finally, Abraham and Joshua left, with handshakes and congratulations all around on their way out.

Now was my time come.

I grabbed a ginger snap from a plate by the sink and began to munch nervously.

Francesca noticed. Her spiritual antenna had fully recovered since Matt's return. If anything, it was sharper than ever.

"Sarah?" she said, looking at me intently.

"Yes, ma'am."

"Go ahead." I knew exactly what she meant, but I didn't know how to start.

Francesca glanced at Matt. "Should we tell her?" she asked.

Matt nodded his head once.

Francesca turned back to me. "Do you honestly suppose we'd even think of leaving Babe behind? On this, the greatest adventure of our summer?"

"You mean she's going? To New York?" I shouted.

"Of course she's going," Matt said. "Mr. Toynbee has already made arrangements with the Waldorf Astoria."

"He has? HOOORRAAAYYY!" I started to dance around the room. I grabbed Babe by the forelegs, and we jigged a few steps. "You're going to New York, you lucky dog."

I worried they wouldn't allow Babe on the train, but Francesca assured me it would all work out, and I believed her.

The next morning, I awoke at the first cock crow, before daylight. I had actually set my alarm clock for four thirty, but I sprang from my little bed at 10 minutes past four full of piss and vinegar and ready to go.

Babe and I ran down the back stairway to the kitchen. While Babe was busy outside, I set about making coffee for Francesca. I set the fine rosewood tray with its porcelain cups. I cut a square of cornbread and set it on a plate, next to a crock of fresh butter. The ritual was once more in place.

Carefully, I carried the tray up the stairs and down the hallway, especially careful to walk down the very center. I stopped in front of Francesca's boudoir and set the tray on the carpet runner.

I thought about knocking but decided that surprise was the order of the day. I opened the door without making a sound, picked up the tray, and stepped into the darkened room. It took a moment for my eyes to adjust to the faint starlight glowing in through the windows.

That's when it hit me. There were two forms lying in Francesca's bed.

I was just about to turn around and run out of the room when Babe bounded through the doorway and pounced on Francesca's bed.

Matt sat up immediately. "What the hell ..." he growled.

My feet were stuck to the floor like cement booties. I couldn't have moved if my life depended on it.

In slow motion, I saw Francesca come fully awake. She raised up her arms to me and said, "Come, child. I have missed you all night long."

I set the tray on the foot of their bed. Without letting myself think, I ran back to the kitchen and found another coffee cup. By the time I arrived back at the boudoir, Francesca and Matt were propped up with pillows and were wearing robes.

I stood at the doorway to her room, curling my toes under. My heart was pounding.

Suddenly, my fear melted away. It could have been the welcoming smiles I saw on both their faces or the cloud of love that enveloped them in that room. It had a magical feeling to it.

I went around to Francesca and kissed her, right on the top of her gray-brown head. Then, I crawled up onto the bed and sat beside Babe. We all had breakfast together.

By seven thirty, Abraham's loaded-to-the-gills taxicab had pulled out of our driveway and onto Thunder Ridge Road. But at the turnoff heading toward town, we kept going.

"Isn't the train station that way?" I asked, pointing.

"Yes," answered Francesca.

Ten minutes later, Abraham stopped at the edge of a grassy field. I was about to ask what the heck was going on when I heard the distinct sound of an airplane coming in from the northeast. Matt got out of the cab and started toward the middle of the field. He took a handkerchief from his jacket pocket and began waving it over his head. I squinted up into the heavens and saw the airplane waggle its wings. It began to circle the field. Lower and lower it sank until finally it touched down and taxied to a stop. The huge man who climbed out of the cockpit was Matt's Canadian friend, Ian Emerson.

"Northern Territories Express, at your service," he boomed.

That's how I came to make my first real trip by air.

The plane was a Twin Beech. Ian had borrowed it from Luke Ahern, another Canuck who had come to America after the war and begun a puddle jumper airline. The plane could seat up to eleven people. That meant there was plenty of room for three adults, one child, one dog and various suitcases.

The nearly 1,000-mile trip took three days. We stopped twice to refuel and spend the night.

During the trip, Ian and Matt took turns piloting, and Francesca even sat in on the controls for short spells. I felt very sophisticated.

When we touched down at La Guardia airport, a limousine awaited us on the tarmac. Since Ian had promised to return the Beachcraft ASAP, he was refueling again practically before we knew it. He and Matt hugged like two long-lost bears.

"I can't thank you enough, Ian," Matt said.

"Don't be silly," Ian said. "It was a lark, a piece of cake." He turned to Francesca. "You took to that flying business, ma'am. Like a duck to water. Matt and I do have some vague plans, you know. When you're both back at Home Farm and settled down a bit, I'd like to come out for a visit. Examine a possible future together. Would that be okay?"

Francesca took his meaty hand in hers. "We'll count on it."

We checked into the Waldorf one day before Mommy and Daddyboys were due to arrive from London. What a posh and lush place that hotel was in those days. The smell of lemon polish wafted down richly carpeted hallways. Huge bouquets of fresh flowers decorated art deco tables nestled in corners on every floor. The bellboys (who hadn't been boys for years and years) had snappy ways and good manners.

The usual routine of registration was waived by the General Manager, George Petrie.

"Mr. Toynbee and *World Travel* have seen to your accommodations and meals," he said as he led us to our room. "Please feel free to make use of our restaurants, bars, and room service. We also have valet and laundry capabilities. Should you need any assistance with any part of your stay with us, contact me personally."

He took a key from his pant pocket and opened a door on the top floor of the hotel.

Matt whistled long and low as soon as he stepped inside. I learned that our room was actually a "suite." It had a little kitchen, three bedrooms, a sitting room and six telephones. The towel racks were heated, and the bathtubs were big enough to fit three grown people. A bottle of champagne stood in a silver ice bucket on a table in the foyer.

Babe and I ran around inspecting everything. There were gold-plated water faucets; velvet-covered couches; walk-in closets and silver cigarette cases filled with cigarettes that stood side-by-side with heavy crystal ashtrays.

Francesca took everything in stride. She somehow fit into this splendid place like a right hand in a right glove. She knew how much to tip the bellboy and how to make arrangements for our bags to be unpacked by somebody else. The bellman offered to walk Babe, but Matt and Francesca and I thought a turn around the city was in order.

It was muggy and hot that September day. I couldn't get over the traffic. There were more cars on one block of Fifth Avenue that afternoon than in the entire city of Lost Nation. Dozens of taxi cabs drove past us. I saw my first delicatessen and tasted my first bagel. The looming spire of the Empire State Building glinted gold in the late-afternoon sun.

I pointed to it and asked, "Isn't that the tallest building in the world?"

Francesca nodded her head. "It would be quite a feat to climb to the top by stairs. Ninety-some stories, I hear."

Matt closed one eye and began to run his finger up the expanse of the building.

"What on earth are you doing, Matt?" Francesca asked.

"Why, counting the stories, Fran. A lot easier from here than inside the building," he drawled with a grin.

She kissed him full on the mouth then, right there in front of the whole of downtown Manhattan. There were hundreds of people hurrying past us, but no one stopped to gawk. I doubt if anyone even noticed.

New Yorkers are a whole different breed of people than those from Lost Nation.

That night, we ordered up room service.

"What a civilized invention," I observed grandly. This made Matt and Francesca laugh.

And think ... you could have just about anything your little heart desired: lobster, steak, lamb, Dover sole, wine, spirits, creamed spinach, spaghetti, baked potatoes, French fries, chocolate éclairs.

"Chocolate éclairs," I said. "What are chocolate éclairs?"

"Order some," said Matt.

In fact, we ordered twice. And the waiter brought a full cart both times. Babe particularly liked the steak tartare.

By bedtime, my eyelids were hanging heavy. Babe and I had a double bed all to ourselves. The spread was raw silk, and the pillows were heavenly soft. Just before I fell asleep, I got up and went over to the window. I sat on the window seat and looked out at the lights of the city for a moment, musing about the summer that was behind me and the rest of my life ahead.

Babe jumped down off the bed and padded over to me. She rested her head in my lap. We'd come a long way together, that was sure. I scratched her head for a moment.

"I love you, Babe," I whispered.

I reached out and opened the window. Then, I got back into bed and slept soundly, with the night sounds of that great city, the Lullaby of Broadway, washing gently over me.

Chapter 36
Reunion

The next morning dawned sullen and wet. Up to then, our adventure to New York City had been one lark after another, so it shouldn't have been surprising that events began to run amok.

Daddyboys and Rachael were scheduled to arrive at LaGuardia in the early evening. That should have given us an entire day to lose ourselves among the noted focal points of the city and still have plenty of time to change clothes and meet their plane.

"Lose ourselves" was the operative phrase.

Our exploration started out innocently enough, shepherded by a driver named Clarence and a limousine provided by Mr. Toynbee. We hit Macy's and Gimbels. We gasped at the sheer size and ornate architecture of St. Paul's Cathedral and were delighted by tiny Trinity Church, the oldest place of worship still extant on Manhattan Island. A heavenly oasis amongst the skyscrapers, the graceful edifice nestles in the middle of a miniscule graveyard. We took turns reading the aged and often irreverent gravestone inscriptions. And, of course, we took a tour to the top of the Empire State Building — elevator, not stairs!

We were dutifully thankful to Mr. Toynbee, who met us at Rockefeller Center at 11:30 for a quick bite. After all, our meanderings had been very civilized, although frankly a Cadillac limousine is no Duisenberg.

"How do you like our fair city, then?" Mr. Toynbee beamed. He was a beamer by nature. He beamed about our trip, about Daddyboys' articles, about his Monte Cristo sandwich. "I can't tell you how proud we at *World Travel* are of Clay Morgan. We feel he has a great future as a writer."

Matt said, "Everything's been swell, Mr. Toynbee. Clarence is a pip — very knowledgeable about the city ... and so forth. Except ..."

"Yes?" Mr. Toynbee beamed.

Matt looked at Francesca and me. Francesca jumped in, beaming every bit as broadly as Mr. Toynbee.

"You see," she began, "we've seen the city, all right ... but we haven't really seen the city."

Mr. Toynbee's beam narrowed slightly just for a moment. "Oh, I see," he said in a way that made me feel he didn't.

Francesca reached across the table and touched Mr. Toynbee gently on the arm. Her tone was conspiratorial. "We'd like to get out on our own this afternoon."

Mr. Toynbee's face fell a quarter inch.

"You mustn't think we don't appreciate all your generous hospitality, Mr. Toynbee," she purred. "But, let's face it, we're simple farm folk. We like the rain." Francesca looked at me for punctuation, and I nodded. "We'd adore to wander a little, for the fun of it. What could possibly happen?"

Mr. Toynbee recovered his beam, though it seemed less beacon-like than before. "Yes, for the fun of it. Hmmm ... Fine. I see ... Well then, why don't I meet you with the car at five thirty? And you can all just go and have fun ... and wander ..." his voice trailed off.

Francesca patted his arm again and turned the conversation around a corner.

Mike, the oldest bellboy of them all, had agreed to walk Babe and make sure she had water. He'd also taken to sneaking steak bones up to her each day after the luncheon rush, and we knew she was in good hands. So we were free to lose ourselves in New York, which is exactly what happened all too literally.

It all came a cropper somewhere around three. We'd found our way on the subway to Battery Park. We took the Staten Island Ferry and glimpsed the Statue of Liberty through the rain from across an increasingly rocky sea. By the time we'd redocked and finished looking around the park, the crowds on the subway had increased exponentially. It was harder to get on and harder to get off. You could feel the mighty swell of humanity pushing you from ahead and behind. We lost both umbrellas but still wore all-encompassing rain slicks.

We missed the express back to mid-town. Then, a man with a French accent gave us expert directions on how to catch the next one at a different station.

Somehow, by five o'clock, we found ourselves back at Battery Park. Francesca and Matt were arguing.

"I knew this was the wrong way," she cried. "Now, we'll never make it back in time."

"Maybe we could catch a cab and go straight to the airport," said Matt with a grump in his voice.

Of course, we had never attempted to hail a taxi at the middle of Manhattan's rush hour in the middle of a thunder and lightening storm. Matt whistled and waved his arm off. Francesca yelled and jumped up and down. We actually got one to stop for us, but a well-schooled taxi thief pulled the old block-and-tackle routine and wrestled it right out from under our noses.

All the rain slicks in the world can not protect a body from rooster tails of water churned up by thousands of automobiles!

By the time we got back to the Waldorf, we closely resembled three drowned rats. I was exhausted. Matt and Francesca were still snapping at each other. As we made our way through the lobby, I noticed a beautifully dressed couple standing with Mr. Petrie and Mr. Toynbee at the registration desk. It took me a moment to recognize them.

"Oh, my," I shouted. "It's them! It's them!"

I ran over and threw my arms around Mommy, who seemed startled. "Sarah, what on earth has happened to you?"

Mr. Toynbee beamed. "I told you there was nothing to worry about."

I turned to Daddyboys, who lofted me into the air.

"We were expecting you two at La Guardia," he said. "Thank God you're here."

Francesca and Mommy embraced with real warmth. Francesca exclaimed over Mommy's outfit. Mommy exclaimed over Francesca's bedraggled state. Daddyboys hugged Francesca with his left arm while still holding me tight with his right arm.

Through it all, Matt stood apart, watching the reunion. He must have been feeling ... what? Like an outsider? Nervous? Downright scared?

Francesca turned to Matt and took his arm. "Rachael? Clay? I'd like to introduce Matthew Mosley. I believe ... you've read about him?"

There was an angular awkwardness about this moment, which made me wonder how much Daddyboys and Mommy really knew about Francesca and Matt. My parents behaved charmingly but were also suddenly on alert.

"Mosley?" asked Daddyboys. "Dan's older brother, right?"

"Yep," answered Matt, almost bashfully. "You're one helluva letter-writer."

They shook hands gingerly, and Clay said, "Oh, thanks."

Matt turned to Rachael and said, "Your little girl is one in a million." Then, he put his arm possessively around Francesca and added, "I know where she gets it."

As Mr. Petrie led us up to the suite, we all de-coated and de-gloved. Francesca managed to keep her left hand, sporting its tell-tale ring, out of sight.

"If there is anything, anything at all I can do for you, don't hesitate to contact me," said Petrie with a bow.

Toynbee took a look at the tension in our party and practically leaped back down the hallway.

"We'll meet at 10 a.m. tomorrow!" he called over his shoulder and never slowed down for an answer.

As we entered the suite, Babe greeted us with her usual brand of enthusiasm.

"Who's this?" Mommy asked, taken aback.

"Babe. Isn't she swell? She can do all kinds of tricks." I flopped down on an ottoman, and Babe jumped up beside me and laid her head on my knees.

"You brought her to New York?" she asked.

"Obviously. She enjoyed the plane ride, and she adores it here. Mike brings her these huge bones."

"Mike? Oh. That's nice," said Mommy. "I don't remember your mentioning a dog in any of your letters."

Francesca nimbly rerouted the conversation. "Let's open this lovely champagne, shall we? Matt, would you?"

After toweling off and settling into the suite's living room, complete with fireplace, we voted unanimously to dine in.

The champagne began to work its magic and set a more congenial mood. Daddyboys, warmed by our presence and relaxed by two glasses of the lovely golden stuff, regaled us with the details of the last leg of their trip.

"Paris is a beautiful city. You can't imagine its grace. But London, it's a powerhouse. The war damage is extensive, of course. But the rebuilding has started and continues round the clock."

"Did you see Buckingham Palace?" I asked.

"Oh, how handsome those guards are," Mommy said, sneaking another look at Babe, who had plopped down by my mother's wing chair. "They dress all in red and wear outrageously high hats with plumes," Mommy continued, moving her feet away from Babe's tongue. "The food is odd, too. They like to cover their meat in pastry shells. And their puddings are a strange texture. Although," she laughed and patted Daddyboys' stomach, "... that didn't stop us from expanding our horizons."

"The Tower is quite a sight," said Daddyboys. "The crown jewels are magnificent and displayed there for everyone to see. But its aspect is still forbidding. I can't imagine the terror Elizabeth the First must have felt on being imprisoned there."

Although Matt was mute during this entire conversation, I could see him getting antsy. He kept shifting his position on the sofa, as though he had a burr in his side. Occasionally, Francesca would casually put her right hand on top of his. This seemed to soothe him.

Mommy and Daddyboys noticed this display of affection. I watched them watch Francesca and Matt, who were also watchful.

Finally, Daddyboys couldn't stand it any longer.

"But enough about us; it would seem there were some hair-raising doings in Lost Nation. Elaborate!"

Francesca and I commenced the story of the arsonist. I started with the fire at the Teems' farm while she filled in the part about Babe's run-in with Eisenstaedt and her subsequent wound.

Mommy looked down at Babe, who was now dozing peacefully, her head resting on Mommy's feet.
"How terrible," she said with real feeling.
I took a deep breath. This dog thing was going to be all right.
Then Francesca and I updated my parents on the rest of our summer escapades: Matt's arrival at Home Farm, the storm and finally, the capture of the escaped convict.
Let's just say it was a prudently edited version of the events.
Matt stood up then and began to pace.
Mommy and Daddyboys looked at Francesca.
"Is there ... anything else?" asked Mommy, fearing there was a great deal more.
Francesca walked over to Matt, who was standing by the door of the suite, looking like he was preparing to bolt.
She took his arm with her left hand. The gemstone glowed purple in the soft lamplight. Mommy's eyes popped out of her head. Daddyboys loosened his tie, as though needing more air.
Matt straightened up and took a deep breath. "Actually," he said, "there is one more thing." He took Francesca in his arms. "We'd like to invite you to our wedding. Two weeks from today at Kitty Hawk, North Carolina."

Chapter 37

That Blessed Union

It was a magnificent day for a wedding. Puffy white clouds lazed across the scraping-blue sky. North Carolina was green that September, as green as the forests and fields of Ireland. Fall was looming but not in evidence, and the humidity had fallen away completely.

I had already begun attending The Pritchard School in Manhattan, but there had been no question of my missing the marriage ceremony, especially since I was the maid of honor. Actually, this title had been bestowed on me as a kind of compromise. Francesca would otherwise have had to choose between Rachael and Maude as her matron-of-honor.

Even so, I was thrilled and scared to death.

Kitty Hawk was the site of the Wright Brothers' first successful manned flight. I guess I was expecting an airdrome or a flight school, or at the very least some large bronze plaque marking the famous spot. But it was just a grassy sand field looking, no doubt, much as it had on the day Orville and Wilbur soared into history. Farmer McFadden, who owned the property, was much taken by the idea of the wedding and joined into the proceedings with gusto.

Maude and Rachael were more nervous than the bride, both acting flighty and chatting up a storm as they helped Francesca prepare. We'd spent Friday evening at a boarding house run by a solidly built woman named Myra, a woman in her seventies bursting with vim and vigor.

"Put down three husbands in my day. That's enough for any woman," she admitted with a wink and a hearty laugh. "But I'm glad to see that other folk haven't given up on that blessed union. Fact is, I'd be tickled to see to the flowers and such. I've got some Queen Elizabeth roses, plenty for a bouquet or two. You just leave it to me."

Francesca had decided to wear her driving ensemble minus her leather helmet. When she unpacked her jodhpurs, Mommy was obviously taken aback.

"Are you sure that's quite ... right?"

"Don't be silly, Rachael," said Maude. "It's Francesca's wedding. Oh, dear, I can hardly believe what I just said. Francesca's wedding!" She fanned herself with her hat for the umpteenth time. "I must be having hot flashes. Sarah, dear, could you possibly find me some lemonade? Oh, my, we'll have to brush those dog hairs off your Capris."

Francesca never added one word to the conversation. She just kept methodically rearranging this and smoothing that. When I could take no more, Babe followed me out of the room, both of us heaving a sigh of relief. Downstairs in the kitchen, Myra was working with her flowers and literally whistling *Dixie*. Uncle Harry, Matt and Daddyboys were sitting around the kitchen table, drinking coffee and exaggerating stories about contrary engines. It seemed to me they were carefully avoiding any talk of the coming nuptials.

Babe went straight over to Matt. She stood on her hind legs and put her paws in his lap, which prompted him to stroke her ears.

Matt had been found to be eminently acceptable by my family on a number of levels. He was a good and kind man, an intelligent man, a good story teller who obviously doted on my grandmother. As for being Francesca's husband ... well ... I guess Francesca, Babe and I were the only ones totally at peace with that idea.

"You're a good dog, Babe, said Matt. He looked up at me then. "Everything okay up there?" he asked, looking totally relaxed.

"Oh, Aunt Maude needs some lemonade. She keeps fanning herself."

"Right there in the ice box, child," said Myra, without looking up. "Glasses are in the cupboard to the right of the sink."

"I believe I could use a glass myself," said Uncle Harry, stroking his neck. "Throat seems awfully dry this morning." He glanced at Matt, who pretended not to notice.

"My baby girl looks like a young lady today," my father said, smiling and looking at me.

"Oh, Daddyboys, don't be silly."

"Come and give me some sugar," said Daddyboys and touched his mouth with his finger.

I kissed him and hugged him then. My, it was wonderful having him around to kiss and hug whenever I felt like it.

"I better get back upstairs with this," I said, motioning to the lemonade, "'cause the natives are getting restless."

All three men laughed loudly.

As Babe and I walked back upstairs, I took a closer look at all the various emotions running through the boarding house that day. Uncle Harry was a little wistful, I thought. Did he feel regret, I wondered. Was he thinking about Grandpap, his beloved brother, and missing him in some way? I know I was. It was comforting to know that Grandpap would have been all for Francesca's happiness.

And Maude, I mused, stopping halfway up the staircase. She seemed genuinely delighted. But I wondered if there was something about Matt's and Francesca's relationship that went missing in her feelings for Harry. Of course, they'd been married forever.

Rachael was uncomfortable with the idea of a step-father a mere twelve years older than herself. Actually, I think she was attracted to Matt in some vague way. An attraction I could understand, as I felt it myself.

I wondered if my mother was troubled by this feeling, as I had been once. I hoped not. She was a simple woman, unused to examining her heart too closely. And she'd always been right as rain about things that were appropriate for her. Now was not the moment to "go down the rabbit hole."

Daddyboys was still riding the crest of the biggest wave of his life. And he'd always maintained a strong tie to Francesca, totally outside his relationship with my mother. To Daddyboys, Francesca wasn't just a mother-in-law; she was friend and confidante. But I could see how Daddyboys might envy Matt's exotic nature and his carefree masculinity.

I am aware that I am delineating emotions I couldn't possibly have understood then. I was, after all, only ten years old. Still, whenever I remember the wedding day, these thoughts, and many others like them, always come flooding over me, a very real part of the sum total of the experience.

I started climbing the stairs again and stopped in front of the door where Babe already awaited me. I could hear more conversation through the door.

"Mother, you're not wearing boots," said Rachael to Francesca anxiously. "All right, all right. But couldn't we clean them up a little?"

Myra had offered to take us all to the field in her Nash station wagon. She'd donned the "only dress I've owned in twenty years"—a bold floral print that made her look even more sturdy, if possible. When Francesca came down the stairs, Myra's eyes bugged.

"That's quite a get-up and no mistake," she said with a grin. "Never had the legs for it myself. Well? Shall we go?"

* * * * *

We were the first to arrive. I'm not sure I was expecting anyone else, and yet, there was a whisper of expectation in the air. The second car on the scene contained the local justice of the peace.

"Orton here. How do. Now, which is the bride and which is the groom?"

Francesca and Matt stepped forward. Justice Orton's eyebrows shot upward.

"I see," he said. "Well ... why don't we step aside here and talk a little about the ceremony." He motioned at Francesca. "This your wedding attire?"

Francesca nodded.

Matt glowed. "Doesn't she look beautiful?" he asked, rhetorically.

"Well, it certainly is appropriate for this place. Now, then ..."

They moved off a little way, and the rest of us stood there, not knowing exactly what to do or say. As Babe was always interested in exploring, we began to walk together across the field. I could smell late-summer jasmine carried on a soft breeze and hear the lazy drone of honey bees. In the distance, I saw a truck driving in our direction. It was Farmer McFadden and his wife, Hattie, coming to join in the festivities.

I lifted my face to the sky and drank in the day. Suddenly, it seemed the buzzing was getting louder, and I looked around for a hive.

The awful thought came to me: could there be a hornet's nest nearby? Yes, it was sure, that drone was getting louder.

Matt suddenly began running toward Myra's station wagon. From the back, he took a long pole. He ran with it to the center of the field and forced it into the loamy dirt. From his aviator jacket pocket, he lifted a long red scarf, which he proceeded to attach to the pole. It looked for all the world like a wind sock.

I looked up into the sky. Planes, maybe twenty or thirty of them, circling, taking turns landing.

One by one, those beautiful mechanical birds, awash in midday sun, waggled their wings and reduced their elevations. At sixty-second intervals, they began to land at Kitty Hawk. It was a grand sight, like a brace of bald eagles floating gently down on air currents.

As the planes landed, their pilots taxied them to the south end of the field. I recognized the leader of the pack — it was The Lady Victoria. Ian had come for the wedding! They had all had come for the wedding!

Babe and I ran to greet them.

Francesca watched the spectacle, stunned but delighted.

Maude and Harry were flabbergasted. "I'll be damned," cried Harry. "This is going to be a day to remember. Come on, Maudie."

Daddyboys and Rachael weren't quite sure what to make of this friendly, though totally unexpected, invasion.

"Are they ... friends of Matt's, then?" Mommy asked to no one in particular.

"This'll make one helluva column," said Daddyboys. He clapped his hands together and whooped, "YeeHAAAWWW!" and started running down the field. Then, he stopped and walked back to Mommy. He took her hand and gave it a little shake. She laughed, and the two of them skipped across the sandy grass together hand-in-hand.

Ian easily picked Matt up and swung him around. "Well, Yank, we made it." Then he gave me a quick kiss on the head and patted Babe.

As the other fliers began to gather around Matt, Babe and me, Francesca materialized in our midst, exuding grace. She touched their faces and took their hands in greeting and sipped from hip flasks. She was in her glory.

It took some minutes to introduce everyone to everyone. When the tone of the afternoon had settled a bit, Justice Orton began to speak.

"Quite a day. Some big kind of love out here in this field. A love of flying, that's sure. The love of one friend for another. Love of a man and a woman." He smiled at the happy couple. "Don't ever remember presiding at a ceremony quite like this before, eh, Mother?" He nodded at Mrs. McFadden, who nodded back. "Expect we'll never see one again. I'm not a preacher, but I think the first thing we ought to do is reflect for a moment on how very lucky we all are to have made it this far."

I watched the pilots and thought about how much some of them had been through. I looked at Francesca and thought about the long span of years, the heartaches and the disappointments and the joys and the troubles that had brought her to this moment. I thought about Matt and Maude and Uncle Harry. I looked for a long moment at my own parents. I knelt down in the grass and hugged Babe.

"All right, then," continued Justice Orton. He turned to Matt and asked, "Matthew Mosley. Do you take this woman, standing there by your side, as your wife for better or worse, richer or poorer, in sickness or health, for as long as you live?"

"You bet I do."

"Well, that's fine. Now, Frances, do you take this man here to be your husband for better or worse, richer or poorer, sickness or health, for as long as you live?"

I started to cry like a baby. But that was okay. I watched as some of those brave pilots wiped tears from their eyes. Justice Orton turned to me. "Crying is a good thing," he advised, patted me on the shoulder and continued. "Well, Frances, what do you say?"

"I do."

"So far, so good." He turned to Ian. "I believe you're the best man, though not any better than the groom. Have you got a ring?"

Ian looked downright puzzled. He shrugged his shoulders.

Justice Orton looked at Matt. "Is there a ring, young man?"

Matt's jaw dropped to his kneecaps. "I didn't think about it." He turned to Francesca and gestured vaguely. "I don't know how it could have slipped my mind."

Francesca began to giggle. She waved her left hand in the air. "Use this ring," she sputtered.

The giggles are terribly contagious, especially in my family. It was just awful. And those damned pilots didn't behave any better than we did. Pretty soon, there were forty raving lunatics out there at Kitty

Hawk, laughing their heads off. Every time Justice Orton began to speak, we all broke down again. He had a bray like a Jenny mule, which was a large part of the problem. My stomach ached terribly, so I threw myself on the grass and covered my ears to see if that would help.

It didn't.

Eventually, after we'd all laughed ourselves hoarse, Justice Orton was able to get us safely back on track. He wiped his eyes with a white bandanna.

"Dear, dear." He looked out at the assemblage sternly. "Now I'm going to ask about that ring again, and I don't want to hear a peep from anybody." He turned to Francesca. "Give Matt that ring, please. What an interesting stone. Now, Matt, you give it back to her and repeat after me: 'With this ring, I thee wed ...' Good. We seem to be getting somewhere."

Justice Orton joined Matt's and Francesca's hands inside of his. "By the power vested in me by the great state of North Carolina, I now pronounce that you are husband and wife. Thank God. Where's the beer?"

The kiss that immediately followed those words was the most powerful and passionate expression of love I have ever witnessed. It was so intimate, so trusting, so full. The union of Francesca and Matt was finally complete.

Chapter 38
Saying Goodbye

January 27, 1986
Buena Vista Convalescent Hospital, Pasadena, California

I drove into the parking lot and parked under an ancient live oak. I turned off my headlights and windshield wipers and sat in my car listening to a Duke Ellington Band rendition of Billy Strayhorn's composition, *Blood Count*.

I looked through the rain toward the low adobe building, which sat back from the street behind an expanse of lawn and flower beds. I knew I should go in; she was waiting for me. But I didn't want her to see me crying.

We'd come a long, long way together, Francesca and I. I'd grown up, and she'd grown old. I was glad Matt hadn't lived to see her in her present state, although she still had the prettiest legs in the county.

I reset the rearview mirror and examined my face. I looked tired. I was tired. I took a deep breath, wiped my eyes and brushed a little blush across my cheeks to relieve the gray tinge of sadness that had recently settled there. Then, I stretched aching muscles, pulled my coat closer around me and got out of the car. It was an effort to move.

The wind was cold. Or maybe it was my soul. I shivered as I ran through the downpour and into the welcoming warmth of the lobby.

Mom and Daddyboys were waiting for me on the sofa by the fireplace. Two or three other families milled around, waiting. Waiting is something you get good at when someone you love is dying.

Dad stood up to greet me. He wore his age well. In fact, I thought he was better-looking than ever. The boyish cast had finally left his features, which had settled into an attractive silver-haired maturity.

Mom was crying. She had cried a lot of tears these past few weeks and looked small sitting there. I kissed them both.

"How is she?" I asked, afraid of the answer.

"Weaker," Dad answered. "They say ... maybe tonight."

Mom gulped back her grief. "Sit down a moment, Sarah, and give me a hug."

We held each other tightly, as if our embrace might hold off the night and what those dark hours would bring.

I sat back. "Is she in pain?" I asked.

Dad shook his head. "Yes," he said, "and she's very ... tired. Ready, I think."

"Oh, Sarah, don't hate me, please, but I can't go back in there. I said my goodbyes. I ... I just can't."

"Mom, Mom, it's okay. You think I don't know ... how hard it is?"

"She wants to see you, I think," said Dad. He sat down beside Mom and took her in his arms. "Alone."

"But I couldn't ..."

"It's all right, Sarah," he soothed. "Your mother and I have always understood your relationship with Frances." He kissed Mom's hair. "You'd better go in. She's been ... waiting for you."

Please don't let me cry, God.

I walked down the silent hallway to Francesca's room. It had a pretty view of the mountains during the day. As I peeked in, I saw that the only light came from a candle by the side of her bed. I'd made that candle for her many years before, when the only presents I could afford were works from my own hands. She looked almost like her old self, lying there so peacefully. She was still a beautiful woman, despite her illness and her 105 years.

"Francesca?" I said softly.

"Sarah? Is that you? Come in. I have missed you all night long."

I walked around the foot of her bed and sat in a chair nearby. She weakly patted the bed.

"Sit here tonight."

I knew my grandmother was in pain. I was afraid I might hurt her. She read my mind.

"Don't be afraid. I need you next to me tonight."

I climbed carefully onto the bed and lay down beside her.

"Better?" I asked.

"Much."

Her breathing was regular but shallow. I stroked her hair softly.

"How is the book coming?" she asked.

"Well. I'm pleased with it."

"Good. I'm sorry I won't get to read it."

I started to protest, "Don't say that ..."

"Ssshhh. It's time, Sweetchild. Past time. I'm ready."

"But I'm not," I said and began to cry. "I was hoping I wouldn't do this."

"Would you have wished to love me less in order to miss me less?"

I shook my head, no. With tears streaming down my face, I breathed in the minty smell I have come to associate with impending death. Some people hate that smell, I know. They're horrified of it, I guess. But it seemed almost pleasant to me as I lay there close to her like that. It was just another part of my grandmother and therefore held no terror for me. In some odd way, I was actually comforted by it.

"I'm glad Matt never saw me this way," she said. "He couldn't have stood it. Most men don't have the capacity to share moments like these. Though your father is holding up wonderfully well."

It was so like her to think of her family even in the waning moments of her life.

"Sarah, Sweetchild. You must take great care with your mother. She's feeling her own mortality rather brutally."

"I will."

"You know," she said, shifting her body closer to mine, "death is the most powerful and intimate experience one person can share with another. I'm glad you're here."

"I love you so much," I whispered.
"I've had a lot of love in my life, haven't I? Cox was a great man, in his wonderfully singular way. He tried to be ... more than he was. For me. I sometimes wonder if he was happy with me."
She closed her eyes and dozed for some minutes.
While she slept, I thought about her life and everything she had been ... everything she had been to me.
Her life with Matt was an adventure, pure and simple. Of course, he taught her to fly. Eventually, she gave up racing cars entirely and concentrated on setting age-bracket flight-distance and speed records. In 1948, they'd opened a small aviation school with Ian not far from Home Farm. People came from all over the United States to learn how to conquer the skies. She had been a marvelous instructor.
In the late 50's, they sold their half of the business to Ian and began to travel. Europe, Africa, the South Pacific. Sometimes Maude and Harry accompanied them, sometimes Mom and Dad. I went along too, as often as I could ... between, during and after my love affairs.
Francesca worried about me. She boosted my spirits when I was ready to be scraped off the floor. She was a steadying influence when I felt like a pinball in the machine of life. She welcomed, and charmed, all the men in my life. She never nagged about great-grandchildren, bless her. She never nagged about anything. Oh, she'd get mad sometimes and push or make suggestions. My God, she was a human being, after all. But I merited her concern the old-fashioned way ... I earned it.
She's the reason I'm a writer. I wrote my first novel about her. Well, not about her exactly, but about a woman with her spirit and her grace. It was a best-seller. She helped to make my fortune. She was the best friend I ever had.
I leaned down and kissed her softly on the cheek. She opened her eyes and smiled.
"You know how I felt about Matt." It wasn't a question.
"Yes, I think so."
"How much I loved him. How he came to be a part of me in the best sense of the word. How we finished each other's sentences and knew each other's deepest secrets."
"Yes," I said again.

"I had a dream about you last night. The great love of your life is just around the corner. You'll know him when you meet him. And you'll think of me. Isn't that lovely?"

I started to cry again. "Yes."

"Sarah, undo the chain from around my neck, would you?"

"Sure."

It was the gold chain on which she wore the sapphire ring Matt had given her.

"I want you to have my second wedding ring. I want you to wear it."

I held it up to the candlelight. It glowed deep blue.

"Take it now. Put it on now," she said.

"Are you sure? You don't want it on when you ... go?"

"No. I want to see it on your finger."

I slipped the ring off its chain and onto my finger. It fit perfectly.

She gave my arm a frail squeeze. "You see. I have loved much in my lifetime. I have been loved much. But no one ever loved me the way you do. And I never loved anyone else the way I love you. You've been a part of my eyes, my heart, my soul. I will ... miss ... you ... Sweetchild."

She fell away from me then. Not gone. Not quite. I pushed the intercom by the side of her bed and asked the nurse to get my mother and father. They were with me in that little room within seconds.

I got up off the bed and knelt down. I still had hold of Francesca's hand; I couldn't seem to let go. Mom and Daddyboys each kissed her on the cheek. Then, we all sat down to wait together.

I'll miss you, too, Francesca.

Francesca of Lost Nation

To order more copies of this book, please visit our website at: www.LuckyCinda.com or e-mail: ldobbins444@gmail.com.

Join our Book Discussion

Who was your favorite character and why?
What was your favorite scene in the book?
Share your thoughts at: www.LuckyCinda.com